DEALING JUSTICE

DARK RIVER SERIES
BOOK 2

J.D. TRAFFORD

TEMPLE BAR PRESS

ALSO BY J.D. TRAFFORD

Little Boy Lost

Good Intentions

Without Precedent

No Time Series, featuring Michael Collins

No Time To Run

No Time To Die

No Time To Hide

Dark River Series

Merchants Bridge

Dealing Justice

Tower Grove, coming fall 2024

This is a work of fiction. Names, characters, organizations, places, events, and incidents are either products of the author's imagination or are used fictitiously. Any resemblance to actual persons, living or dead, or actual events is purely coincidental.

Text copyright @ 2023 by J.D. Trafford

All rights reserved.

No part of this book may be reproduced, or stored in a retrieval system, or transmitted in any form or by any means, electronic, mechanical, photocopying, recording, or otherwise, without express written permission of the publisher.

Published by Temple Bar Press, Saint Paul, MN.

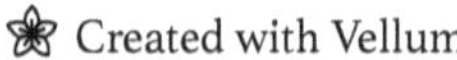 Created with Vellum

To my constant readers, you are the best.

-J.D.

DEALING JUSTICE
Dark River Series, Book 2

J.D. Trafford

1

I should've been doing much better on the day the judge died. My partner at the FBI, Charlie Matthews, would say the death of Judge Griggs was and always will be irrelevant. He'd tell me this all started, later, at the hospital as my father struggled to breathe and my mother ran to go get the nurse, leaving the two of us alone. Matthews would say what happened to the judge was just a rabbit hole, a misdirection - except I don't think so.

The two may not be directly connected, but they are certainly interwoven. I cannot think or talk about one without thinking or talking about the other, because what I did on that morning—the morning I appeared for a hearing in front of Judge David C. Griggs— and the countless, questionable decisions that followed don't make any sense in isolation. The two cannot be compartmentalized.

Life doesn't work that way, at least my life doesn't work that way. It's messy. If I'm going to do this, really explain what happened, then I must tell it all, not just the pieces or the parts that make me sound good or heroic. That's why I'm starting here, and I apologize in advance if it's a waste of time, but honesty is important to me, and everybody needs to know my head was still scrambled that morning, even though it had been more than a year since I'd been shot at Merchants Bridge and, yet, miraculously healed.

Every week, I went to see Dr. Dan, and that morning was no different. His assistant, first, checked to make sure my insurance was still valid. Then she'd run my credit card through the little machine on her desk to extract the co-pay from my bank account, and then I waited for the honor and privilege of sitting on Dr. Dan's couch.

This is what I did. I never canceled. It didn't matter what was going on at work. I took the time to take care of myself, like a good little girl. I faithfully did what I was expected to do. I lay prostrate before the psychiatric gods. I begged for them to heal me, as Dr. Dan prescribed me one more pill after another. Upon his advice, I'd stopped looking for the man with the white beard and Irish lilt and stopped returning Gray's calls. Gray and I had been inseparable for a time, but now we were apart. Our kiss also may have had something to do with it.

Dr. Dan and I talked about that night at Merchants Bridge, session after session. There would be an occasional side-quest into the sexual harassment I'd experienced as a young female cop, but we'd soon return to what I saw and experienced lying on the ground, bleeding to death, and being healed by an old man who appeared out of nowhere. Dr. Dan, eventually, opined that I did not see what I saw or experience what I often referred to as "wrinkles in reality." I like this term a lot, by the way, because it sounds less crazy than miracles and ghosts and supernatural powers.

Over time, our sessions had become more adversarial, and Dr. Dan's platitudes became more frequent and even more obnoxious. "Trust the process," he said as sleep became even harder for me to find. "You cannot control this," Dr. Dan said after I told him I was being followed. Then, the morning the judge died, he said, "This process is not linear, Amy, surely you understand that."

And I responded, "Linear? I'm not asking for a straight line. Two steps forward, one step back would be a miracle, but I'm still in the same place. Nothing has changed. I'm stuck." I remember this clearly. I wanted to be normal so badly, it hurt. I wanted Dr. Dan to fix me, but I knew deep down he couldn't.

The bell rang before we finished. I walked out the door with tears streaming down my cheeks and cried all the way to the courthouse. Like I said, I should have been doing much better on that day. I should've been able to make better decisions for myself and protect the people around me, but I didn't.

———

So here it goes, I was under oath, sitting in the witness chair at the federal courthouse in downtown St. Louis. Colton Steele strutted and preened in front of me. He held up a large plastic bag containing a gun in one hand; the other held a smaller bag containing seven bullets.

Steele said, "I'd like to offer Exhibits Twelve and Thirteen into evidence."

There was no objection, and so Steele, a rising star in the United States Attorney's Office, took the items up to the bench. He placed each in front of Judge Griggs with as much drama as he could squeeze out of the task, twisting his wrist at just the right moment so as to allow his sterling silver and pearl cufflinks to reflect the overhead light. The movement created a momentary flash, *ka-pow*. Steele, then, walked back to the prosecutor's table.

As he did so, I glanced at the clock at the far end of the courtroom, praying it soon would be over. I hated testifying. This was not unique amongst law enforcement officers, regardless of rank or jurisdiction. Nobody enjoyed being under the microscope, but my dislike was different.

It actually made me physically ill. This wasn't because of my horrible session with Dr. Dan earlier that morning, or even Merchants Bridge. I'd always struggled with testifying. Luckily, as a low-level patrol officer working the night shift, most of those cases were pretty minor, and I could manage it with a stiff drink and some breathing exercises. I didn't need to be a compelling witness when talking about a guy running a red light, a kid stealing sneakers, or a woman who had too much wine at an office party and drove her SUV into a lamppost. I was passable, and everybody seemed to be okay with that, but these cases were serious.

I was an agent at the FBI. The defendants weren't looking at fifteen days in the local jail; they were facing years, if not decades, in a federal prison. Lives and careers were on the line. With higher stakes, the expectations also grew.

Colton Steele had spent hours prepping me. It didn't matter that this was just a preliminary hearing, a pro-forma motion to suppress some drugs and a gun found after an arrest. It didn't matter that there was no jury, no members of the media, no weeping victims, nor friends of the defendant. He and the other prosecutors expected a performance from me, a perfectly executed dance.

I think the problem was and has always been that I was convinced, at some point during the proceeding, I'd be publicly exposed as a fraud, an imposter. This could occur in a myriad of different ways: a prosecutor could inadvertently let it slip that my father pulled some strings and got me into the police academy or Matthews vouched for me during the hiring process when others at the FBI had doubts; or maybe a judge was going to castigate me for mishandling evidence or flouting some protocol I'd never heard of; or perhaps a clever defense attorney would probe the real reasons why I left the St. Louis Police Department or inquire into my mental health.

These were the thoughts that crowded my head and tied my stomach in knots as Colton Steele continued to question me. He asked, "Did you inform Mr. Marsh of his Miranda rights?"

"I did," I said, a little too softly, which caused the court reporter to look up from her steno machine and ask me to repeat my answer. I sat up a little straighter. "I did...um...I did read him his rights."

"And did Mr. Marsh waive his right to an attorney, and also his right to remain silent?"

"Initially he waived it, but halfway through the interview, he asked to stop, and so we stopped."

It was then I remembered my father had an appointment to see his oncologist. In my angst over Dr. Dan and the hearing, I'd forgotten he was going in for lab work and a consultation. Both he and my mother assured me it was minor, nothing to worry about, but cancer was still cancer. I looked up at the clock and wondered whether his appointment was already over.

"Agent Wirth, did you hear my question?" One of Steele's perfect brows was raised, and then his expression tightened into one of annoyance.

I had not heard the question. "I'm sorry. Could you repeat it?"

"The conversation with the defendant," Steele said. "Was it recorded?"

"Yes."

The moment those words were said, Steele placed an envelope in front of me. "Marked as Exhibit Fourteen is what the United States proffers as a recording of the conversation between Agent Amy Wirth and Defendant Jeremiah Marsh." He pointed at the envelope. "Do you recognize that?"

"Yes." I picked up the envelope and examined it. My signature was across the seal. "This contains a flash drive of a video recording of my conversation with the defendant."

"And did you watch this video prior to testifying today?"

"Yes, a few days ago, I watched the video. Then I placed the flash drive back into the envelope and re-sealed it."

"And is that seal unbroken?"

"Yes, it is unbroken."

"And is this," Colton Steele held up a half-dozen stapled sheets of paper high into the air as if they were stone tablets delivered to him by the Almighty, "a true and accurate transcription of the video?"

"I think so..." my voice trailed, again, "but I'd actually have to see it." The judge's law clerk suppressed a laugh, but Steele was unfazed. His performance continued, despite me.

"Of course." He bowed his head slightly, then handed me the papers with another flourish. I couldn't help thinking Colton Steele was the most pompous asshole I'd ever met, and in my job, that's saying a lot.

He turned to Judge Griggs. "Let the record reflect, Your Honor, that I have given to Agent Wirth what I have marked as Exhibit Fourteen-A." Steele gave me a moment to flip through the pages of the transcript. "I'll ask the question, again, now that you have reviewed it." He tilted his head to the side with a little smirk. "Is Exhibit Fourteen-A a true and accurate transcript of Exhibit Fourteen, the video?"

"It is."

Colton Steele, then, offered both into evidence without objection and asked the judge for permission to "publish," meaning to play the recording.

Judge Griggs nodded, then pressed a button on a small monitor that controlled the courtroom's video and audio. Various screens throughout the courtroom lit up as the video began to play.

Along with everyone else, Judge Griggs watched the interview with little expression. He was in his mid-fifties and was now in his seventh year serving as a federal district court judge. Griggs was childhood friends with Missouri's senior senator, and during his confirmation hearings, people had been worried about whether Griggs was only a political hack, a man who would be forever indebted to his friend and the machine that had granted him a job for which he could never be fired.

During his time on the bench, however, Judge Griggs, had distinguished himself largely by not distinguishing himself at all. His criminal sentences were neither harsh nor lenient. His rulings in civil cases were also even-handed. He avoided courthouse gossip. He treated attorneys, staff, and his fellow judges with respect, and Griggs was careful to avoid any case that could be considered by anyone as remotely "political."

When asked about this by a reporter, Judge Griggs merely pointed to the Rules of Judicial Conduct. The rules require recusal whenever there is actual bias or the *appearance* of bias. "Given my close friendship with the senator, it's not a stretch to conclude that one of the parties may feel like I am biased against them or closed minded to their position, even when I am not. Appearances matter to the integrity of the system of justice. Ultimately, getting a decision right is important, but procedural fairness—how parties feel about the method in which the decision is made—is even more important to our collective faith in the rule of law than the ultimate decision."

It's that reputation and even-handed demeanor that made the following sequence of events so surprising. When the video finished, Judge Griggs announced it was now time to take our morning recess. He gathered all the exhibits, picked them up, and exited the courtroom with his law clerk and court reporter. Five minutes later, there was a gunshot and the sound of a woman screaming.

———

SOME COWERED UNDER the tables or ran toward the exit, but I did the opposite. I unholstered my gun and went toward the sound. In hindsight, this was surprising. I think Dr. Dan and I would have both predicted I'd either be the first person out the door or curled up in the corner with my eyes shut. There was, however, no flashback to that cold night at Merchants Bridge. There wasn't time to ruminate about how I was perceived by my colleagues or to doubt my own abilities. There was an active shooter, and when there's an active shooter, every second mattered.

I knew I had to cut off the path to the courthouse's public areas. Even if I couldn't take down the shooter, it might give others enough time to escape to safety. As I crossed the room, I saw Colton Steele. He was hiding under a table.

"Get up, and get the others out." I grabbed Steele, pulled him to his feet, and shoved him toward the exit. "Did you hear me? Get these people out."

I couldn't waste any more time on him. I ran up a few steps, past the area where administrative staff sat during hearings, and then to the door behind the judge's bench. It led to a back hallway. Two U.S. Marshals followed me, with their guns drawn as well. The door was locked, but a marshal pressed his key card against a black box. The door clicked open, and I was the first to go through it.

The back hallway was empty and quiet now.

We moved together, past several conference rooms, toward Judge Griggs's chambers. Halfway, a woman stumbled into the hall, crying for help. Adrenaline was running so high, I almost shot her, but by the grace of God, I made the split-second decision to wait.

She was the court reporter. Her face was twisted in a knot of anguish and fear. Then she pointed. "The judge!" she screamed, then repeated it over and over. "The judge. The judge. The judge."

I directed one of the marshals to stay with her and continued inside, with the second marshal following behind into the suite. The first area was small, like a waiting area: four chairs and a table with magazines. Beyond it were workstations for the judge's staff, a conference room, and then in the back was the door to the judge's chambers.

I didn't see anyone upon entry, but I heard a soft whimper. We took a few, slow, cautious steps further inside. Then I saw him. The law clerk sat on the floor, back to the wall. His legs folded, pulled tight against his chest. His head buried in his hands. His body shaking.

There was no blood on him, no apparent weapon, but as far as I knew, he could be the shooter. I directed the second marshal to search the clerk, while I called out to the judge.

"Griggs."

Still no answer. Although the shooting hadn't continued, there was no guarantee the danger had passed. I wasn't going to assume anything.

"Judge Griggs, are you okay?" I stepped closer to the door. "Is anybody else in there with you?"

Gun extended, I counted to three under my breath and crossed the threshold to work the room. Nobody in the corners, behind the couch, or in the bathroom.

It was clear.

There was only Judge Griggs, slumped in a large brown leather chair. A bullet hole under his chin, and the back of his head gone. Shards of bone, clumps of hair, blood and brain were scattered on the ceiling and wall behind him.

On the judge's desk was a picture of his family and two clear evidence bags. Both were empty. On the floor was Exhibit 12, the gun that had been offered into evidence that morning. Nearby was a spent shell casing I assumed was one of the seven bullets, which Colton Steele had entered into evidence as

Exhibit 13, with his cufflinks flashing. I figured the other six bullets would be found in the gun.

I backed out, slowly. There was nothing left for me to do, and I didn't want to contaminate the scene any more than I already had.

In the hallway, I passed the marshal who'd been tending to the court reporter. "It's clear." I pointed at the door. "Make sure nobody goes in. The techs need to tear that place apart." Then I continued, not waiting for a response.

I kept walking until I found a bathroom at the far end of the hall. Once the door closed behind me and I was alone, my whole body began to shake, just like the court reporter and law clerk. The more I tried to calm down, the harder I shook.

At the sink, I set my gun down on the counter and turned on the faucet. I splashed cold water on my face. I told myself it was over, then I splashed even more water on my face, again and again, until my breathing returned to normal.

I took a paper towel and dried myself. Then I looked at the mirror, examining the person staring back, feeling like I'd seen something in Judge Griggs's chambers, but maybe not. Maybe I hadn't seen anything, but instead felt it. I closed my eyes and tried to picture the room, but it didn't take long for my concentration to break. It was interrupted by my doubts and insecurities, surfacing, again.

Would my father have done it differently? How could I have done it better? What mistakes had I made?

The vibration of my cell phone brought me out of the trance. I pulled it from my pocket and sighed when I saw whose name appeared on the screen. It was a call I couldn't ignore.

I tapped the screen and put the phone to my ear and said, "Hello, Chief."

2

———

T he bureau chief was Anna Marie Parks, but nobody called her Ms. Parks, and certainly nobody called her Anna. To her face, agents addressed her as "Chief." When she was not in the room, she was called "Carrot" or "*The Carrot*."

Her nickname was not because she had red hair, but because carrots were the only thing anyone at the agency had ever seen her eat. She was also an exercise fanatic. Therefore, she physically resembled a carrot as well, with a thin, bird-like frame topped with a head that appeared too large for her body and an even larger nest of curly, dirty blonde hair that shot out in every direction, as if she'd been recently electrocuted.

"What a mess."

She tossed aside the initial reports. The Carrot did not like messes, and for that reason she did not like me. Messes seemed to follow me wherever I went.

The Carrot shook her head. "How the hell did a live gun get into a federal courthouse?"

I felt myself shrink under her harsh gaze. "It was evidence,"

I said softly. "The gun that Judge Griggs used to kill himself was the gun we retrieved during Marsh's arrest."

Her lips puckered and face tightened, considering this information. Then the Carrot's eyes narrowed. "So, what you're really telling me is that the firearm wasn't disabled?"

"It was disabled." The response came quick, a little too fast and sharp.

Doubts crept into my head. *Had I really checked it?* It was hard to imagine the gun wasn't disabled. It was standard protocol. Perhaps I just wanted the gun to be disabled, so my memory had made it so.

Matthews sensed the trouble, and he stepped in before I said something stupid or agreed I'd made a mistake, when I hadn't. He was a veteran agent, and therefore had more credibility with the Chief.

"The gun lock was on the whole time. It was all standard—fourteen-inch cable running through the open slide and down through the magazine— there's no way it could've been fired. If you want me to dig up the pictures of it, I will, but I can assure you when the gun entered the courthouse, it was disabled."

The Carrot folded her thin arms across her chest. He'd softened her, but she remained unimpressed. "But Agent Matthews, obviously it wasn't entirely disabled because—"

"Because Judge Griggs removed the lock," Matthews said.

"And how did he get the key?"

When Matthews didn't have an immediate response, I rejoined the conversation like a kid hoping to disrupt an argument between Mom and Dad. "There wasn't a key," I said. "It was a combination lock. Somebody must've given him the combination, or he just knew it."

The Carrot stared at me as if I had just said something insane. "And how exactly would a federal judge know the combination to our lock?"

"Because all of our gun locks have the same combination: three-one-four," I said.

"So, you're telling me the most sophisticated combination the Federal Bureau of Investigation can come up with is the telephone area code for the City of St. Louis?"

"I was told that's how it's always been." I shrugged. "Easy to remember."

The Carrot emitted a grunt, like she'd just been punched in the gut. Then she looked at Matthews. "What do you think?"

"I think Wirth was smart to keep that last part out of the initial report. And we should make damn sure it stays out of any future reports."

The Carrot nodded, but it was obvious she wasn't completely buying Matthews's attempts to build me up. She didn't believe I was savvy enough to keep that information out of my initial report, and if that was what the Carrot was thinking, she'd be right. I wasn't that savvy or aware of the political ramifications.

Matthews continued. "If anybody asks, you can say 'the investigation is ongoing' or 'we need to talk to the family first.' That should keep the reporters at a distance for now. In a few days, it'll be forgotten. If it's not, then just tell everybody there's a confidential internal review of our procedures, or something like that. Most people don't even know we have gun safety protocols."

"The judges know....and they aren't going to forget. And the U.S. Marshals would love to hang us out to dry on this." The room settled into an awkward silence as the Carrot formulated defenses and strategies in her head. Eventually, she said, "The truth is that it doesn't matter. If a person really wants to kill themself, they'll find a way... but I can't say that." The Carrot jotted down some notes on a legal pad, then looked at Matthews. "Because it's a federal judge doing it in a federal courthouse, we'll claim primary jurisdiction. Keep the marshals and local cops out. You two will be assigned, because I want to limit the number of people involved. I don't see a need to devote much, if any, further resources to it. Wait a few weeks, file a final report, and close it out."

The Carrot then turned in her chair to the computer behind her. With her back to us, the Carrot began to scroll through her emails and peck out a few responses. The meeting, evidently, was over.

Taking the hint, Matthews stood, but I wasn't done. "So, just to clarify, you don't want any further investigation?"

In my periphery, I saw Matthews's eyes widen, mystified as to why I had reengaged.

The Carrot's shoulders slumped. Then, without turning to face us, she gave her directive in a clipped, monotone voice, "You are to conduct a thorough and professional investigation, Agent Wirth...I hope that is clear. That is always my expectation."

"Yes, Chief."

Then the Carrot continued, now weighing her words carefully. "I do, however, understand if nothing surprising comes of your investigation. We must always balance how to expend our limited resources, given our heavy caseload. So, as always, I leave it to *your* discretion." The Carrot then dismissed me with a flick of her hand.

This time, I said nothing. If I had attempted to speak, Matthews likely would've put his hand over my mouth and dragged me away.

We walked in silence back to our shared office. However, once inside, and with the door closed, Matthews made his displeasure known.

"You didn't have to do that."

"Do what?"

"You know what," Matthews said. "You didn't have to ask the Carrot for clarification."

"That's exactly why I did it." I put my hands on my hips, conjuring a little self-righteous indignation of my own. "Whenever there's something that doesn't feel right, it's our job to follow the trail, and this doesn't feel right."

"Hey," Matthews held out his hands in surrender. "Save it. You don't have to lecture me on that."

"I know." I backed down quickly. Matthews was the last person who needed a lecture from me. "It's just the politics of it all." I sat down in the chair across from him. "One of my buttons, you know? Whenever somebody tries to tell me how or who to investigate, it gets my back up. I can't get my dad's voice out of my head. 'Real cops follow the case, lazy cops close 'em.'"

"Optics, not politics," Matthews said. "The Carrot isn't worried about politics. She's worried about whether or not she's going to be embarrassed, and about whether the bureau is going to lose credibility. That's why you scare her so much. She doesn't think you understand that."

"What about you? Do you think I don't understand that?"

"Is that a trick question?" Matthews smiled. "You know I think you've got great instincts, Wirth, better than most, but maybe you should start thinking for yourself instead of thinking about what your dad would or would not do. You gotta pick your battles to survive in this place."

"And Judge Griggs isn't a fight you want to pick?"

Matthews considered this. "Not really, no."

"Because you don't think anything is there?"

"I didn't say that," Matthews said. "A federal judge doesn't just shoot himself in the head because he's having a bad day, not in the way he did it. That was a statement of some sort. He didn't need to use that particular gun. This is Missouri, could've gotten a gun anywhere. He also didn't need to do it at the courthouse, and he certainly didn't need to do it during work hours, as opposed to in the evening, when there were less people around...all of those were choices he made." Matthews leaned back, then conceded the point. "It raises red flags for me, too."

"But you're okay walking away?"

"I'm not walking away. I just don't think it's worth investing a lot of time in it, because the one person who can tell you why, for certain, is dead, and anybody else who knows anything isn't likely to talk."

"So, you're saying the Carrot was right about that. Clean it up and close it out in a few weeks."

"Unfortunately," Matthews said, resigned. "The Carrot is often right about stuff like that, which is how she got to where she is, and why it won't be too long before she's in Washington, D.C., with the big dogs. Rumor has it the President really wants a woman to run the FBI."

"It still doesn't seem right, letting it go."

Matthews's eyes softened, and his tone did the same. "Go home. Get some rest," he said. "I'll open the lines of communication with the court administrator and medical examiner. That's basic stuff the Carrot can't get too upset about, and then we'll go from there. We'll take it a step at a time."

I said, "We need to talk to the wife." It came out too sharp, something that had been happening a lot lately. When I saw Matthews wince, I hated myself for being unable to control the crap that sometimes came out of my mouth.

Matthews, still kind, humored me. "Fine, but that can wait until tomorrow morning. I mean it, go home and get some sleep. We'll go see the wife first thing."

3

———

My apartment was above one of the many antique shops that lined Cherokee Street, on the city's south side. It wasn't the nicest apartment in St. Louis, but it certainly wasn't the worst. The owner of the one hundred and twenty year-old building lived just a few blocks away. He was a friendly guy, responsive whenever anything broke, which was often, and kept the rent affordable.

The apartment's best feature was a little balcony off the back. It overlooked a garden the antique shop had filled with birdbaths, eclectic sculptures, and architectural remnants of the many old houses and buildings that had been torn down throughout the city. On the far side of the garden was a small, neglected shack made of stone. It looked like something out of a Hans Christian Andersen fairy tale.

I'd strung some white twinkle lights along the railing and outfitted the space with a small, wooden table and chair. It was where I liked to have coffee in the morning and a glass of wine at night. It was quiet, and as I sat on my perch above the garden, I often felt like I was overseeing the excavation of some strange archeological site in the distant future, imagining myself as an anthropologist struggling to decipher what I'd found, and what it revealed about the values of a once powerful, fallen civilization.

I'd then be standing in front of a virtual lecture hall filled with eager students from around the world. Behind me, a holographic picture of the courtyard would be displayed. "As near as I can surmise," I'd say with a British accent, of course, because people---even in the future---who spoke with a British accent always sounded far more intelligent than a cop's daughter from Missouri, "I believe there were a series of massive earthquakes or other natural disasters in places like Detroit, St. Louis, Cleveland, Flint, and Youngstown, which occurred in the mid to late twentieth century. What else could explain such devastation? What else would cause so much debris in these cities, which had, up until that point, given every other indication of prosperity?"

This night, however, I was not a professor opining to eager students in a lecture hall. I was an exhausted daughter trying to listen with patience as my mother talked in circles.

"He's fine," she said.

"So you don't want me to come down there?" I held the phone closer to my ear.

"You are always welcome, sweetie, but maybe this is not the best time." It was a very Midwestern way of telling me to mind my own business.

She then attempted to explain the doctor's prognosis from that morning's appointment, but my father kept yelling, interrupting her. The back and forth between my parents made the whole conversation incomprehensible.

There was beeping in the background, and then the sound of another voice. "Where are you?" I asked.

My mother began to answer, but then her voice trailed and whatever she said was muffled.

"So do you want me to come down or not?"

"Well, I think under the circumstances, coming down would be—"

My father, Jack Wirth, yelled in the background, "No, tell her no." His voice sounded like the engine of a muscle car, deepened from his years of cigarettes and playing the blues in smokey bars.

"Why don't you just give the phone to Dad?" I said. "Let me talk to Dad."

"Fine." There was a long pause.

The transition was filled with grunts, more growls, and side comments. Then my father had the phone. "You're not coming down here. It's stupid. It's not a big deal. The cost of a plane ticket is outrageous, and you've got a lot going on."

"I can get time off work."

"You're still in the two-year probationary period, and you need to start out strong, show them you appreciate the opportunity."

"I know, Dad."

"Do you? Because I didn't take one single day of vacation for seven years when I first got the badge, and that cemented my reputation for the rest of my time on the force," he said, "and having that reputation meant I got the benefit of the doubt when things went sideways - and things inevitably go sideways, Tiger. You know that better than most, I—"

"But this next appointment sounds—"

He interrupted, "There is no next appointment."

"Mom had said you have an important appointment in a couple days, but she hasn't really told me what it was all about."

Her father forced a laugh. "Your mother gets confused sometimes. Her heart is in the right place, but you need to just let me handle it. Everything is under control."

"It doesn't seem like it's under control," I said. "I want to be there and hear what the doctor says, not get everything secondhand."

"You don't trust what I'm saying? I tell the truth. The truth is all you got in this world. That's the North Star, kiddo. Follow it..."

"Wherever it leads," Wirth finished her father's sentence. "Follow it wherever it leads." She'd heard that, as well as so many other Jack-isms, she could publish a book. "I got it, Dad. It's just...your life. I love you, and I want to know exactly what's going on. I want to be able to ask the doctor questions, and I don't think you're getting all the information you need to make---"

He cut me off again. "I'm doing everything I can." My father sounded more tired now. "And I am saying to you—very seriously—that you should wait." He took a deep breath. "Listen, Tiger, don't go burning up your sick leave on this. Your mother and I just have a little disagreement over what comes next, that's all. I'll see you soon. I promise you that."

That promise seemed like an attempt simply to placate me, and it worked, because I wanted it to work. I was exhausted after everything that had happened that day, and I backed off, even though, in hindsight, I shouldn't have. Deep down, I knew I was making a mistake, but I didn't have the energy to keep arguing with him.

"Fine," I said, "but I want a full report."

"And you'll get one," my father said, which turned out to be one of many lies he told me that night.

I hung up the phone and set it down on the little wooden table next to me. I then sat on the balcony for a long time, listening to the sounds of the city and working through a bottle of wine, one glass at a time. When I'd finished it off, I went back inside and sat on my sofa with my cat, Mister Bones.

I scrolled through various websites on my laptop as he nestled next to me. The national news was dominated by a gigantic ice shelf in Antarctica that was melting faster than previously believed. With Congress in recess and the President on vacation in Hawaii, the "Doomsday Glacier" was getting a lot of coverage. There were a lot of people arguing about what it meant for sea levels, the jet stream, and the survival of the planet. There was no mention of Judge Griggs, but the local websites were different.

His suicide was much more prominent. Nearly every story featured video of and quotes from Colton Steele, describing the chaos and how he bravely escorted court staff and members of the public to safety. He was the hero of the day.

My name wasn't mentioned, which was infuriating, but probably for the best. I was still a new kid at the bureau, and I understood all too well headlines often resulted in resentment, and even harassment, from more experienced colleagues.

In my head, I heard my father say, "Be careful not to be the tallest flower in the garden, Tiger. It's dangerous, because the tallest flower is the first to get picked off." It was a classic Jack-ism yet, another pearl of wisdom from the big man.

I clicked a button on the browser, and my bookmarks appeared. At the top of the list was the link for "Full House Poker." I hesitated for a moment, thinking about whether it was really a good time to play. I was in the hole for over $600, and if I wanted to get back to even, I'd need to be mentally sharp - and I was definitely not sharp. After drinking a full bottle of wine, I was numb and drunk, but I logged on, anyway and started playing.

This does not make sense, but nothing about my behavior and decisions during this time were logical. One would think that after not sleeping well, if at all, in the days leading up to my testimony and everything that had happened at the court-house, I'd crash the moment my head touched the pillow, but that wasn't correct. There were things that came to visit me in the dark. They didn't haunt me every night, but surely they would come that night. In fact, I knew they would. They always came when I was low, and I was feeling quite low that night.

So, I played poker for as long as I could to keep these unwanted visitors away, but they came as I knew they would.

The beginning of my hauntings were often different. Locations, people, time of day, and the activity varied when the dreams began. Even the mood was different, the intensity. Often they began with something fun, like a fancy dinner party, dance, or swimming down in the Ozarks. It would then darken, and there'd be a gun fired in the darkness, a burst of light, and a stab of pain.

Sometimes I woke up at that point, but not this time. I was down on the cold ground. A bearded man held me, mumbling prayers with a slight Irish lilt. It was a person Gray and I had come to call the Irish Santa. He was protecting me as the men began to crowd.

This was another point in the sequence when I'd often wake up, but not this time. It was different that night. I was pinned, unable to break away from some invisible bonds that prevented me from moving or raising my arms in defense. The crowd laughed at me. Some grabbed their crotches, taunting and making crude remarks.

Then he came for me, speaking different languages, ancient languages. I didn't understand, but I was afraid. It ebbed and flowed. I am tortured and I witness others who are tortured as well, stripped of their skin. These were people I love, but I could do nothing to protect them.

Then the man leaned over me. His face was obscured as the others urged him to continue. I didn't understand the old tongues, but I knew they all wanted him to "do it." That much was clear. They were thirsty for a feast. He put his hand on my breast and stomach, then pushed hard. I couldn't breathe, and the walls of the cave turned crimson, painted with thousands of handprints circling up to heaven, and still I couldn't breathe.

4

———

That's when I woke up. It was as if a bucket of water had been poured onto me. My pajamas were soaked through. I was cold and clammy. My hair was twisted into a tangle. It was a quarter to eight. I'd overslept but felt as though I hadn't slept at all.

I picked up my phone, texted Matthews, and stumbled out of bed. In the bathroom, I shoved six different pills into my mouth, then looked back at the various articles of clothing covering my bedroom floor.

Which ones were the least dirty?

Forty minutes later, I'm at a Waffle House in Saint Charles. Matthews, of course, had already arrived when I pulled into the parking lot. He was in a booth, sipping coffee and admiring what he called "the Waffle House Vista." Regardless of where we were in Missouri or southern Illinois, the vista's components remained the same: a parking lot comprised of crumbling pavement with weeds rising through the cracks, a highway of some variety, a gas station nearby with diesel and showers, and a couple semi-trucks delivering crap that would likely end up on a shelf at Wal-Mart or a Dollar General within a day or two.

There were certainly better places to eat breakfast, but Matthews liked the vista and loved Waffle House coffee for some reason. This one happened to be close to where Matthews lived, and Judge Griggs's house was just another ten miles to the west.

The plan was to meet, assign roles, and identify priorities for the interview, then hopefully be back in the city with enough time for one of us to talk with the court administrator.

"Good morning." I slid into the booth, and the old plastic cushion squeaked and farted beneath me.

"You're late, again."

I glanced at my watch and attempted to play it off. "I could accuse you of being early, or I could blame traffic," I said. "Whatever excuse works better for you...I'm always open to suggestions."

The edge of Matthews's mouth curled into a tight smile. Then kindly, like a big brother, he said, "You don't look like you slept at all, and it seems to be a recurring look."

"I don't like this new drug Dr. Dan has been prescribing me," I said.

"How new?"

"I don't know. A week or so, maybe a month."

The whole thing was a lie, but a good one. I'd much rather blame the medication than admit how much alcohol I was drinking, and how much time I spent gambling money I didn't have on the Internet.

"Well, this has been going on for longer than a month. I say this just in case you're wondering when I started to notice. Are you talking to your doctor about it?"

In my head, I cycled through various responses that ranged from sincere to witty, but instead I nodded, signaled to the waitress for coffee, and changed the subject. "Anything interesting from the techs?"

Matthews was kind enough to follow my lead. He was a good guy, and he wasn't going to push, at least not after what had happened the day before.

"It's more like what they didn't find," he said, "no suicide note, which is odd, but they did find a five million-dollar life insurance policy in the desk drawer."

"Maybe that was his note."

The waitress arrived with a thick ceramic mug filled with coffee and set it down in front of me. She asked, "You ready to order?" while removing a pencil from behind her ear.

I said, "Two eggs, two cakes, and bacon."

To the waitress, Matthews said, "Biscuits and gravy." To me, he said, "Don't tell my wife."

I returned with a dutiful nod of the head, as I always did when Matthews wanted to conceal his poor dietary choices from his better half. Then we waited as the waitress scribbled it all down and walked back to the kitchen before continuing our discussion.

"Here's the interesting thing about this insurance policy," Matthews said, "It was taken out a little over a year ago, almost to the day, meaning the suicide clause had just expired."

"I thought those were two years?"

"Two is more standard," Matthews said, "but some are one, really depends."

"So, you think Judge Griggs was planning to commit suicide for over a year and was just waiting for a policy clause to expire?"

"Probably one of the few people who actually read his policy," Matthews said. "He was a judge after all."

"It seems...I don't know, like, very methodical."

I thought about my own darkness, what it was like to feel alone in a crowded room, and lately there hadn't even been many crowded rooms. I had no family in the area, no boyfriend, and not really any friends of any kind except for Gray, and I didn't think we were friends anymore. My fault, not his.

I watched as a tanker truck arrived at the gas station on the other side of the road. A man in coveralls lifted a round iron plate in the cement, then shoved a white tube into the hole.

"Amy." Matthews snapped his fingers, bringing me back to the present. "Earth to Amy."

"Sorry, I was just thinking." I picked up my mug of coffee and took a sip, grimacing at its bitterness. "How can you like this stuff?" I put down the mug.

"It cleans you out," Mathews said. "Makes you run smooth all day, like flushing a radiator."

"It tastes like it was ground between the butt cheeks of German trolls."

"That's oddly specific." Matthews laughed. "Now stop messing around and tell me what you're thinking."

"He could've just been depressed, but another alternative was that something else happened a year ago, something that scared him, and he wanted a way out."

"Possibly." Matthews nodded as the waitress approached with our plates of food. "I guess we'll know more when we talk with his wife."

———

THE JUDGE'S house was just off Highway C. It was once farmland and had now been subdivided into twenty-acre lots where rich people could pretend to be farmers. We pulled onto a crushed rock driveway. Matthews drove up toward the house, which was tucked a quarter of a mile back.

There were four vehicles parked off to the side near a pole barn and two women on a porch swing. Each had the same profile, similar posture. One was middle-aged, and one was older. I figured it was the judge's wife and her mother.

We'd decided over breakfast I'd take the lead, not knowing exactly how Christine Griggs would react to personal questions from a black, male FBI agent. There was no reason to assume she'd have a problem with Matthews, but we also knew people were more likely to open up to others who looked like them, something deep within our reptilian brains.

"Mrs. Griggs?" I stepped onto the porch first. "Sorry to disturb you, but I believe one of our colleagues let you know we'd be stopping by this morning."

The younger woman nodded, then looked at the older one. "It's okay, Mom," Christine said. "I'll be okay."

Her mother rose. She touched Christine's shoulder, gave it a squeeze, then disappeared into the house. Then Christine Griggs gestured toward the two empty chairs opposite the porch swing.

"Have a seat. We should get it over with."

I thanked her, and as we settled in, I formally introduced myself, then Matthews. I complimented her on the house and commented on the beauty of the land. It was hard to believe we were less than an hour from downtown St. Louis. As the small talk ran its course, Matthews sensed the end and discreetly removed a small notebook from his pocket, along with a pen.

The interview then began in earnest. I started with basic biographical information. They were easy questions, intended to make her feel more at ease. With each one, however, Christine Griggs did not become more relaxed. Her eyes narrowed, and the tiny lines on her face became harder as her grip tightened on her cup of tea. It was as if she was bracing herself for impact.

She was a pretty woman, which was a combination of effort and money. She had the physique of a distance runner, probably yoga a couple times a week as well. Her teeth were whitened, hair highlighted, and eyebrows plucked. On her finger was a diamond ring with a stone that could likely be seen from outer space.

After asking where she'd first met the judge, I was about to go on to the next question when Christine Griggs held up her hand, then said in a whisper, "Can you just get to the point?"

"The point?" I responded.

Sadness welled up in Christine Griggs's eyes, but there was also anger. "Obviously, David killed himself, and you want to know why he did it. The answer to that question is, I have no idea." She gestured to the expensive house, manicured front yard, and expensive cars. "What possible reason would he have to kill himself? He had everything. *We* had everything."

"I'm sorry for the intrusion, ma'am. I'm just---"

"Just doing your job." A tear escaped and ran down her cheek. Christine Griggs wiped it away. "And you want to know if I was surprised, and the answer to that question is yes. I'm in shock...why he'd do this to himself or me or our children. I have no clue."

She blinked, and more tears escaped, but this time she made no effort to wipe them away. Her stare instead drifted over to Matthews. She looked at the notebook in his hand, open and a page half-filled with writing, then bowed her head and cried openly.

I waited, letting her have the time, and eventually the crying slowed. Christine Griggs gathered herself, then asked, "Are we done?"

I said, "We have a few more questions, but we can come back."

"No, let's do this." She sniffled and wiped her nose. "I frankly don't ever want to see you again," a beat, then, "no offense."

"We understand." I looked at Matthews. He nodded, so I

continued. "Based on what you just told us, there was no note and no warning?"

"Nothing obvious." She sighed. "He has...or had, I guess, a stressful job. It's a lot of pressure, more than people realize. Pressure to clear cases within a certain number of days, pressure to settle cases, and pressure to do the right thing while also getting it legally right...a lot of pressure. He'd often joke he was the 'village executioner' and a little piece of his soul disappeared every day he put on the robe. His humanity was being stripped away every time he sent another human being into a concrete box."

"Was he seeing a therapist or taking any medication for depression or anxiety?"

"No, but he was certainly counting the days until retirement. There was no way he was going to be one of those judges who works for the rest of their lives. He was always checking our retirement accounts, looking at places in Panama and Asia...I think he would've retired tomorrow if I said it was okay, but we're not that old, and I didn't want to move. I love it here, but if I'd have known he was this unhappy...of course, he could've quit, and we would've figured it out."

"Had anybody threatened him? Did he gamble or have large debts?"

"He didn't gamble, and he had no debts. He hated debt."

I made a mental note that Christine Griggs had not answered the question about threats but moved on. I decided that would be something I'd talk about with Matthews later.

"Did you know he took out a life insurance policy about a year ago?"

"He did what?" Outwardly, nothing had changed, but it was obvious she was thinking about her answer, calculating. Then Christine said, "Maybe he mentioned it." She glanced down and away. "Maybe...I don't know for sure."

I looked over at Matthews. He gave a slight nod, agreeing to one more push. So, I pushed.

"A year ago, something happened, correct?"

Christine didn't answer. It was in the way the question was phrased that seemed to give her pause, a suggestion I knew something did, in fact, happen a year ago and it would be a mistake for her to lie. She bought herself a little more time with a question of her own.

"A year ago?"

"That's when the insurance policy was taken out, and I believe there was an event, a catalyst that happened. Correct?"

Christine set her cup to the side and leaned back, thinking, or at least pretending to think. Then, "Nothing specific comes to mind...our daughter was in an accident, a car accident. Maybe that had something to do with it?"

"A bad accident?"

"The car was totaled. She had a broken nose from the airbag, cracked rib," Christine said, then added, "that's the only thing I can think of. Things like that happen, makes you reevaluate. Maybe he thought, *What would happen if I was in a car accident or something?* I really don't know. He took care of the money, not me."

Then Christine Griggs stood. The interview was over, regardless of whether or not I wanted to ask her more questions.

———

BECAUSE I HAD STOPPED along the way for real coffee and a snack, Matthews got back to the FBI bureau station first. He was already at his desk when I walked through the door. Matthews was working on turning his handwritten notes of our conversation with Christine Griggs into a formal report for the file.

"What did you get for me?" he asked without looking up from his computer screen. His fingers continued to *click* and *clack* on the keyboard.

"Oat milk latte for me, and I demanded the darkest, oldest, most burnt-tasting coffee they had for you, no cream."

"Sounds delicious."

Matthews flipped a page on his notepad and continued typing, while I walked over to my side of the office. Our two desks were pressed against one another in the middle of the small room. Whiteboards and bulletin boards hung on the back wall, with a narrow table below and a couple filing cabinets.

Each side was a mirror image of the other, except my side was cluttered. Paper was strewn across the top of my desk. A half-dozen, square, sticky notes adorned the edges of my computer screen, and my file cabinet was so stuffed, it did not fully close. Matthews's side of the office was spotless. If he hadn't actually been there, a visitor would likely assume his half was unoccupied.

The office was like a physical manifestation of our different styles and approach. Probably our partnership's greatest strength, a tension that often drew out the best, but I often wondered how long it could last. Two people couldn't pull in opposite directions forever. Eventually, the rubber band snapped.

I watched and waited as Matthews saved his report and finally looked at me, signaling he was ready to talk. He'd worked cases for over twenty years, a veteran law enforcement officer. Although we had the same title, Charlie Matthews was, without question, the lead agent in this partnership.

He asked, "So, where are we at?"

I'd been thinking about how to answer that question the entire drive back to the city. "I want the autopsy report, phone records, credit card records, and bank statements." When I saw

Matthews open his mouth to question, I held up my hand. "I know. It probably won't amount to anything, but it feels wrong to just close it. We owe it to them to take a good look."

"Who's *them*?" Matthews asked. "The Carrot wants this turned around quickly. The judge's wife wants the case closed, sooner rather than later, and as for me..." He pointed at the stack of files on his desk. "These are just some of the referrals I've gotten in this morning." Matthews ran his thumb along the edges of the folders. "Must be six new ones, in addition to forty or fifty more that came in over the past three weeks, and I know my voicemail box is full of prosecutors wanting a status update on almost every single one."

I'd anticipated this argument, and I was ready with a snappy response. "But do any of those cases involve the death of a federal district court judge?"

"Maybe not," Matthews said, "but there are certainly high-profile cases in our stack, and unlike Griggs, these have actual evidence of a crime." He folded his arms across his chest. "This was just a suicide, Amy. It's tragic, but not a crime."

"Until we know what was going on in the background, we can't say that for sure. I agree it was a suicide, but there's something else, too."

By the look on his face, I could tell Matthews's frustration was growing, but he wasn't somebody who yelled. Instead, he laid out the facts, which I had to appreciate.

"Amy, come on," he said. "You know regardless of what you discover about his background, or his family's background, all we have is a suicide at the end of the day."

"What if he was being blackmailed? Extorted?"

Matthews closed his eyes, then shifted tactics. "I'm going to call these prosecutors back and tell them to call you directly. I'll tell them you can answer all their questions. I've been shielding you from some of this, but I think you have to learn that our most valuable resource is our time, and it doesn't seem like you recognize that. Every minute we spend on one case is a minute we don't spend on another."

"Now you sound like the Carrot."

"I don't care," Matthews said. "I've worked for worse bureau chiefs than her."

"But if we peel back the layers of the onion just a little," I said, "it may uncover something else...I don't know what, but we won't ever know if we don't—"

"And while you're 'peeling onions,'" Matthew said, "our stack grows. The trail will get cold on these other cases, witnesses will disappear, memories will get foggy and faded." Matthews picked up the cup of coffee I'd brought for him and took a sip. "The prosecutors annoy the hell out of me - and so does the Carrot, don't misunderstand - but they have every reason to want us to move on these. Criminal cases are not wine; they don't get better with age."

"I know that." I was about to continue to protest, but my cell phone rang. I looked down at the screen, and it was my mother. To Matthews, "I better get this." Then I got up, walked out of our office, and into the hallway. "What's going on, Mom? Is Dad okay?"

"He won't listen to me." She was crying, and I thought to myself, *How many people have I seen or heard crying in the last forty-eight hours, including myself?* "He left. I don't know where he is."

"What do you mean, you don't know where he is?"

"He's very sick, and he won't listen to me or the doctors. You have to talk to him. You need to call him and tell him to go back to the hospital."

"Mom, I'm in the middle of a meeting right now...wait, hospital?"

"Yes, he's been in the hospital." The pitch of her voice grew higher, panicked. "You need to call him. He won't take my calls.

This can't wait. He's going to die, Amy. He needs to get back to the hospital right away."

"Die? I thought these were just a few tests?" This didn't make any sense. "What are you talking about, Mom? Where is he?"

"I told you. I don't know. We got into another argument, and I left. I needed a break, and when I got back to his room, he was gone. I don't know where he went, and he won't—"

Two beeps. "Hold on, Mom." I looked at the screen and saw the Caller ID. "It's him on the other line. I'm going to talk to Dad now, then I'll call you back." I disconnected from my mother, and the line clicked over.

"Amy, this is your dad." There was a lot of background noise, people talking, and somebody making announcements over an intercom system.

"Mom is panicked. Where are you right now?"

He didn't answer my question. "Consider this a peremptory strike," my father said. His voice was soft and weak. "I don't know what your mom has been telling you, but I don't want you getting all riled up. She's always been very dramatic, and she's been a little funny in the head lately."

"Dad, I'm not riled up. I'm just concerned and confused. Mom says you left the hospital and the doctor wants you back. I didn't even know you were in the hospital."

"Well, I'm not going back, and I'm not going to die in a hospital." The background noise escalated. There was a series of bells, then more announcements. "We can talk about this some more in a few hours. My plane is boarding."

"What do you mean your plane is boarding?"

"I'm in the Charlotte airport. It's the connecting flight, and I'll be arriving in about two and half hours."

"Here?"

"Yes, check your email," my father said. "I sent you the flight information, and I'll see you at the airport when I arrive."

"Dad, if you're that sick, you shouldn't be flying anywhere. You should—"

"I have to use my time wisely, Tiger," he said. "And it can't be in a hospital bed. I've got a few things to set right."

"What do you need to set right?" I asked, but my father didn't answer. He had already disconnected.

5

———

I waited near the baggage carousels at the St. Louis International Airport. Once a hub, the number and size of the planes coming in and out had decreased as various airlines merged in the 1980s and 1990s, but it was still busy. I found a bench and watched as people emerged from a long corridor.

It'd been close to a year since I'd seen my dad. Attempts at video chatting during the pandemic were always politely declined, and I knew better than to push it. Such attempts would not work. My father was stubborn, and he considered it his best trait. The higher the frustration, the more he dug himself in.

The electronic signs indicated the flight from Charlotte had landed, and I watched as people slowly began to gather around the carousel where luggage from his flight was supposed to be delivered. I checked my phone, but there were no calls or texts. I began to wonder. Perhaps my father had changed his mind.

A blue light flashed, accompanied by the sound of a buzzer, warning people the metal carousel was about to turn. A single suitcase coasted down the slide. There was a pause, then another. Soon, the bags began arriving in earnest.

I looked down the corridor and still didn't see my father. Then I looked at the growing number of people at the carousel and didn't see him there either. Just in case he may have snuck past me, I got up and walked through the crowd. I didn't find him. I stepped back, pulled out my phone, and called him, but my father didn't answer.

The bags kept coming. People yanked them off the carousel and went on their way. I remained, still looking for my father. I called him again, but there was still no answer. So, I called my mother instead. She answered on the first ring.

Without preamble, she asked, "Is everything okay?"

"Not really," I said. "His flight landed about twenty minutes ago, and I don't see him anywhere. I've called, and I get no answer. How about you?"

"All I know is that he said he was flying up." My mother's voice cracked. "That's all I know...he's very sick, dear. You must understand that."

"Okay." I hung up the phone, and that's when I saw a TSA agent standing near an information desk in the distance. I thought maybe he could help.

The agent was about fifty yards away. I walked toward him, then out of the corner of my eye I saw a small old man. He was coming out of the corridor, moving slowly with a cane.

Wrong guy, I thought and continued walking toward the agent by the information desk. Then I stopped and looked again.

I now recognized the black fedora hat, but the rest was all wrong. My father, Jack Wirth, was a giant of a man. He was six-foot-three and easily 240 pounds. His snakeskin cowboy boots tacked on another two inches. He towered over people. He had presence. Everybody knew Jack, and if they hadn't noticed him when he entered a room, they certainly noticed him when he let loose his deep, booming laugh, which was often.

This little old man, I thought, was an imposter. A con artist who had stolen my father's signature fedora. The man walking toward me looked as if he could be blown away the moment he left the building. His clothes, all of which hung off him like bed sheets, looked as if they could catch a strong wind and carry him away like a kite.

But he kept coming toward me. His eyes were sunk deep. His skin was paper thin, creased in a hundred ways. Now just six feet away, his mouth opened.

"Well, don't just stand there." He pointed his cane at the carousel, no longer crowded with people. "Go grab my bag, and let's go get a beer."

———

AT MY FATHER'S INSISTENCE, we stopped at The Royal Bar, off Kingshighway, a street name that lost its apostrophe and space sometime in the early 1900s and never got it back. In front were probably fifteen Harley Davidson motorcycles, and the parking lot was also filled with half a dozen classic muscle cars. Some had the hoods open, with owners nearby hanging out, smoking, and talking about what they'd done to bring these vehicles back to life.

My father, however, didn't choose the Royal because of motorcycles or muscle cars. The Royal was one of the places he would go for open mic night on Wednesdays, prior to retiring down to Florida. He wanted to see the place again, and if what my mother said was true, it'd be his last time.

Inside, the bar wasn't too crowded. We found a table in the corner. From there, my father could see the stage and hear the music, but we'd also be able to have a conversation.

"Let me get our drinks," I said. "You stay here."

My father didn't complain about me serving him. He looked exhausted, too tired to protest, but at least he had a smile on his face. I went up to the bar. I handed the bartender my credit card and ordered two Buds.

"I don't want to open a tab." I looked back, checking on my dad. "Hopefully, this'll be quick."

Upon returning to the table, I put one of the pint glasses in front of him, and he greedily took a sip. I sat down and did the same. After a minute or two, I leaned in close.

"You want to tell me why you're here, and not in a hospital down in Florida?"

"Unfinished business," he said.

"Revenge?"

I meant it as a joke, but my father didn't laugh. He worked it over, tumbling it around in his head until he was finally ready to spit out an answer. It was just one word.

"Maybe."

He took another drink, and when he was done, my father closed his eyes and took a deep breath, savoring one of the cheapest beers on tap as if it was made by craftsmen in tiny batches. His eyes were closed for so long, I thought he may have fallen asleep.

Then he whispered, "Follow the case wherever it goes...I didn't do that with this one." It was more to himself than to me.

"Dad," I put my hand on his arm, "I don't think you're in any condition to be solving cold cases right now."

His eyes opened, and he looked at me with a hard stare. "Well, that's exactly what I'm doing. You're supposed to live life with no regrets, right? Well, I regret this. I regret everything about it."

"You're sick, Dad. You need to rest. You need to get treatment. I'm putting you on the first plane back to Florida tomorrow. You need to be with Mom."

He grunted and looked away in disgust. "You can't do that. I may be old, but I still have my mind, and I have work to do."

There was no way I was going to let him win that easily, but I decided a tactical retreat was my best option. I'd get my dad comfortable and let him lower his guard. Then I'd either come back stronger that night or the next day, after we'd had a decent night's sleep.

"So what's this case?"

"I can't talk about it with you," he said.

"You're being ridiculous." I took away my hand, irritation growing. "I can't believe there's an old case you'd...." I stopped myself, but my father continued for me.

"...spend my dying days chasing? Is that what you were going to say?"

He was right, but I said nothing.

"I supposedly lived by a code," my father said. "I certainly told everybody I did...be fearless." His shoulders slumped, and when he looked at me, he showed me contrition for the first time in his life. "But the truth is, I was afraid of this one, Tiger. What it'd do to me and everybody I loved. It scared me. Walking away from it has been my biggest regret. That's why I'm back."

He said nothing more.

———

WHILE MY FATHER slept in my bed, I lay on the sofa, waiting for the drugs to hit. The length of time varied, but usually the sleeping pills took no more than twenty minutes. I checked my watch, and it had already been thirty. Still no sleep.

Mister Bones sat on top of the recliner, finding my behavior quite peculiar. After dark, this area of the apartment was usually his domain, and as the cat watched me roll from one side to the other, it was clear he was not happy about my presence.

I looked at the cat and said, "It's just for one night."

Mister Bones would hear none of it. He stretched, making sure to dig his claws deep into the top of a chair's already fraying fabric, then jumped down. He trotted away, in search of privacy, his nose held high in disgust.

This left me alone. I tried the various relaxation techniques that had been recommended by Dr. Dan during our many sessions. None of them worked. As hard as I tried to clear my mind, thoughts about my father would only disappear for a second before returning.

I worried about whether he was suffering from dementia in addition to cancer. Dementia could explain his sudden obsession with an old case, and I wondered whether such a case even existed. I wondered whether he was even safe with me for one night. Perhaps he'd wander off.

Had I locked the doors? What if he tried to crawl out a window?

Until I'd seen him, I had no idea how far the cancer had progressed.

There was so much I didn't know. He and my mother had talked about treatment, but I never asked about the details. I figured it was once or twice a week at the hospital, for an hour. Now I wondered whether it was daily, perhaps he needed 24-hour nursing care. I knew nothing.

I realized I had been in denial. That's why I didn't visit them in Florida. That's why I didn't demand my mother tell me all the details.

Did he even have a will or a health care directive?

I didn't know that either. Until I saw my father walk into the baggage claim area with the assistance of a cane, I thought he was immortal. My father was larger than life, a superhero. He'd won more commendations as a cop than anyone else in the history of the St. Louis Police Department. Everybody knew him, either personally or by reputation.

Growing up, he was my protector and mentor, and when he spoke to me, it was like I was the only other person in the world. His singular focus was on me. Nothing was more important than to hear my thoughts and ideas. He lived to push me forward, and I wanted nothing more than to make him proud.

Then I thought about the man in the other room. Some elements remained, but in many ways, my father—the giant who swept me off my feet and raised me up onto his shoulders—was already dead.

And when I woke up the next morning, that final thought that came to me right before I had drifted off to sleep was, unfortunately, far more accurate than it seemed at the time.

6

─────

Bacon fried on the stove. It was meant to be a surprise. My father loved bacon and eggs. Add a couple slices of toast with strawberry jam, and he'd look at me and say, "The rest of the day is downhill from here, Tiger."

That's what he called me. Not "sweetie," "pumpkin," or "darlin'," like a lot of other dads. Jack Wirth called his daughter "tiger," because that's how he wanted me to act. His girl wasn't going to spend three hours on her hair and make-up. His girl wasn't going to watch princess movies, and his girl certainly wasn't going to take dance lessons. Instead, he signed me up for karate and bought me my own gun at the age of nine.

That was what I was thinking about just before I found him, what it was like growing up as a little girl in the house Jack Wirth built. When the smell of bacon didn't wake him up, which I figured it would, I knocked on the bedroom door. When he didn't answer, I opened it a few inches. Then I walked around the foot of the bed to the side where he was sleeping.

"Dad." I touched his shoulder, gently. "Dad, I've got your favorites ready for you." I paused and waited. When he still didn't move, I squeezed his shoulder. "C'mon on, Dad. Time to wake up."

There was nothing.

I screamed at him, but no response. I pulled away the sheets, then stepped back, praying I would see his chest rise and fall. Instead, all I could see was the pool of urine and blood beneath him, and an overwhelming smell of feces.

I turned, almost tripped over Mister Bones, and ran into the other room as the cat screeched at me. I dialed 911, then went back and began pounding on my father's chest.

I WAS TOLD they lost him in the ambulance but the defibrillator brought my father back to life. Then they lost him, again, as he was rolled into the emergency room at Barnes Jewish Hospital. A tube was shoved down his throat, which supplied oxygen, then the defibrillator brought him back to life a second time.

By the time I arrived, he was already stabilized. They had my father up in the intensive care unit, but he wasn't awake. They'd put him in a medically induced coma, whatever that meant. To me, it just looked like a bunch of machines and wires.

I called my mother, relayed what little information I had, then bought her a plane ticket to St. Louis. After that, there wasn't anything left for me to do. I could only wait.

SEVEN HOURS LATER, I found myself back at the St. Louis International Airport, sitting on the same bench where I had waited for my father the day before. The whole time, I replayed everything that had been said and done, trying to figure out how I could've done things differently.

Even though nothing came to mind, and the outcome had been inevitable, I still felt guilty. I looked up at the large screen mounted on the wall. The plane had landed. Remembering how long it had taken my father to walk from the gate to the baggage carousels, I settled in for a long wait, but my mother was much faster. She actually spotted me first, rather than the other way around. She waved her hand in the air, then hustled over to the bench. I stood and hugged her for a long time, then we parted and I was able to take a good long look at her.

Much to my surprise, my mom didn't seem to have aged at all. Whereas my father had shrunk, my mother seemed to be standing taller. Her skin tan, her muscles a bit more toned, more fit. Her eyes sparkled.

"I can't believe your father did this to you...to us." She shook her head, the scowl intensifying.

"Why didn't you tell me he had gotten that bad? I didn't even recognize him."

"You know your father," she said. "With your new job, he didn't want to burden you, made me promise." She looked away, unable to hold my eye, but I understood. My dad could do that to people, especially those closest to him.

We started walking toward the exit, and my mom continued as she put her arm around me. "I felt like I needed to honor his wishes, his privacy, but that wasn't fair to you. I certainly had no idea he was going to discharge himself from the hospital. No idea he was going to come here."

"He told me he had unfinished business," I said. "Something about an old case. He didn't give me any details."

My mother stopped just before the revolving doors. "An old case?" She shook her head. "Are you sure?"

"That's what he told me," I said, "but now I'm wondering whether he was all there, you know?"

My mother neither agreed nor disagreed. She said, "He's been in the hospital getting treatment for months. We were at the end of the line. I wanted him to go into hospice, and he wanted to go home. That's what our argument was about. I had to take a break, and while I was gone, he left." She looked around and shook her head. "And now he's here."

———

WE MET with a team of doctors in a conference room. We were told my father's medical files had been sent electronically from his treating physicians in Florida and reviewed. They were now being summarized to us by a young female oncologist. She was a resident, measuring her words carefully as she described the next steps and decisions that would ultimately need to be made. In short, none of the options she identified sounded good to me.

The doctor actually reminded me of myself, a young woman proving she was tough enough to handle the rigors of the job as her supervisors listened and evaluated her performance.

She said, "Right now, as you know, your husband has been intubated and is in a medically induced coma. You're going to need to decide when to remove the breathing tube. By keeping it in, you give the body an opportunity to rest and recuperate. However, it can't stay in forever. Every day he's in the bed means the risk of infection increases and muscles deteriorate. As a rule of thumb, every day he's in the coma means another week of recovery."

She paused, waited a few beats for either me or my mother to ask a question, then continued when no questions were asked. "After that, the underlying cancer is still there. Through Washington University, we have some experimental drug trials going on, but I don't think the doctors who had been treating your husband over the past six months were wrong to recommend hospice. All of the traditional treatments have been unsuccessful, and he doesn't fit the profile related to most of the drug trials."

The young doctor continued. She began to talk about the experimental treatments in greater detail, but I couldn't focus. The words washed over me, white noise as my anger toward both my mother and father grew.

Six months of treatment. *How could they have kept this information from me?* I'd known my father was diagnosed with cancer, but both of them minimized it. They lied. They said the doctors had it all under control, just needed to do some tests. I could've visited him, spent time with my father before the cancer spread too far, but missed the opportunity.

There were good memories that could've been made, conversations that could've been had. Instead, my final memory of my father outside of a hospital would be of him limping down an airport corridor, drinking a beer in a dive bar, and nearly dying in my bed.

"What do you think?" My mother asked.

The question pulled me back into the room. "What?"

"The next steps," she asked. "What do you think of the next steps?"

I took a deep breath and began to massage my temples. "I don't know, Mom. Do whatever you think is right." I pushed back from the table and walked out of the room.

7

—————

My father was kept on the ventilator for one more day, but that was enough. Neither my mother nor I could stand looking at him like that for any longer. He was a larger-than-life man, now shrunk down to nothing and kept alive by a half-dozen gadgets that pumped stuff into his body from plastic bags on poles.

A nurse handed a clipboard to my mother. I watched her sign, then silently watched the nurse scurry away with the executed consent form. I reached out my hand. Saying nothing, my mother took it and squeezed. In a few minutes, the doctors would remove the tube and disconnect the machines. I knew there were some who would consider our decision as too rash.

How could they lose faith so quickly?

But neither my mother nor I believed in an interventionist God who saved only those that had earned the right to be saved and let die those that deserved to die.

Although I was sure there was a thin layer between the known and unknown, because I'd felt its presence—experienced its wrinkles in reality— this was different. I could imagine no God passing judgment on either my mother or me for showing mercy, refusing to prolong the inevitable and allowing nature to take its course, however long or fast.

A doctor came into the family waiting room about an hour later. He told us everything had been removed. "Your husband is very sick," he said to my mother. "It's wait and see."

And so we waited.

There was no change until early the next morning. My mother was asleep on my shoulder. I was watching a generic rom com about a businesswoman who returned to the small town where she grew up, to save her family's independent clothing store on Main Street. It was being pushed out by the new big box store near the highway.

The nurse arrived a little after 5:00 a.m. "His eyes are open," she said. "Come."

We followed her through the large sliding glass doors that separated the intensive care unit from the rest of the hospital, past the nursing station, then to my father's room. I hadn't expected him to be dancing around his bed, singing, "Oh what a beautiful morning," but I couldn't help feeling a little disappointed.

When the nurse had told us he'd opened his eyes, she was not being efficient with her words. "Open eyes" was not shorthand for a myriad of other signs of life. That was it. My father's eyes were simply open. Except for the absence of the life-sustaining equipment, everything else was the same.

"You should talk to him." The nurse stepped aside to allow us to approach his bed.

My mother didn't hesitate. She took my father's hand in hers, and with the other she touched his pale face, then moved closer and began to talk.

He did not respond. My father just stared up at the ceiling. His dry and cracked lips never moved. My mother kept on saying, "I love you, Jack. I love you." But there was still no response. I watched for a few more seconds but couldn't take it anymore. This was not the plan. My hands balled up into fists, face turning red. He was supposed to either live or die, not be...whatever this was. I turned away. My mother could do whatever she wanted, but I couldn't stay.

I began to walk out of the room, stopping at the curtain only to collect myself, and that's where I was when I heard his voice. It wasn't the deep growl of a bear. It was much softer, and a little slurred, but it was his.

He said, "Tiger."

GIVEN THE CANCER, nobody's hopes were particularly high that he would ever be strong enough to walk again, or even go home. The oncologist gave him a few weeks to live, at most.

"He is a very sick man," he kept saying.

The neurologist also stated that, at some point, my father had suffered a stroke and was at risk for another, but at least he was talking a little. That was one of the bright spots: he was talking. His voice was soft, usually just a few words at a time, but he was there. He could smile, and even laugh. These were such simple things. So easy to take for granted, but I was thankful.

From a chair in the corner of his room, I watched as my mother sat by his bedside for hours. She'd read him articles from the *Post-Dispatch*, and they'd chat a little, meaning my mom would do most of the talking about politics, the weather, and, most importantly, if the Cardinals had a shot at the World Series. Then my dad would say a word or two in response.

It was on the sixth day my dad asked my mom to get him a cup of ice chips. When she was gone, he lifted his head and looked at me. His face was scrunched up, like he'd eaten something sour.

"Made a mess... I know."

I got up and walked over to him. "But you're here." I touched his cheek, gently, then sat down in the chair where my mother had been sitting. "I wasn't ready for you to go. When things were really bad, I tried to push that to the side, because it seemed selfish, but it was true. I wanted a chance to say goodbye."

My father closed his eyes, and I wondered for a second whether he'd gone to sleep. It was just like what he had done at the Royal Bar after his escape from the hospital, drifted away mid-conversation. I waited, glancing at the door to see if my mother had returned, and when I looked back at him, his eyes were now open.

"I'm sorry. I'm sorry...have to ask you this, but..." His breathing was heavy now, a pause between every word he spoke. "The case," he said, "help me."

I stood, like a shock of electricity had been shot up my back. The chair nearly tipped over. "The case? Help?" My voice trembled and turned toward the dramatic. "That's why you wanted this special, private moment with your only beloved child...to talk about some stupid case?"

"Not stupid," my father said softly, but I didn't wait to hear any more.

"Mom and I have just gone through hell because of you, because you got on a plane and flew halfway across the country, only to almost die hundreds of miles away from your devoted wife. If mom knew you were talking to me about this, she'd—"

"She'd what?"

We both looked at the doorway where she now stood, holding a cup of ice. My mother's skeptical gaze shifted from my father to me, then back again.

"What were you two talking about, Amy?" she asked. "I could hear the yelling all the way down the hall."

Neither of us answered the question.

I then looked at my father and shook my head, disappointed. "Ask him," I said. "I'll be back tonight. I need a break."

My dad grabbed my wrist. "Don't go, Amy," he said, "you have to find who killed her. Stop him. You must. There's many more, and...much more to come." It was probably the longest string of words my father had said since waking up from his coma, but then his eyes rolled back into his head and his whole body jerked and started to convulse.

"What's happening?" I looked at my mom, afraid. She still stood in the doorway. "I think...he's having another seizure or something. Get the nurse. Get the doctors."

———

WE WAITED FOR AN UPDATE, and eventually a doctor came to see me and my mother in the waiting room. I don't know what he told us, because I wasn't listening. So many emotions swirled inside of me, my brain couldn't process anything. It was as if I was submerged underwater. All I wanted to do was see my father one last time before he died.

Eventually, we were led back to his room. My mother immediately went to my father's bedside to hold his hand, stroke his hair, and whisper comfort in his ear.

My father's eyes were wide. His breathing shallow. The only other noise was the staccato beep of the heart monitor. Although he was in bed, not moving, his heart was racing. What should've been 60 or 70 beats per minute was up to 120, then 134.

Most of the machines, wires, and tubes were back. A nurse was in the process of changing one of the plastic bags so it could continue to feed painkillers into my father's arm, one drip at a time. Her face was tight. Her movements focused. This was the final watch.

My dad turned his head toward me. "It hurts....glass, shards of glass."

"I know." I looked at the nurse, who was now pressing a button to release even more drugs into the stream. "They're working on it, Dad."

My father's eyes closed again. The beeps from the heart monitor spiked up to 140, then 145 beats per minute. He groaned in pain. His whole face knotted. Then his heart slowed, a slight recovery.

The shards of glass tumbling around in his body appeared to have stopped, but I was sure they'd start churning, again.

"Dad?"

"Tiger." He looked at me, his eyes now wide and clear. "I love you."

"I love you, too."

"Forgive me." He raised an arm in the air, gesturing to the room. "This...forgive me."

"This? It's not your fault," I said. "You have cancer, Dad, it's not-"

"No." His voice came out clear and strong as his heart rate spiked again. His jaw clenched as the churn of glass resumed. He fought through the pain. "The girl...Kasi..." Each word was a struggle as his heart rate reached 160, then 165. He closed his eyes. His heart rate started to plummet. "Forgive me."

I stepped away from my father's bedside. There was a chair in the corner of the room, small with minimal padding. The ICU was not a place for comfort. I sat down, attempting to process as my mother comforted my father in his final minutes of life.

He looked at her. "I love you." His muscles relaxed, and he sunk deeper into the bed. My mother held him close; he looked peaceful. Perhaps I was just projecting calm and peace when there was none, but I didn't think so. That's how he looked.

The incessant beeps from the heart rate monitor continued

to slow. There were no more spikes. The numbers dropped, steadily. It was like a train slowing as it pulled into the station.

I watched the numbers fall. At 45 beats per minute, the background on the monitor changed color to yellow, and there was a high-pitched tone.

The doctor gestured toward it, and the nurse muted the machine. The tone was gone, but I could still see the numbers continue to drop—35...33...32...29...it was silent in the room, except for the sound of my father struggling for air. His body jerked.

"It's okay, Jack." The numbers kept dropping as my mother leaned over, practically laying in the bed with him. "It's going to be over soon." She held his hand—5...4...3...2...1—then kissed him on the cheek.

8

It was well past nine when I got back from the hospital. There had been more forms to sign, and we had to make other arrangements. It was the beginning of the business-end of death, the cold administration of winding down a life, comprised of hundreds of decisions, from the mundane to the emotional. A funeral home had to be scheduled to come and pick up my father's body. Relatives and friends needed to be notified, along with banks, the Social Security administration, and insurance companies. Then there was the size and scope of the memorial service. It was all overwhelming, and I was exhausted.

Mister Bones greeted me at the door. He purred as he pushed his body against my leg, back and forth. "Hungry, little buddy?" I scratched behind his ears, then went to the kitchen to get him some food.

With his bowl filled, I lay down on the couch and doom-scrolled through various news feeds on my cell phone. The political outrage was the same, each party accusing the other of crimes and cover-ups. Meanwhile, the droughts continued. There were riots in the Middle East and India over food prices as grain and flour became more scarce as the war continued in Eastern Europe. Then there was the glacier. Various pundits argued, while climate experts estimated the days, minutes, and seconds until it fell into the sea. The truth was that nobody knew.

It was all an attempt to decompress, but a failed attempt. I put aside the phone, picked up the laptop from the coffee table, and went out to the balcony after retrieving a bottle of wine from the kitchen. I knew I shouldn't drink or gamble, but I couldn't stop myself. I typed in my login code and password, then pulled up the website for Full House Poker. Along the top of the screen, it stated I was now, "-$250." This was still a lot, but it was better than being more than six hundred in the hole. I clicked the "deal" button and started the chase.

A round of Texas Hold-Em began with people from all over the world. To my right, at the virtual table, was the male avatar from a person in Japan. Next to him was someone from Canada. Then there was a person from Los Angeles, and another from Germany.

Soon, I was lost in the game. My troubles faded into the background as the cards were dealt, and one round blurred into another, then another. Players dropped off, replaced by new ones, but the game continued.

I went up, and I went down, but I didn't pay much attention to that. I was too busy working through the odds, studying the cards that were shown and what remained in the deck. My father's death was pushed to a distant corner in my head.

The clink of the virtual chips moved to and from the center of the screen, and the cards flying from the dealer to each player was soothing, almost hypnotic. Time passed, but I wasn't aware of how much time had passed until a box appeared in the center of my screen. The battery was under 10%, and I either needed to shut down or plug in. I looked at the time; it was past 2:20 a.m. I'd been playing for more than four hours.

I checked my balance at the top of the screen, and my heart sunk. Rather than getting out of the hole, I was deeper in debt. I now owed the virtual casino over $1,800. I didn't know what to do.

You're supposed to quit when you're ahead, not while you're behind, I thought.

Another round was about to start, and the virtual dealer asked me if I wanted to continue. A timer began to count down, and it reminded me of the numbers dropping on the heart rate monitor next to my father's hospital bed as he died.

Then a light turned on in the shed below me on the other side of the courtyard. It was the first time I'd ever seen it lit. I didn't even know it had electricity. What was once my quiet archaeological site was now something different. The balcony where I went to be alone, now exposed.

I saw movement inside, shadows bending the colors in the window.

Was someone now living there?

The movement stopped, then a woman stood in the window. She looked up at me. It wasn't just that I saw her, I *felt* her. It was as if she were talking to me, calming my nerves and answering my questions:

Fear not, fear not, for I am no trespasser, nor a thief. No need to call the police, Amy, for I am just an old, tired woman who wants to keep you safe. It is hard for you to trust, but you will soon understand. You must finish the job.

I turned off my laptop and went inside, deciding I was done for the night. I was exhausted and had to be hallucinating. It was far past my bedtime.

I changed into my least dirty pajamas, then went into the bathroom. I dutifully took my handful of nighttime meds and brushed my teeth, as I thought about the person in the shed.

Why now? Why did they appear tonight?

Then I walked to my bedroom and saw my father's suitcase in the corner.

It had been there the whole time, untouched. I wanted to open it, but I resisted the urge. Maybe it was conditioning. I'd been taught to show deference, even awe, of my father for the entirety of my life. Perhaps it would be a violation of trust, like swiping money from the top of his dresser or sneaking some of his "good" whiskey to impress a friend.

Maybe I resisted because I was in denial, an attempt to rewrite my own memory. An attempt to pretend my father had come to St. Louis in his fragile condition only to see me, his daughter, not settle an old score or investigate an old case.

His crazy trip was merely a failure to cope with his illness, the temporary insanity of an otherwise honorable man. It was easy to pretend there was no "unfinished business," except providing closure to the people who loved him the most. There was no case. It was just a figment of his imagination, as well as mine. That's what I told myself, but I knew it wasn't true.

What had the old woman said? Something about a job.

I stopped pretending, and I put the suitcase on my new bed. The old, stained mattress had been hauled away by the men who'd delivered the new one. The soiled sheets had been tossed in a dumpster out back. I pressed a button. Latches sprung open, metal hitting metal like the clicking of a gun's hammer. When I flipped open the top, I knew it wasn't idle curiosity I was satisfying. I was hunting.

What was so important that he was willing to die for it?

I began with the clothes. One by one, I searched the pockets or anything else that may have been folded inside. I searched the suitcase's various zippered compartments, examined his shoes, and dumped out his toiletry bag. Although unlikely, I even tested the suitcase's lining to see if it might pull away, revealing a hiding place, but there was nothing there.

I stepped back, unsatisfied. I stared at the emptied suitcase on my bed in disbelief. I was certain my father would not have come with nothing. Then I realized where it was. I may have searched the suitcase, but that wasn't everything he brought with him. I walked out of the bedroom toward the front door. Adjacent to it was a closet.

I opened the closet door, and there it was: my father's suit coat. I took it down off the hook, reached inside the front breast pocket, and removed a small leather book with my father's initials embossed on the cover. I knew this book very well, darkened by time and worn by use. Inside was a pencil and spiral notepad, fastened to the leather binding with a clip.

I opened the book. On the first piece of paper was a case number. I recognized the format from my days at the St. Louis Police Department. My father had also written, "Kasi Barnes." Below that was a phone number, as well as the name of his old partner, Frank Perelli.

There it was, all the information I needed to get started. I could now attempt to fulfill my father's dying wish, finish the case that killed him. My palms grew sweaty, and my father's old notebook from his days as a homicide investigator felt odd in my hands. I wasn't worthy of holding it. I was afraid.

This is all wrong, I thought, then tossed it in the garbage.

EVELYN

The old woman with long dreadlocks, which today were the color orange and tomorrow may be different, sat on a park bench. It wasn't one of the city's famous parks. It was very small, a pocket of green with old trees and a modest playground. It was a neighborhood park, and she knew the regulars and their rhythms.

During the day, parents used it to entertain their young children, burn their energy so they'd be "ready" for the dreaded nap. In the early evening, the dog owners would take over. Some of them referred to it as "happy hour" and came with a cocktail, along with their plastic poop bags, drinking while the dogs jumped on one another and chased rubber balls.

At night, however, it was abandoned. The park's lights cast the scene in a deep, amber glow, as if frozen in time. This old woman with long dreadlocks liked it that way the best, sitting alone on the bench after dark and feeding her birds. They were there for her. They were her children.

She tossed a handful of sunflower seeds to those who had gathered before her to share their stories. They brought her news from all corners of the city. She listened to them as they scrambled and pecked. They were good birds and loyal, but they were also scared.

If she were to die, what would happen to them? If she did nothing, how many more innocent people would be killed? There were rules, of course. Everybody knew the rules, and she'd seen what happens to those who break them. Could she do it? Evelyn wasn't sure.

She tossed another handful of seeds onto the sidewalk, then turned her head toward Amy Wirth's apartment and considered her options.

9

The funeral was at St. Stephens Catholic Church, in South City. It was a Friday afternoon, and the small sanctuary was full. Attendees could be easily divided into one of three categories: cops, musicians, or family.

The priest had asked me to speak on behalf of the family, but I declined. I knew I couldn't do it. I'd just break down. Even if everything was written out and all I had to do was read, I'd still only get about thirty seconds into the eulogy before choking up, at best. Tears at funerals were natural and expected, but complete emotional breakdowns were not really what anybody wanted to see.

For my entire life, Jack Wirth was my rock. My father was my mentor and protector. He was a man known for his honesty, blunt and unvarnished. It was his guiding principle. He would follow a case wherever it would go, regardless of whether it would damage his career or challenge the powerful. He was fearless. He was a man I thought I could never live up to, and how could I talk about that in front of all of these people?

Perelli did the eulogy instead. He, like many of the other

cops in attendance, wore his full dress uniform. Badge and shoes polished to a high shine.

"Jack and Frank," he began. "That was us, like we were one. But let me tell you, when people said, 'We need Jack and Frank on this case,' what they were really saying was that they needed Jack on the case. I was just along for the ride."

Perelli took a handkerchief out of his pocket and wiped his nose, collecting himself. "He was an unbelievable detective. I don't know how many cases he closed, but I doubt anybody in the history of the department ever closed more. Jack Wirth was like a dog with a bone. Once he got ahold of a case, he didn't give up until it was solved."

Perelli then told a few classic stories about my father. I'd heard them many times before. I knew the pacing and punchlines and felt myself drifting away as those around me smiled and laughed in all the right places. The bigger Perelli built up my father, the smaller I felt.

When he was done, the priest began his homily. It was about death and self-reflection and eternal life. After Merchants Bridge, I've thought a lot about life and death, both my own and others. I couldn't even count the number of times I'd discussed it with Dr. Dan.

As a cop and the daughter of a cop, you feel it, the weight of it. This comes at you differently depending on the day. Of course, it's heaviest and most obvious when someone dies. A life was taken without warning. Tears were shed. Families must be notified with late night phone calls or knocks on doors, entire worlds destroyed.

Then there were the bodies. Crime scenes were tragic but don't really surprise much of anyone. There is no shock. They've become ubiquitous on television shows and movies. The autopsy, however, was different. The morgue was free of pretense and drama. It's a place where people go from human to animal.

The medical examiner removes any external reminder of the person who once were. The life lived is irrelevant. The body stripped of clothes and jewelry. Precious expressions of individuality placed in a paper sack, and the skin of the deceased scrubbed clean. If he or she were shot, a long, stiff pole is pushed through the entrance wound and out the other side to determine the angle the bullet passed through the body. Organs are cut out and weighed. Then the body is sewn back together, placed in a long plastic bag, and put in a freezer.

There is no hierarchy in the morgue. Rich and poor, good and bad are treated the same, and everyone eventually ends up in the same place, either in the ground or in a jar filled with ash. That, I think, is the most disturbing, and perhaps why the belief in some form of after-life, heaven, or reincarnation is so pervasive, crossing cultures over millennia. It's just too horrible to imagine the life that we were given is the only life we will ever get.

These were the frightening thoughts I have when haunted in my dreams.

As the priest talked about my father and heaven, he seemed so sure of himself. I looked down and realized my arms were folded across my chest, skeptical. I have no idea whether heaven exists. In many ways, I hope there is a heaven. It'd be nice to talk to my father again. We've still got lots of things to discuss.

But I'm doubtful, very doubtful.

The more I thought about it as I sat on the cold, hard, wooden pew, the only eternal life that I think exists was not found in the clouds, but in the people left behind. The effect of our daily interactions was the long tail through the generations, following the dead long after they're gone. Thus, instead of talking about eternal life, I wished the priest would be talking about our eternal legacy.

What was my father's eternal legacy? What were the lessons he passed down to me? What was I supposed to carry on after his death?

I thought about all the Jack-isms, those little life lessons he was constantly trying to impart on me. Then I thought about the leather book, now in my garbage. Certainly, who I was now was not the legacy that my father wanted to leave. I was supposed to embrace and embody him, true eternal life.

I needed to change. I needed to be stronger, and I needed to figure out how to find justice for Kasi, whoever that was. I needed to carry on his work so that he could have eternal life.

10

F riends and family gathered in the Blue Star after the funeral. It was a legendary blues club that opened in the 1970s in the basement of an old department store on Washington Avenue. For decades, it was often the only nightlife in that part of town, riding out the city's highs and lows like a ship in the ocean. As the empty buildings were converted into condos, the Blue Star began to rise once again. The addition of a Wednesday night burlesque show didn't hurt either.

My mother and I stood at the door, receiving people as the room filled. Four men stood on stage. They were all older, hair either white or gone, with growing bellies and shrinking butts. I couldn't remember their names, but I knew they were part of a loose collective that used to play with my father before he moved to Florida.

After forty minutes of greeting and listening to condolences, the people stopped coming through the line. I gave my mother a hug, then led her from the front door over to a table away from the stage. My aunts were already settled in with plates of mostaccioli and toasted ravioli with various cocktails to wash it all down.

I directed her to an empty chair next to Aunt Janice and told her I'd be back with some food. "Just hang on."

As I walked across the room to the buffet, I looked for Perelli. I didn't see him on my first pass, but as I walked back with a full plate of food, I saw him at the bar, laughing with a couple of retired cops who looked vaguely familiar. I put the plate down on the table in front of my mother, then I told her I'd be right back for some drinks.

I went to the bar, ordered a Manhattan for her, and waited for a moment to talk to Perelli, alone. The band finished "Goin' Down Slow," by St. Louis Jimmy Oden, and slid into a rendition of "My Babe," by Little Walter. By the time they began a tune from Howlin' Wolf, Perelli was alone.

I glanced over my shoulder to make sure there was nobody behind me and approached. "I need to talk to you about a case my dad was working on when he died," I said. "I need to talk to you about Kasi Barnes."

Perelli shook his head. "I'll tell you what I told your pops when he called, ain't nothing good is going to come from that. It was tragic, but," he shrugged his shoulders, "it happens. Addicts overdose. Happens every day."

I leaned in closer. "My dad wanted to make it right. What did he mean by that? There must be something there."

"Your dad *wanted* something to be there, something more, because he felt guilty for maybe closing it a little too quick. But just because you want it, don't mean how it is, you know?" Perelli's eyes softened, then he whispered, "Leave it alone, kid. You got your own career and your own cases, chasing ghosts ain't a good use of your time."

"What about following the truth wherever it leads, regardless of the consequences, collateral damage be damned?"

Perelli smiled a little, some nostalgia. "Now you're sounding just like your old man."

I knew he was softening, so I kept pushing. "My dad didn't want to leave it alone. That's why he flew here. It didn't matter if he was dying, this is what he wanted, and he asked me to do this for him."

Perelli took a step back and rubbed the back of his neck, considering what he should do. "You probably know your dad asked me to pull the file," he said. "Jack called me up a couple weeks ago, and he was all hyped up. Says I gotta pull it right away. It coulda raised some eyebrows around the department— me pulling it without a sign-off from one of the boys up in homicide—but I managed to get it outta the archives nice and smooth, since that's where I work now."

"So you've got it?"

Perelli nodded. "I got it," he said, "and if you stop by the crypt, I'll give it to you, and I hope to hell you know what you're doing."

MATTHEWS WAS PRETTY easy to find. He stood alone against the back wall, drinking a beer and listening to the music. Since he was FBI, most of the cops in attendance either didn't know him or stayed away.

"Thanks for coming."

I joined him on the wall. We didn't talk, just listened to the band, which had now shifted into a medley of Stevie Ray Vaughn covers. I nursed my beer through "Cold Shot" and "Pride and Joy," finishing it halfway through "Little Wing."

The band announced they were taking a break, and the volume of the room quieted. Matthews said, "I know what you're going through. My pops died about thirteen years ago, mom passed about three years after that. It's a weird feeling when a parent dies, like somebody cut a string or let loose an anchor. The holidays are when it really hits you...like I said, a weird feeling."

I looked over at my mother, still at the table with her sisters. "I wish she'd move back here from Florida, but she probably won't."

"It's early. Give her time." Matthews held up his empty glass. "Another?"

I nodded, and Matthews flagged down a waitress and ordered more of the same. As she went to the bar to retrieve our order, I asked, "Did your dad have a dying wish?"

"Like other than saying he was proud of me and wishing me a happy life?" Matthews shook his head. "Nah."

I thought about whether to tell him more. Matthews was my partner, but he wasn't really my friend. I didn't have any friends. Working the dog shift as a patrol cop made it difficult to maintain friendships with normal people. You sleep when they're awake, and you're awake when they're asleep. Theoretically, I was supposed to bond with my brothers and sisters in blue, but that ended when I had recorded another officer planting evidence with my body-worn camera. After that, I was a traitor.

When the waitress returned with our drinks, and after Matthews put a twenty on her tray, I took a breath and told him part of the story. I told him about my father's decision to keep the severity of his illness a secret from me, his surprise trip to St. Louis, and his unfinished business, as well as his final request for me to find who killed Kasi Barnes.

It took a second or two for Matthews to say anything after I'd dumped it all on him. His eyes squinted, seeming a little confused. Then, "Why didn't you tell me this stuff before?"

I wondered the same. "I'm a private person." The answer sounded weak and was, in fact, weak. I took a large drink, buying some time, then said, "I think I have to change some things if I'm going to figure it out," I said. "I need to be more like him."

I could tell Matthews didn't like the idea, but he didn't say it outright. Instead, he looked over to where my mother was sitting and nodded in her direction. "Does she know? You should talk to her before you do anything."

"Her? I'm not sure, but I doubt it. My dad was independent. He'd go it alone, and so should I...I just need to put my head down and break through some walls, wherever it leads."

"Like you're doing with the judge?"

"No," I said. "I need to do even better than that. I'm getting nowhere with Judge Griggs."

"Okay, if that's what you want." He stepped back, giving me room, while also watching the band begin to gather on-stage to start their second set. "Speaking of Judge Griggs, we've got just about everything we can get without a warrant or his wife's consent, including the calls to and from his chambers, work emails, and calendar. That kind of stuff."

"Anything interesting?"

"Haven't had time to really go through it," Matthews said. "I skimmed what the techs sent over, and nothing popped out. I thought you could take the lead, since you've got the passion for it."

"Can you send the files to me tonight?"

"Tonight? I thought you'd take some time off."

"I wasn't planning to," I said. "I've already been out of the office enough lately, and sitting at home being sad all the time isn't healthy."

"Well, putting it in a box and shoving it away isn't particularly healthy either, but I'll send it over to you."

"Good," I said. "We can talk about it tomorrow morning."

"What about Dr. Dan?" Matthews said. "You have an appointment tomorrow."

"Not anymore," I said. "I'm taking a therapy break. It wasn't helping, maybe I'll start going to somebody different in a few months. I don't know. My dad was always skeptical of that stuff, and I'm thinking he was right. Who's to say whether all these drugs he's prescribed me are even working?" I didn't look at Matthews, because I didn't want to see his reaction.

The band began playing "Reconsider Baby," by Lowell Fulson. I should've recognized this as a big, flashing neon sign telling me that what I was about to do was a mistake. I was the baby who needed to reconsider, but I missed it. I was going to run through some walls, instead. Consequences be damned.

IT DIDN'T SURPRISE me that my mother did not want to stay, booking a flight back to Florida that departed a few hours after the memorial service. She never liked St. Louis. My mother spent most of her early life in Nashville.

From the stories she told me, I got the picture they were upper middle class. Her father—my grandfather—managed an auto parts store not far from the Vanderbilt campus. My grandmother managed the household, living in a modest but well-kept bungalow in the Inglewood neighborhood. Along with her brother and three sisters, my mother excelled at school. She was president of various clubs, and she was popular enough to be on the student council.

In the middle of her junior year of high school, the entire family moved. It was abrupt. Although nobody ever came out and said it, my understanding was that my grandfather was accused of stealing some money from the store. They left quickly for St. Louis. No farewell parties or long goodbyes.

They settled in the Dutchtown neighborhood in South City. It was a difficult transition. At her new school, my mother was like a queen bee who'd been pushed out of the hive. No longer relevant. The cliques were already established. Who ate where and with whom in the lunchroom was set, and she resented it. She didn't belong anywhere. She went from knowing everyone to knowing nobody.

According to family lore, one day my father saw my mother eating alone in the cafeteria and sat down beside her. He was captain of the football team and baseball team, Mr. Popular. "If it wasn't for your father," my mother would say, "I'm pretty sure I'd have run away, gone back to Nashville, even if I had to sleep outside in a park."

My mother told this story hundreds of times, emphasizing different aspects depending on the situation and life lesson to be imparted on me. The end, however, was always the same. "Your father is the only good thing about this place." This "place" meaning St. Louis. The city was far too hard and dirty for her. Nashville, by contrast, was civilized.

So, when we arrived at the airport, I doubted she would ever return. She'd been living in a hotel for weeks, and my mother was ready to go back to Florida and leave St. Louis in the past.

Before she opened the door to get out of the car, however, my mother paused. She put her hand on my knee. "I'm so sorry you had to go through this." I saw emotion rise up in her, but my mother kept it from fully coming to the surface. She was a proud and reserved woman, far too private for such displays, even with her own daughter.

"I don't know why he came back here." My mother looked away as she said this, and I wondered if that was really true.

I, obviously, wasn't privy to my parent's private conversations, but I had assumed there had been a confrontation at some point about Kasi Barnes, but maybe not. My mother was of a different generation, more deferential. My father was and forever would be the golden boy who sat next to her in the lunchroom, bringing her into the fold, his friends becoming her friends, saving her.

Knowing he was dying, perhaps my mother never asked, never wanting to taint that ideal image she had of him. With me, this topic had been avoided both before and after my father's death, but it lurked in the background of every conversation. I then thought of Matthews. He told me to talk to her, so I tried.

"Do you remember our argument between Dad and me, when you went to get the ice?"

My mother said nothing.

"Do you want to know? Do you really want to know why he came back?"

My mother sighed and looked at the floor. "I'm tired, Amy, really tired." She bit her lower lip as she thought about her answer. Then, "I think that's between you two. If Jack wanted me to know, then he would've told me."

"This isn't the nineteen fifties anymore."

"No, it's not the nineteen fifties, not even the nineteen nineties," my mother said. "But whatever brought him back to St. Louis was not good, and I'd rather not know right now. I'd rather just remember him as he lived, not as he died."

With that, the conversation was done. We said our goodbyes, and I watched her disappear into the terminal. It was a missed opportunity. The conversation should not have ended. I recognize that now.

FROM THE AIRPORT, I went to my apartment on Cherokee Street. I scooped some food into Mister Bones' bowl, then got back in my car and drove to the office. The building was quiet when I arrived. Most of the lights were off.

I sat behind my desk and booted up my computer. Matthews had promised to send the documents to me, and he was a man of his word. I opened the file. The first was a list of all the telephone calls made to and from the judge's chambers over the past two years. One column indicated the date and time. The second was the duration, and the third was the telephone number.

I looked at it briefly, but there was no point in spending much time with it. The calls only had meaning once a name or business associated with the incoming or outgoing telephone number was identified. Luckily, the FBI had a computer program to do that. I thought about running it through the system but then decided to wait. Most of the numbers were internal to the court system, and I figured the others were also work-related. I was more interested in calls and texts to and from his personal cell phone, but we didn't have those.

The next document was a preliminary catalog of the judge's chambers. The techs did not bother to catalog everything, but they did identify the contents of the judge's trash, wallet, and what was in and on his desk. At the direction of the chief judge, the techs did not search the file cabinets in the outer office for confidentiality reasons, and given our limited resources, it was "deemed unnecessary at this time."

Each item on the inventory was given a number, unique barcode that could be scanned and tracked, and hyperlink to one or more photographs associated with the item. Most of it was expected. There were proposed orders that were submitted by attorneys with motions pending before the judge. There were legal research memoranda drafted by the judge's law clerk, as well as mundane documents related to the mechanics of the law factory: proposed court policies, meeting agendas, and hearing schedules.

What remained were the personal items. Judge Griggs, like most people, brought some of his home life to the office. There were letters from his daughter's college about tuition. A reunion invitation from the Country Day school where Griggs had attended high school, and a group of documents in an electronic folder labeled "bills." This was what I had begun reviewing when I noticed the Carrot. I felt myself jump in surprise.

She stood in the doorway to my office. I had no idea how long she had been watching.

"You scared me to death." I put my hand on my heart, hoping the pounding would subside. "I thought I was the only one still in the building."

"No," the Carrot said. "I'm most productive at night. No meetings. Nobody dropping in. No expectation that I'm going to suddenly respond to an email." She nodded toward my computer. "What are you working on?"

"Me?" I had to think fast, knowing the Carrot wanted the Judge Griggs file closed. "Blue tags," I said. "Colton Steele has a bunch of trials coming up; just trying to locate some of our witnesses who haven't been returning his calls."

"Good." The Carrot nodded, appearing to be satisfied with my answer. She turned, began to walk away, then stopped. She looked back at me. "I'm sorry to hear about your father, Agent Wirth. Losing a parent can be difficult." That was the most warmth and empathy I'd ever seen the Carrot exhibit. Nobody would ever call it effusive, but it was genuine.

"Thank you," I said.

"The funeral was today, correct?"

"It was."

"But now you're here." She looked at her watch. "I am not somebody who should lecture anyone about work-life balance, Agent Wirth, but I think it'd be best if you went home and got some rest. People make bad decisions when they're tired." Then she added, "Your two-year review is coming up shortly, and you really need to finish strong."

This last part caused my stomach to flip.

11

E ven though I didn't take any of my bedtime pills, I was out within seconds of my head hitting the pillow. That was good, but the dreams still came. This time, I was lying down on the wet, cold cobblestones that ran along the edges of the Mississippi near the Gateway Arch, undeveloped strips that flooded in the spring. My arms were chained above my head. A man held my feet. Another leaned over me. His face was obscured.

"Give it to me," he said, "like you did in the video."

It was a reference to a video that had circulated around the St. Louis Police Department of a woman having sex in the back of a squad car. Her face could not be seen, but she had the same color hair. The title of the video was "Our hero likes it ruff."

"It wasn't me," I pleaded. "That wasn't me."

Then he put his hand on my breast and pushed hard. The other hand pushed even harder on my stomach. I had no choice but to exhale. All of his weight was upon me. His legs molted into a long tail. Like a snake, it wrapped around me, squeezing even harder. I fought for breath.

My eyes searched for someone to help, but there was no one. He pressed harder and harder. I tried to scream, but there was no sound. I felt a rush to my face as the oxygen was finally depleted. As I blacked out, the last thing I saw were two hand prints on an ancient wall.

That's when I woke up. My bed sheets were soaked with sweat once again. I looked at the clock. It was a quarter past ten. Sunlight shone through the window.

I got up, my muscles sore. I walked into the kitchen and got a glass of cold water. I drank it, then another. I looked out the window and saw the pigeon on the balcony's railing. It watched me, processing everything. I slid the glass door open, but the pigeon did not move. Even after stepping toward it, the pigeon remained. I reached out, edging close, but just as the bird was about to jump into my hand, the old woman called for it with a snap.

I looked down at the courtyard. Her hands were raised. Her orange dreadlocks hung loose. She snapped her fingers a second time, and the pigeon glided down and landed on her shoulder. With a nod, the old woman waved at me, then turned to go back into the shed.

Her presence should have been concerning, even creepy. Nobody likes to be watched, and there was no doubt she was watching me. Dr. Dan and I had many conversations about my paranoia. After Merchant's Bridge, I was convinced I was being followed and still in danger, but for some reason I was not disturbed by this old woman. Her presence was almost comforting, a testament to my loneliness perhaps.

As I turned away from the window, I felt a warmth within myself I hadn't known for years. It wasn't a transformation. I was still me, with all of my flaws, but something was different. I felt like my brain was processing a little faster, and I had more energy.

Rather than log onto my laptop or scroll on my phone, I

went to the garbage and pulled out my father's leather note-book. Then I went to my bedroom and fished some old workout clothes from the bottom of my drawer.

I went for a run. It didn't last long. Twenty minutes later, I was back in my apartment. I was sweaty. My lungs burned, and my left knee felt a little unstable. I figured the pain would only grow throughout the day, but as I walked past a mirror on my way to the shower, I noticed there was a smile on my face.

Maybe running through walls was going to be a good thing?

———

I CALLED Matthews on my drive over to see Perelli in a place we called "The Crypt." It was the nickname given to a windowless, temperature-controlled storage facility where evidence was kept for thousands of pending and closed cases. It wasn't the only such facility, but it was the largest. After my dad retired from the police force, Perelli had accepted an opportunity to manage it. In terms of status within the department, Perelli's move to the crypt was a demotion---going from homicide to being a glorified librarian---but he didn't see it that way. He got regular hours, and as a manager, his rank and pay increased.

Matthews picked up on the second ring as I drove west on the highway toward Forest Park. "I reviewed some of the stuff you sent me last night. How closely have you looked at them?"

"Not very," Matthews said, "I'm working on our real cases, remember?" He laughed a little, as if he was kidding, but there was an edge to it.

"I know. I know. You're a saint, and I owe you." I was feeling good, and I wasn't going to let Mathews guilt-trip me. "I'm thinking it might be drugs. And not just the regular stuff, some-thing like cocaine."

"And you are basing that on what?" Matthews, as always, played the devil's advocate. "As I recall the autopsy, there was a lot of stuff in his system when he died, but it was prescribed, no hard stuff like that."

I countered. "Cocaine goes through the system fast," I said. "If he did it a couple days before the suicide, it wouldn't still be in his system."

Matthews was silent, thinking. Then, "It'd be in his hair. We could ask the medical examiner to test his hair. That'll go back about three months."

I nodded as I pulled into the crypt's parking lot. "Can we do that without getting the Carrot all bent out of shape?"

"I think so," Matthews said. "She wouldn't be happy about it...if she found out, but I doubt she'd find out. We'll just keep it out of the daily chrono unless something turns up. If the hair follicle test is negative, we'll just bury it in the file and move on."

"Sounds good." I put the car in park and turned off the engine. "If Judge Griggs had a drug problem, there are a lot of people who may want to exploit that."

"Maybe," Matthews said, still unconvinced, "or he was just a depressed guy with a drug problem. That's not unusual. In fact, it's a good explanation as to why he did it."

"Are you gonna contact the medical examiner for the hair follicle, or do you want me to do it?"

"I ain't touching this, Amy. You can keep going, but just remember our deal."

"I know." I got out of the car, the phone still pressed to my ear. "I've got until the public memorial, and then we close it."

"Exactly," Matthews said. "And don't do something you're going to regret in the meantime. The probationary review is just on the horizon."

I thought of the Carrot. She'd said the same thing last night.

"I'll be careful, and we'll talk soon. I'll be in the office in about an hour, probably less."

PERELLI LOOKED up from his cell phone when I entered the room. He sat on the other side of a large sheet of bulletproof glass. Perelli was wearing wireless earbuds and appeared to be watching a movie on his laptop. When he noticed me, he smiled, quickly closed the laptop, and waved me closer.

The Crypt was a gigantic evidence locker. Officers and investigators brought evidence to the window where it was processed, a barcode was scanned, and then it was placed on the appropriate shelf. Each step was documented, so a chain of custody was established if the evidence was ever proffered as an exhibit in court or there were allegations of evidence tampering.

Although the procedural safeguards had improved over the decades, there were still issues. Every four years or so, a newspaper article would appear on the front page of the *Post-Dispatch* about a failure. Usually, it was a gun that was supposed to be securely stored in the Crypt but somehow ended up back on the street, brandished in a robbery, or used in a drive-by. An investigation would be announced by a somber-faced politician, then nothing would come of it.

"There she is," Perelli said, "my little Jack in a Dress."

This was a joke Frank Perelli had told for as long as I could remember. He thought it was hilarious, but as a teenage girl, it was horrifying. As an adult woman, it was merely insulting. It didn't matter to Perelli that I didn't really look much like my father and rarely wore a dress; he told the joke anyway, ignoring my obvious annoyance.

"When we talked yesterday, you never mentioned whether you liked your new job with the Feebies?"

"Not so new anymore, but I'm settling in."

"Gotta be a better fit," Perelli said. "You were too smart for this place."

I didn't know if Perelli was aware that I'd been sexually harassed on an almost daily basis while I was an investigator with the St. Louis Police Department, but I played along. "I agree. I am too smart for this place." I forced a smile and tilted my head to the side, playing nice. Then I got to the point. "You said you had the file?"

Perelli nodded. "I still think you're wasting your time, but I got it." I expected him to disappear into the back to retrieve one or more boxes of evidence and multiple binders. In my mind, I'd imagined the case of Kasi Barnes must've been complex. Any investigation that would prompt my father to do what he had done, nearly dying in the process, had to be big.

Perelli instead went into his pocket and retrieved a jump drive. "Here it is." He pushed the small black plastic rectangle through the opening in the window.

I knew digital storage could hold a lot of documents and images, but I was still surprised everything could fit on a jump drive.

"There's nothing else?"

"Nope," Perelli said. "Everything else, clothes and stuff, was likely returned to the family or destroyed."

"Destroyed?" It didn't make any sense. If the investigation was unsolved, evidence of the crime should've been kept, regardless of the age of the case. Forensic science was always improving. Cases were only closed once they were solved.

Perelli noticed the confused look on my face and clarified. "We closed it, your dad and me." He shrugged. "Just let me know if you need my help in some way or you figure something out." He looked around. "Ain't much going on around here, so I could use a little excitement."

"I will," I said. "I'll keep you in the loop." Then I hustled away, with the jump drive in my pocket.

———

When I walked in the door, Matthews pointed at a can of Diet Coke and brown sack on the top of my desk. "How'd you know I forgot to eat?"

"Let's just say my investigative skills are next level." Matthews gave me a sympathetic smile as he watched me open the bag from Rooster and pull out one of their Ham & Jam sandwiches. "Figured you needed somebody to take care of you."

"You're the best."

I bit into the sandwich, and a tiny piece of egg rolled down my chin and onto the desk. I didn't care, only then realizing how hungry I was. I wasn't sure when I had last eaten.

"I saw the Carrot last night when I was in here working late. Has she said anything to you about me?"

"Don't worry about the Carrot." Matthews avoided the question. "Just do the work." He pointed at the corner of my desk. There must've been twenty folders. "These are more blue tag files. I hereby bestow them upon you, my lady." He made a curling gesture with his hand and bowed his head.

"And what did I ever do to deserve this high honor?"

"You work with me, of course," Matthews said, then paused so I knew he wasn't just joking around. "Seriously, though, I think you need to take it easy with everything you've been through. These files are flexible, so you can do them during the day or in the evening from just about anywhere. It's simple work. All you need to do is make contact with these witnesses, then verify contact information and let them know about the trial date. If they hesitate or squirm, don't push it. Let the attorneys know, and they'll handle it. Document everything." Then he tilted his head toward the Carrot's office. "If she snoops around, I've got you covered."

I was going to turn down the offer, but then I thought about the jump drive in my pocket. The blue tag files would give me some time, but I wouldn't use it to relax. I'd use it to figure who Kasi Barnes really was.

"That's really nice of you, Matthews. I appreciate it." I, then, decided to reciprocate. "What can I do for you?"

Matthews's face turned into a big grin. "I thought you might never ask. Your favorite prosecutor is going to finish picking a jury in the next hour or so, and I'm supposed to go over to the courthouse and babysit a witness. Colton Steele wants me to make sure the guy doesn't leave. He also wants me to be present if defense counsel or some private investigator tries to question the witness before he testifies."

"For the rest of the day?"

"Most likely."

I thought about it, then agreed. "I can do it."

"Seriously?"

"Sure, it's not a problem."

12

My agreement to spend the afternoon at the courthouse was not entirely altruistic. I figured while I was waiting I could review the Kasi Barnes file on my laptop and formulate a plan. I also wanted an opportunity to go back to Judge Griggs's chambers. I wanted to see it again, but not because I thought the techs had missed critical evidence.

I wanted to see it again because it might help me make sense of it all. My memories of that chaotic morning were fragments, dominated by the faces and sounds of people in panic and grief, including my own emotions. I thought going back might help me put it into an orderly and sterile chronology, view the scene objectively.

When I arrived, a U.S. Marshal let me into the courtroom after I showed him my credentials. We didn't get far before my pulse quickened as the memories of that morning came back. I thought of my dad and pushed aside those emotions. It was what he would've done.

I followed the marshal down the aisle. There was an oak divider with a brass bar along the top that separated the public gallery from counsel tables. The marshal pushed open the low, ornamental gate and held it for me. I walked through. It was where the phrase "passing the bar" came from. With the exception of witnesses, only attorneys were allowed on the other side of that brass bar.

We walked to the side door by the bench, which led to the judge's chambers. I remembered yanking Colton Steele off the ground, then pulling my gun, convinced there was a mass shooter on the loose.

The marshal pressed his card against the magnetic reader, and we entered the back hallway. It was dark and stale, obviously abandoned, a place now cursed. The air left a bitter taste on the tip of my tongue.

I remembered the woman who fell into the hallway, hysterical. My finger had begun to press down on the trigger, but I'd resisted the urge to pull. Then I saw the door to the judge's suite and walked toward it, pausing at the threshold.

"You good?" the Marshal asked. His voice, to me, sounded distant, like I was at the bottom of a deep well. Grotesque images of Judge Griggs—him slumped over and the back wall splattered with a stew of blood, hair, and brain tissue—flashed before me. My stomach turned.

The marshal said, "Unless you got a reason to go back into the courtroom, Agent Wirth, I'll let you be. You can see yourself out."

I gave a slight nod, without looking at him. "Fine."

As the marshal walked away, I went inside, and the air changed again. It was not merely stale. It was thick and harsh. The bleach and lemon cleanser cut my throat as I tried to breathe. I covered my nose and mouth with my hand, an attempt to give myself some time to adjust, but it didn't help much. I then walked further inside.

The desks for the law clerk and court reporter were largely undisturbed, frozen in time. It would have looked as if Judge

Griggs's staff had simply gone to lunch, except for the remnants of the clerk's morning coffee. It had now thickened and generated an island of mold at its center.

The door to Judge Griggs's chambers had yellow tape, instructing people to "not cross." The door, however, wasn't sealed. This angered me. The investigation was active. Although it'd likely be closed soon, it was still a serious breach in protocol. Anybody with a magnetic pass-card could have come into chambers, removed whatever they wanted, and left. Nobody the wiser.

I opened the door and ducked under the tape. The chemical odor grew even harsher, and I began to gag and cough. It was a smell that wasn't going to go away any time soon. My guess was that the entire room would be gutted the moment the case was officially closed, banishing any remnant of Judge Griggs and what had happened there.

I started to feel lightheaded. I wanted out but forced myself to take a closer look, and I realized how desperately I wanted to find anything that could give me a lead, a little direction. I walked over to the judge's large desk.

I also wanted to know "Why?" Perhaps my own past flirtations with ending my life played a role. I just couldn't accept the idea that a married man with children, wealthy, and at the pinnacle of his profession would commit suicide for no reason at all. There had to be more. If there wasn't anything more, then why did I—somebody who was alone and far from successful—still live?

In the top drawer, I found nothing but office supplies, while the middle drawer contained a box of protein bars, snacks, and a bag of taffy. The lower drawer had personnel files related to the judge's clerk and court reporter, as well as brochures for the federal health insurance program.

I thought that was it.

As I closed the lower drawer, however, I noticed something.

It was black. Almost completely covered, it could've been mistaken as a shadow. I pushed one of the files aside and took a picture of it with my phone. Then I picked it up and held it in my hand. The object was a casino chip. "Expedition" was printed on the edge, which was the name of the biggest casino in downtown St. Louis, a reference to the Gateway Arch, Lewis & Clark, and the city's role as the starting point for pioneers traveling west.

I knew of the Expedition, although I'd never been inside. I preferred losing money and going into debt from the comfort of my couch, thereby avoiding the shame and disappointed looks of the people around me as I went deeper into the hole.

I smiled. This was what I wanted. It was a path forward for my investigation. I put the chip back in the drawer, and as I did, my phone rang.

It was Matthews. I didn't have an opportunity to tell him about the poker chip. Colton Steele had called him, upset, wondering where he was. Matthews had told Steele that I was covering it, but Steele was still mad, threatening to call the Carrot if nobody arrived in the next three minutes.

I looked at my watch, realizing how much time had passed. They were right. I was late. To Matthews, I said, "I got it covered." Then I rushed out the door.

———

I DID AS EXPECTED. After a tongue lashing from Colton Steele, I sat with the witness in a small conference room for two hours. While the witness read a copy of the *Wall Street Journal*, I took the jump drive out of my pocket and reviewed the Kasi Barnes file on my laptop.

I began with the photographs. My peers would likely consider this to be an unusual place to start. Most cops followed the mantra of the old Dragnet detective, Joe Friday:

"Just the facts, ma'am." Start with the "what" and "when," and from there delve into the "who" and "why." They'd begin with sterile reports, working chronologically from the first responding officer to the interviews and statements, and from there to the catalog of physical evidence collected along with the autopsy report. Photographs would only be viewed in conjunction with these steps, if at all. Sometimes there wasn't a reason to look at the photographs, and if there was no reason, why unsettle things?

I worked in reverse. I usually went directly to the crime scene photographs. Seeing the person who died—an actual life prematurely lost, a human being—was important. It provided me with motivation and context. A connection was created by that simple act of viewing a victim as a human being, rather than viewing the victim as secondary to the crime.

That desire to understand the victim was probably why I couldn't bring myself to close the Judge Griggs suicide file. I didn't know him yet. He eluded me, and I, for some reason, felt compelled to go deeper into his life before I'd accept that he simply put a bullet through his brain because he was depressed.

Perhaps my father felt the same way about Kasi Barnes as I did about Judge Griggs. He never knew her and therefore couldn't accept that it was a tragedy, not a crime. I thought about my conversation with Perelli after the funeral, when I was asking him for the file. He told me my father wanted something to be there that wasn't.

He then added, "Addicts overdose. Happens every day." Nothing special.

I clicked the folder icon. My screen then populated with over a hundred photographs. The thumbnail images looked like loose pieces of a jigsaw puzzle. I selected one at random, and it filled the screen.

I recognized the location right away, because was in my

dream. It was along the sloping edge of the Mississippi River, where barges still loaded and unloaded on their way toward the Gulf of Mexico. Long ago, the plants and trees were removed and replaced by large cobblestones, now smoothed by time and the constant encroachment of water, icing in the winter and rising in the spring. To the left, a streetlight was on, but unnecessary. The honey gauze of an early sun illuminated the body without need of assistance.

There were no obscuring shadows, no mystery as to what was on display. She lay on her back. Her hair was wet, as well as the thin dress that covered some, but not all, of her body. Her skin was pale white. Her hair black. No obvious sign of sexual assault.

I clicked another photograph. This was a closer view. Her eyes were open, one brown and one green. Black mascara ran from the edges. The upper ear pierced four times. The lobe gauged, stretched with a black plug. Kasi Barnes was not shot or stabbed or strangled. Just as Perelli told me, there was no mystery. The holes and tracks up her arm told the story, and when I read the toxicology report, it was confirmed. She died of an overdose.

Overdose deaths were routine. When I worked the dog shift, some nights I'd respond to two or three suspected overdoses per night. Sometimes the person would die, but often I or somebody else could bring the person back from the dead with a shot of naltrexone. If the person passed, a file was generated, and reports were written that were nearly identical to the one for Kasi Barnes. That's because overdose case reports were recycled. Cops simply cut and pasted from a template, replacing one junkie's name with another, sprinkling in some original details, and it was done.

What "unfinished business" could my father possibly have with Kasi Barnes?

In the moment, I couldn't think of why, of all the cases my

dad handled over his career, he came back to St. Louis for this one. As he lay dying in the hospital, this was the one he asked me to solve. He told me to find the person who killed this young woman. He told me to stop him, and "there's more."

I thought, this was just like my investigation of Judge Griggs's suicide. Everybody wanted the case closed and to move on, but there was more to it. That's probably what bothered my dad so much. He wanted to follow the case wherever it led, and he didn't get the opportunity. In the hospital, he told me there were other victims.

He said, "There's more," meaning it's bigger than just Kasi Barnes, but she's somehow the key. If I find out who sold her the drugs, I'd be able to build a much bigger case. That had to be it. That's what I needed to do.

I closed the folder with the crime scene photographs and started reading the police reports, as well as the case chronology. I needed to figure out that next move while I felt this energy, a renewed kinship with my dad. Maybe we weren't so different. We had the same instincts, I thought, us against the world, and we'd find justice long after others had quit.

It took about two hours, but I worked through the entire file by the time a paralegal with the United States Attorney's Office eventually knocked on the door. The woman came inside.

She asked, "All good in here?"

"Nobody came to bother us," I said.

"Excellent."

The paralegal then told the witness they were ready for his testimony. He folded his newspaper, stood, put it under his arm, and walked out the door.

That was it. I was done for the day. I looked down at my laptop, thinking about shutting it down and then thinking about my dad again. For over a year, I'd gone to Dr. Dan to cure me. My father was totally against the "head shrinks." When I told him I didn't have a choice and the FBI was requiring it after what had happened at Merchant's Bridge, he told me just to "check the box and get out." At the time, I remember rolling my eyes. He could be such a dinosaur, and I knew he'd go bananas if I told him how many drugs I took in a day.

Now looking back on it, I think my dad was right. Dr. Dan had no incentive to stop, billing my insurance every week. All the while, he was pushing me away from my father, sowing doubts about how I'd been raised, scoffing at the little pearls of wisdom my dad had imparted over the years. In the process, my confidence was going down, not up. My nighttime hauntings became more intense, not less, and my career was going in the toilet. I felt it. Matthews was worried about me. We both knew the Carrot was looking for reasons to get rid of me at the review hearing.

"Therapy is for other people," my dad had said. "We're unique. You and me, we're people of action in a passive world. Don't ever forget that, Tiger. Meditation and navel-gazing don't solve cases, but good ol' fashioned shoe leather always gets the job done."

Exactly, I thought, good old fashioned shoe leather. I went back to the electronic files on my laptop and scanned the reports for a name. Then I found it: Heather Barnes. She was Kasi's mother but never formally interviewed. I'd start with her, but not before a quick trip to the casino.

13

The Expedition Casino was wedged between a highway and bridge, about a quarter of a mile away from the Gateway Arch. It was consistent with the architecture of the late 1990s, as if there was a secret government bonus for anybody who incorporated a ridiculous amount of blue, mirrored glass into their design. The casino's most prominent feature was a curved, twelve-story tower. It was likely intended to reflect the majesty of the meandering river. To me, it looked more like a shark fin, warning the happy little gamblers who strolled inside they were about to be eaten.

I knew I'd need a subpoena to get any official information from the casino. So, my goal was to establish relationships. If Judge Griggs was gambling thousands of dollars, he'd be a familiar face to the staff. A little extra tip to a waitress might go a long way towards helping me understand what happened to him.

The problem with this plan was that it required money. As the slot machines beeped and dinged, I tried to do some quick calculations in my head. I, of course, already owed the online casino quite a bit. My checking account balance was thin, under $200. Of my six credit cards, I knew two or three were maxed out, and I tried to remember the one with the most available for a cash advance.

I'd gotten my first credit card during college orientation. There was a table outside the student union. A cute guy offered a free T-shirt and $75 just to sign up. "You don't even need to use it," he'd said, like a drug dealer offering a free hit.

Over the years, I'd get emails notifying me I was eligible to increase my credit limit. I'd accepted some, but not all of them. "Was it twelve thousand dollars?" I asked myself as I got in line for the cashier. "No, more like fifteen thousand."

Now I was at the window, and I realized the teller was a little person standing on a box so he'd be the right height for the counter.

"How much?" the teller asked.

My rational brain told me I should calculate the exact amount I was willing to lose, not a penny more. My emotional brain, however, thought about how good it would feel to win, and how much easier it would be playing against people in real life rather than an avatar on a computer screen. It was the classic trope seen in countless cartoons and movies, an angel and a devil on opposite shoulders, whispering conflicting advice into each ear.

The cashier repeated the question. "What amount of chips do you need, ma'am?"

I hesitated, then handed the cashier that old college credit card that just happened to be in the back of my wallet. "A thousand."

The cashier's eyes lowered, slightly. It was like he already knew that was what I was going to do, only waiting for confirmation. "I'll need to see your driver's license before running the card."

I gave it to him. He matched the name and signatures, then

handed the license back to me. "You'll need to enter your PIN," he said after sliding the card through the magnetic reader.

I did as I was told, holding my breath as I waited for the little screen to confirm the transaction. Seconds ticked by, which felt like hours. A sick feeling formed in the pit of my stomach as I felt the eyes of all the people behind me. They were surely watching and judging.

I was about to press the red button to cancel the transaction when the machine beeped. The little man handed my card back to me and removed a variety of chips from his drawer, denominations of $10, $25, and $50. He pushed all of them through the window, except one. It was black, worth $100. Just like the chip I'd found in Judge Griggs's drawer.

As the little man's eyes darted around, he made a slight nod toward a camera recording our every move. Then, out of the corner of his mouth, he whispered, "This one, Miss Amy, is special, just like you." He slid the chip towards me, but not all the way. His index finger remained on top of it.

Closing his eyes, the little man moved his lips, speaking silently while his finger ran clockwise around the edge. He repeated the motion twice around, counter-clockwise once, then twice around again. Then he opened his eyes, leaned toward me, and spoke softly, but it didn't sound like a whisper. It was as if he spoke into a microphone.

His words echoed in my head. "Don't use it right away."

The little man tapped the middle of the chip six times. Then he pulled his hand back, as if the chip was on fire.

"Wait until you *really* need to change your luck, Miss Amy. Keep it separate from the others."

This all should have been very disturbing, but I somehow felt lighter, like I was in on the joke. I couldn't help smiling, wondering how many others he'd performed this routine for. The little man vibrated with energy. His patter was entertaining and hypnotic, like a carnival hustler, and it likely resulted in some very nice tips.

"Thank you." I picked up the black chip and did as I was told, placing it in a separate pocket.

"Good girl." The little man nodded and winked, then looked past me at the line of people who had been waiting. "Next."

———

ALTHOUGH I'D DONE plenty of gambling online, too much, I'd done very little in real life. I'd gone to a few police conferences where there was gambling attached to the convention center or nearby. One was in Nashville, another in Illinois.

Even as the number of casinos in St. Louis grew, I stayed away. I did not like the cigarette smoke, and the clientele was depressing. I hated seeing their glazed expressions as the casino methodically took their money, death by a thousand cuts. I was particularly disturbed by the slot zombies. All of these people sitting in a row, staring at a screen, tapping a button for hours and hours. They probably bothered me the most because they reminded me of myself, sitting in my apartment, staring at my laptop with a glass of wine, and tapping the keys to be dealt another hand.

At least the Expedition didn't allow smoking. I walked over to a low-stakes poker table. Forty minutes later, I was up $100. An hour after that, I was down $250. A waitress kept bringing me free drinks, and I held steady for quite some time, even as different players joined and left the table.

My attempts to make small talk with the dealer and various servers didn't get very far, and at the two-hour mark, my plan to get insight into Judge Griggs or even locate somebody who could identify him had failed. I was also losing badly, going eleven hands in a row without a win.

In front of me on the green felt, there was only one five-dollar chip and one ten-dollar chip. In my pocket was the black chip I was supposed to keep until my luck needed to change. That was all I had left. Almost a thousand dollars had disappeared, soon to be accruing interest on my credit card at over 28%, along with my debt to Full House Poker.

I put the five-dollar chip into the pot, and the cards were dealt. The other players eyed me. They'd watched my pile of chips shrink, and they certainly sensed my desperation. Blood was in the water, and now they'd go in for the kill.

A man with a bushy mustache raised $10 and called. With a pair of kings, I felt pretty good. It would've been stupid to fold. So, I put my last $10 chip into the pot and called it. One by one, everybody revealed their cards.

The woman to my right won the hand with two pairs, and I got up from the table. The realization of what I'd just done began to sink in. I'd come to The Expedition broke, and I was going to walk out even deeper in debt - and without any information about Judge Griggs.

I was an idiot.

I walked across the casino toward the cashier. I had to stop. My plan was to cash in my one remaining black chip. I didn't want to leave the casino with nothing in my pocket. That would be pathetic.

As I walked past a craps table, I noticed a group of people having a great time playing roulette. They were young and beautiful, probably there as part of a bridal party. The dealer saw me, and we exchanged a look.

He was thin and athletic, built like a long-distance runner. His jaw was square. His hair was dark brown, and his eyes were piercing blue.

"Want to give it a try?" he asked as I approached.

I stopped. "I don't know how to play."

"It's easy," he said. "We'll all teach you."

The angel and devil reappeared on my shoulders, each whispering different advice. Then I thought of my dad, another one of his favorite sayings being, "You can't win if you don't play." This advice was intended to encourage me to take chances in life; reach for that next rung on the ladder or try something new. My father never said it in the context of gambling money that I didn't have or could afford to lose, but in the moment I didn't care. I was going to run through that wall. I started to tell myself this was what my dad would do, but I stopped. This wasn't true. I was his legacy. I was his eternal life. Running through this wall wasn't something he would do; it was something *we* would do together. I was an extension of him.

"Okay," I said, joining the group.

The cute dealer, whose name tag said his name was John, brightened. The bridal party cheered. A waitress appeared from nowhere, and suddenly I was on the edge of the table with a drink in one hand and my black one-hundred dollar chip in the other.

I watched them play, while the dealer explained my options and the odds. "If you want to stay here for a little while, I'd just bet on black or bet on red. You won't get rich, but the odds are fifty-fifty, and you'll get free booze along the way."

"And if I bet on a number?"

The dealer hesitated. "High risk, high reward." He ran his hand through his hair, gave me a smile. "You can do whatever you want," John said, "but my personal preference is that you stay a while."

My heart fluttered. That sounds ridiculous, like I was some middle-school girl, but that was exactly what happened. I, too, wanted to stay a while. I was about to ask him to break my black chip into smaller denominations when I happened to see the little man who'd been working at the cashier window. His jacket was on, and it looked like he was going home.

His eyes, however, were on me, locked and staring. As if reading my mind, he shook his head, then I heard him say, "Don't do it." It was loud, just like before, as if there was a speaker in my head. Intellectually, I knew I didn't really hear him say it, because he was about twenty or thirty feet away. The crowd in the casino may have thinned, but there were still people talking and machines dinging everywhere. I know it didn't make any sense. I know I didn't actually hear him say it, but I did.

I laid the black chip on the green felt. "I'm all in on Black Four."

"Seriously?"

John did not approve, but the bridal party certainly did. They all cheered.

A woman wearing a fake diamond tiara, likely the bride-to-be, said, "She's our lucky charm. I got a tingle."

The guy on the other side said, "High roller."

"So you're sure?" John asked.

I nodded. "Go big or go home," which was another Jack-ism.

"Okay."

John used his stick to push my chip to a black circle with the number 4 on it. My father was born on the fourth of December, and I figured it was as good as any other choice.

The dealer then moved the other chips around to their places, and he spun the roulette wheel. Everybody around the table started clapping their hands, whooping and hollering as the silver marble bounced from one number to another.

The wheel slowed, and so did the marble. It bounced, then bounced twice more, then finally settled on Black 4.

The crowd erupted as John called it out. "Black Four Winner." He took a large stack of chips out and placed them on the table. Then he pushed them toward me as others slapped my back and gave me high fives.

I was stunned, staring at what now appeared directly in front of me. My $100 had turned into $3,500. Nobody at the table wanted me to leave now, and John looked particularly happy when I decided to stick around. For the rest of the night, I stayed away from anything too risky. Only small bets on whether the marble would land on red or black, just as John had originally advised.

Although I was no longer taking big risks, my luck remained, winning far more than I lost. The crowd at the table grew, and soon people were simply copying whatever I did.

An hour and a half later, another dealer, not nearly as good looking as John, approached. John saw him, then gave everyone a final broad smile.

"That's the end of my shift, folks, but Max will take good care of you."

Everybody gave John a round of applause as he stepped away from the roulette table. A few in the bridal party gave him a tip. I looked down at my pile of chips.

"Hang on," I said. "You need to help me cash these out."

The bride-to-be made a kissy sound, while the others laughed. I didn't care. I was thoroughly buzzed from the free drinks, even though they were ridiculously watered down. My inhibitions were gone.

"Just to the window, then you can go home," I said, then added in a flirty, unfamiliar voice, "Unless you don't want to."

———

I WAITED at the bar for him to change out of his uniform, continuing to be served free booze because John had told the bartender I was with him. When he tapped me on the shoulder, it was quite the transformation. The formal attire was gone, and John looked like he was ready to hike up a mountain.

"Sorry that took so long, but I hate wearing that tuxedo." He sat down across from me. "So first of all, congratulations. I've been working here a long time, and it's rare to be in the presence of an actual winner."

I laughed, knowing the absurdity of the statement. "A winner," I said, "that's me." I motioned for the waitress. "Now let me buy you a drink."

It was his turn to laugh. "I drink for free."

"Even better," I said. The waitress took John's order, then left us alone with one another.

He asked, "So what are you going to do with it?"

I thought about the $4,600 that had just been electronically transferred into my bank account. "I know I should say I'm going to take an exotic vacation, but sadly, it's just going to pay off a bunch of debts." I kept it vague, never mentioning it was almost entirely gambling debts. "The rest will be for taxes and a little cushion. I've never had much of a financial cushion, so that'll be nice."

"I understand," John said. "You may have assumed I'm one of those really rich casino employees. You know the type. A guy who's really a billionaire that works here just for fun, but the truth is, I only work here because it fits my class schedule. They're open twenty-four-seven, so it's about as flexible as a job can be."

"Where are you a student?"

"Finishing up at UMSL," John said, pronouncing the acronym for the University of Missouri-St. Louis as "Umm-sul," rather than saying the letters. "It's taken me a long time. I bounced around a few places, took multiple gap years, dabbled in carpentry...sort of waiting and biding time for my brain to grow up. How about you?"

"Traditional," I said. "Graduated high school, and then four years straight at Wash U."

"That's a great school." His eyebrows rose, impressed. "And after graduating?"

"This and that." I dodged the question. My experience was that most men didn't really want to go out with a woman who carries a gun. I shifted the focus back onto him. "So, you never said what you're studying."

"Teaching," John said. "I like the outdoors and figure it'd be nice to travel in the summers. I love going out west, but it's super expensive, so I'm rehabbing an old Airstream."

I teased, "You're a hipster."

"Not quite." He watched as the waitress approached and delivered his drink, then watched her leave. Once she was out of earshot, he said, "Can I ask you something you might take offense at?"

I paused, trying to figure out where this was going. Such questions rarely ended well. "I guess."

"Can I take you home tonight?"

I laughed. The laughter came out in a burst. "Well, that's pretty forward."

John held out his hands. "No," his face reddened, "it's not like that...well, I mean, maybe, but..." He shrugged. "You've had a lot to drink, and...I mean, it's not like you're falling over or passed out, but it's probably not going to be good for you to drive."

"I can call an Uber." It came out a bit harsher than I had intended.

"Of course," John said. "Totally up to you."

"Right," I said, warming back up. I hadn't been with a man in a long time and was a bit nervous about even the possibility. Then I reminded myself that this was the new me. It was time to stop meditating and navel-gazing and start living life.

We finished our drinks, becoming even more flirty along the way. Then I pushed the cocktail glass to the side and took his hand.

"Okay, Johnny boy. You can take me home, but only if you withhold judgment about how messy my apartment is."

———

MISTER BONES barely lifted his head as we entered. The cat was far too tired to offer us anything more than a half-opened eye and annoyed flick of his tail. I turned on a small lamp so I could guide John to my bedroom but otherwise kept the lights off.

As he kissed the nape of my neck, I kept thinking, *I never do this.* But "this" was exactly what I was doing. There were so many emotions swirling inside my head. I was simultaneously grieving the loss of my father, the bittersweet joy of being an FBI agent after being run out of the St. Louis Police Department, figuring out the next steps in both my father's case and my own, the jubilation of crawling my way out of debt with a lucky chip, and now this.

For the first time in years, if ever, I let myself go. I allowed myself to be in the present, to be free. All that mattered to me was making the most of that specific moment in time.

We struggled to get our pants off, fumbling with the belts and zippers. It was never as smooth as in the movies when clothes seemed to disappear magically. We bumped and kissed, stumbled and grabbed, smiling the whole time.

Then we were in the bed, laughing and pawing at one another like we were teenagers in the back of a car.

———

IN THE MORNING, I opened my eyes to the sun. I hadn't closed the shades the night before, and it cast an unfiltered light into the room. I reached out for John, but he wasn't there. His side of the bed was empty, and my mood sank.

I figured it was just going to be a hook-up, but that didn't prevent the feeling of disappointment. I thought I remembered him mentioning an early morning class. Maybe that was it, or maybe he had just been laying the groundwork for his great escape.

I got up and put on some semi-clean pajamas before wandering into the other room. Mister Bones immediately began meowing at me, his bowl empty. I decided he could wait. Instead, I looked around the apartment for a note, playing it cool.

I never found one.

It was a somewhat bitter end to what had been a great evening. I shuffled back into the kitchen to get the cat some food, feeling increasingly hungover with every step. As I reached for the drawer where it was stored, my head began to spin. I almost threw up but managed to hold it back.

After filling Mister Bones' food dish, I realized I was out of coffee. This was not good. I sat down on the couch, considering my options, when I heard a buzz from the ancient intercom system.

Now what? I thought as I walked over to it and pressed the button.

"Hey, it's John." His voice sounded tinny through the speaker. "You were out of coffee and...just about everything else. I got some stuff for breakfast."

My face brightened at the sound of his voice. The hangover that had weighed me down just moments ago disappeared, and I wanted to confess my love to him on the spot.

Instead, I pressed the button to unlock the door and said, "You're my hero."

EVELYN

She readied a pot of boiling water while keeping an eye on Wirth's apartment. Except for the figures briefly passing in front of the second story windows, she could not see what was going on inside, but she could feel it. What she felt made her happy.

Amy Wirth's aura had always been blue, projecting a deep vein of freethinking and intuition. These characteristics were her greatest strengths, if only she could trust herself. The young woman's energy had been so muddied by pain, she could not fully access her talents.

The old woman brushed away her long dreadlocks, now purple, then removed two cups from the shelf. Her parrot watched from above as Evelyn placed a tea bag in each cup and filled them with hot water.

While the tea steeped, the old woman opened the window that faced a crumbling alley, which ran parallel to Cherokee Street. She called. A crow responded, then she gave her instructions to it. Another responded further away, and the message transmitted from one tree to the next.

Her wrinkled lips curled into a tight, satisfied smile. Then she closed the window, retrieved her cups of tea, and placed them on the table at the same time as there was a knock on the door.

"It's unlocked."

The door opened, and a man with a white beard and full head of white hair stepped inside. "An unlocked door." His words, sung with an Irish lilt, sounding both playful and serious. "You're too trustful, Evelyn, always have been."

"I can hold my own, Pike."

She sat down, then pointed at the empty chair across from her. The man with the white beard walked across the small space, covering it in just a few steps, and sat down.

The woman stirred a little honey into her tea. "Figured you'd be coming to visit me." Her eyes twinkled. "It's been a bit of time since you've scolded me for stepping out of line. I've missed your little lectures."

"I don't control you, Evelyn. You know that, but there are others that certainly will if you continue down this path."

She shrugged, then folded her arms across her narrow chest, like a toddler refusing to eat her broccoli. "I'm old. What can they do to me? I'm not afraid of death." This was a lie, but it was a good lie. It made her feel strong.

"Understood," Pike said. "But it's not just you they can hurt. They can take away the things you love." He looked at the parrot, then at some of the pigeons who had congregated on Evelyn's windowsill. Then Pike pointed at his throat. "Imagine never being able to call them again; to lose that gift, Evelyn. The thing that gives you the most joy. They can take those away." Pike saw a slight tremble run through his friend, but Evelyn recovered quickly.

She stiffened and shot back, "You were out of line with the lawyer, and even more risky when you saved the woman I now protect in your absence. What's the difference?" She took another sip of tea. "Or is this a 'do as I say, not as I do' situation?"

"I paid dearly for that; surely you've heard." Pike raised his left arm so Evelyn could see the place where his hand once was, the hand he had used to heal, now gone forever.

"I'm sorry." Evelyn looked away, biting her lip. "I guess I'd heard rumors, but there are always rumors amongst us."

"Well, now you know why I'm concerned about that little stunt you and Cain pulled, and where it's going to lead."

"You did what you did because they needed to be protected, and she still needs protection, a little help now and again is fine. She needed a change of luck. That's what we're doing here. That's all."

"Don't try and kid a kidder, Evelyn," Pike said. "This isn't just about a little protection and giving someone a dash of luck."

"I don't know what exactly you're insinuating, but we—"

"Come now, Evelyn." Pike's voice lowered. Each word was spoken with all the rough edges smoothed away. "You and Cain are hunting again, and the man you're hunting is both powerful and connected to those who are even more powerful than you can imagine."

There was a long silence. Then Evelyn's defenses lowered and she spoke in a more conspiratorial tone. "Well, let's just say, hypothetically, we were doing something like that." She was not ready to fully confess, but she wasn't going to cede the fight either. "There is right, and there is wrong. Maybe *we* can't directly stop him, because of his father, but the young woman living in that apartment certainly can if she finds herself in the right situation."

Pike looked beyond Evelyn, through the window, and up at what was Amy Wirth's apartment. "Her?"

"We don't have many options," Evelyn said. "Her father was too old, and I believe you saved her for a reason. It wasn't just a random act of kindness, Pike. You knew what you were doing when you went to Merchant's Bridge. You always know."

"That…" Pike closed his eyes and lowered his head. The torture that followed those actions resurfaced, taking him back to that very dark place. He thought of what they made him confess, what they made him promise. Then he opened his eyes, wary. "That was a mistake, Evelyn."

"It was not a mistake, and you know it." She nodded toward Pike's missing hand. "Cain and I will not allow your sacrifices to be for nothing."

"Please don't do this for me." Tears welled in Pike's eyes. "I couldn't live with the guilt…I was told to bring you a message, a warning, and you must heed it, Evelyn. You must be thoughtful. This person you are hunting. He doesn't change anything, the die has been cast, and there are hundreds, if not thousands more just like him. People trying to hasten the end, consolidate the line, and you and Cain can't hunt them all."

"I agree," Evelyn said. "But this one would send a message to the others in hiding, others who share our values. Cain and I have thought it through, and we've made a specific decision not to let this monster roam free."

14

As we washed the breakfast dishes, John and I chatted easily. I talked about growing up in the city as the daughter of a cop, and John shared his experiences growing up on a farm in a small town in west-central Illinois. He mentioned his town wasn't even on most maps and that the Casey's gas station also served as the local grocery store, pizza place, hardware store, and donut shop.

"It was actually pretty tough for me," John said as he picked up another plate to dry. "I have dyslexia, and it took a long time to really learn how to read. Special ed started an hour earlier than the rest of the classes, so I rode on a bus with a lot of kids who had Down syndrome or were in wheelchairs. Got bullied pretty bad." John put the plate in the cabinet. "I guess that's why I want to be a teacher, in addition to the summers."

He took another plate from me. "How about you? You went to Wash U, and then what?"

I knew the question was coming and even considered lying to him or shading the truth. In the past, I'd told men I worked for the "government shuffling paper," and that was often a sufficient response for a little while, but I took a chance this time.

"I'm an FBI agent."

"Whoa." John stopped drying the plate. "You're serious...the FBI? As in, the Federal Bureau of Investigation?"

I nodded, studying John's reaction. Except for the initial surprise, he didn't give any indication that he was going to run for the door. He put the last plate back in the cabinet and asked. "So, do you have a gun?"

"I have many guns," I replied. "It's kind of a requirement of the job."

"That's cool." John closed the cabinet, then turned to face me. "Cool, as in..." He looked me up and down. "Like, super sexy."

It was, at least, said half in jest, but I couldn't stop myself from blushing.

HE DROVE me back to the casino, and we located my car. I kissed John one last time, thanked him for the breakfast, and we exchanged phone numbers. He waited until I got into my car, making sure it started and I was safe before driving away.

It was a nice gesture, and I allowed myself to wonder if there may be a future beyond the hook-up. This was what I thought about on my way to work.

When I arrived, the office was empty. Matthews had a meeting with a forensic accountant related to one of our other cases. He wouldn't be back until the afternoon, which gave me a little more freedom.

I logged on to the Internet and checked my account. Last night's casino winnings had already posted and were available. I was always bad with money, so I didn't wait until any of the payments were due. I pressed a few buttons, and within a few minutes my debts were paid. I was in the clear.

I leaned back, placed my hands behind my head, and stared at the screen: Balance Due: $0

I took a mental picture, convincing myself this was the end. I swore I would never gamble again. I'd never go into debt again. That was the old me, and it was time to leave her behind.

Then I thought about everything else that had happened in the last twenty-four hours. I had started my investigation to figure out what happened to Kasi Barnes. I had made some progress related to Judge Griggs's suicide, and I had met a seemingly functional man who might be interested in having a relationship with me.

Not too bad.

My pity party was over. No meds. No Dr. Dan. No self-loathing. No self-doubt. This was the new me, and I liked it. Running through walls was fun.

———

Matthews arrived late that afternoon, looking stressed and tired from spending so much time with Colton Steele. He dropped down into his chair, heavy.

"I've dealt with a lot of U.S. Attorneys over the years, but that guy has to be the worst."

I finished documenting my latest interactions with a witness on an Excel spreadsheet related to the blue tag files and turned to face him. "Sounds like you need a beer," I said. "And I need your guidance."

Matthews shook his head, grimacing. "I just got here," he said. "Haven't even checked my messages."

I told him his messages could wait. "What you really need is to take a break with me."

"What's your proposal?"

"A beer at O'Brien's, right now."

He looked at his watch. "I thought you were afraid of

checking out a little early, worried you might get caught by the Carrot?"

"It's a new me."

"Fine," Matthews said. "Let's go."

———

The pub was large, with many booths and tables, designed to accommodate throngs of people who congregated there before and after Blues hockey games and St. Louis City soccer matches. On this weekday afternoon, however, Maggie O'Briens was mostly empty. There were no games scheduled for that night, and it was a little too early for the after-work crowd.

We walked to a booth in the far corner for privacy, and along the way the bartender greeted us. "The usual?" Sandy asked.

Matthews gave her a thumbs up, and we settled in. I opened a menu and began searching for something to eat, and Matthews did the same. When our drinks arrived, we placed an order for loaded nachos just to get us started and began to debrief our day. I let Matthews go first, because I wanted to seem mature and objective about what I'd found in Judge Griggs's desk drawer, even though I was like a four-year-old with a secret.

Matthews noticed my bouncing leg about halfway through a story about how Colton Steele had insulted a key confidential informant and paused mid-sentence. "Okay, I think you're going to explode." He pretended to sigh but was amused by my behavior. "Let's declare an intermission on my rants against Colton Steele, and you can just tell me about your day." I feigned reluctance, but Matthews would have none of it. "Cough it up, rookie."

"Only if you insist." I wiggled in anticipation. I couldn't

remember the last time I'd felt so much energy, to be so alive, and we both laughed.

An older couple across the room turned, and Sandy, the bartender, shook her head at us. I knew FBI agents were supposed to be stoic and serious all the time, but sometimes the pressure found a way to relieve itself. I cracked. Then Matthews cracked, and we couldn't stop laughing. It sent everything sideways, and despite my excitement, I never actually told Matthews what I'd found in Judge Griggs's desk drawer until halfway through the nachos.

"It's interesting," Matthews said. "And a bit surprising. Judge Griggs had the reputation of a Boy Scout...in fact, I think he was an actual Boy Scout, an Eagle Scout or something like that."

"If he had a gambling problem, that helps explain the suicide, and it might've been something that was being exploited by people who had business before the court."

"Like blackmail."

"Exactly."

"What about your theory that he had a drug problem? Where did that go? You sounded pretty sure, and now you're off in a completely different direction."

"It's still possible. He could have a drug problem and a gambling problem," I said. "I sent an email to the medical examiner, requesting the hair follicle test, but I haven't heard back." I grabbed some nachos off the platter and moved them onto my plate. "The gambling, I think, is better."

"But his wife said he didn't gamble," Matthews said. "It could've just been a souvenir from a conference or a night out with the guys, something he forgot was in his pocket and tossed it in a drawer."

"We need to get all of his credit card and bank statements to really know." I waved at Sandy to get another round of beer, then continued. "With that casino chip, I think we have enough to subpoena the banks, and maybe even the casino."

Mathews was about to respond when Sandy arrived, and he waited until she was gone to tell me what was on his mind.

"It's good work, don't get me wrong," he said, "but what's the basis for a subpoena? There's no crime here. It's a suicide, and now you've probably figured out a possible reason why, which, when there isn't a note, is more than most families ever get."

"But he did it in the courthouse," I said. "You told me that might be a message. He was trying to tell us something."

"Like what?"

"I don't know, exactly," I said. "He was a smart guy, and he had everything. It's just wrong. I feel like he wanted us to investigate, to intervene somehow."

"Do you hear yourself? You just said he had everything, but then a few minutes ago you were talking about mental health medications, then you went to possible drug addiction, and now we've got a secret gambling addiction that was financially ruining him and his family, along with somebody blackmailing him. That isn't somebody who had everything, and frankly, it sounds farfetched."

"I know, but there has to be more to it than that."

"But sometimes there's not. It's just a suicide, Amy. There's only so much we can do. And we have other cases to work on. I got a roofing company that's operating out of Alton and doing all sorts of bad stuff. It's a scam, and I need your help on it."

I slouched into a pout. "There has to be a way."

"You've got a week until the memorial service," Matthews said. "That was the deal. You've got a week."

"I know," I said. "Until then, I'll keep going."

Matthews rolled his eyes. "Let me guess: you're running through walls."

I smiled. "It's actually working pretty well so far."

"If you say so," Matthews said, "but I still need your help on that new roofing company case, and you still need to be working through those blue tag files."

"I promise, but can we at least try and get a warrant for the judge's financials?"

"It's a waste of time," Matthews said. "They'll never go for it."

"Let's just try," I begged, and Matthews relented.

15

———

Amber Brenner was one of the nicest attorneys at the U.S. Attorney's Office, but she wasn't nice enough to draft and submit a subpoena for me to get Judge Griggs's financial records. She agreed with Matthews. I didn't have enough, especially without the permission of the judge's wife. Evidently, even dead people have a constitutional right to privacy, which was news to me.

The rest of the week followed a familiar pattern. During the day, Matthews and I met with attorneys and former employees of Kalvin Storm Chasers, the roofing company accused of exploiting undocumented immigrants and scamming customers. Between meetings and over lunch, I'd work the blue tag files, and then in the evening I connected with John.

We'd have dinner or coffee, if he had the evening off. When he was working, I'd show up when his shift was over at the casino. I was never tempted to gamble. We'd have a drink and hang out. Then we'd usually end up in bed together at the end of the night.

That's where I was on Thursday: in bed with John. He was

asleep, but I could not put my mind to rest. I turned onto my side and looked at him.

Were we in love? Or more importantly, was I in love?

It all seemed too easy, and in the darkness of the room, my thoughts turned skeptical. It'd been my experience that men, at some point, expired like a piece of fruit. Maybe they didn't turn rotten, but the sweetness turned sour as what was once exciting turned banal.

I looked at him, naked beside me, and I couldn't help wondering when he'd go bad. If it was going to happen, I wanted it to happen now, before the pain would be too much. Breaking it off would save both of us the torture of a long goodbye.

I didn't want us to get comfortable. I didn't want to move in together and start making sacrifices and compromises that inevitably turned into tiny seeds of resentment. Resentment that would grow over months and years until it was all-consuming.

I closed my eyes, squeezing them shut, and told myself to stop it. This was just my brain playing tricks on me. Living without meds meant living without guardrails. I took a shallow breath through my nose and told myself to stop it again, calmer this time.

You're running through walls, remember? Living in the moment.

Jack Wirth would never self-destruct. He'd keep going. He'd keep his eyes on the prize.

The prize? I thought about Kasi Barnes and my father's final wish to find the person responsible for her death. *What was I doing to keep that going?*

Days had passed since I'd done anything to locate Heather Barnes, the girl's mother, and obtain some information that would help me find the person who killed her daughter. Then there was Judge Griggs. I'd promised Matthews I'd write the report and close out the case after the memorial. That was the deal.

I looked at the clock. It was 2:00 a.m. The judge's public memorial was in one day. I felt a knot tighten in my stomach and my hands begin to shake.

I got up and went into the bathroom. I opened the medicine cabinet. I knew it was empty, but I needed to see it. I needed confirmation, to know the big bottle of Xanax was gone. All of it was gone. No pills, no safety net. I just needed to calm myself down and focus.

I walked back into the bedroom. John was still asleep. He hadn't moved at all. I pulled a pair of pajamas out of my drawer, and as I put them on, I committed to a plan. In the morning, I'd tell John we couldn't see each other for just a few days. I had deadlines, and something needed to give. I was sure he'd understand, but I was wrong.

John looked confused. The hair that shot out in every direction didn't help. He looked at me from the other side of the table, a half-eaten English muffin on his plate and mug of coffee in his hand.

"Just to be clear, you're saying you're not breaking up with me, but yet you don't want to see me."

Sensing I was on the precipice of totally screwing up the best relationship that had happened to me in years, I tried to clarify. "It's not a break, exactly." My voice grew higher, and the words tumbled out. "We're definitely not taking a break. I've just fallen behind at work, and I need to catch up. That's it, honestly. It's about me being selfish. I'm up for review soon, and I need to show some progress on these cases."

"I can help, you know? Like, somehow. Didn't you say that judge was a gambler?"

I thought about my original plan of befriending casino staff, seeing if any of the dealers or waitresses remembered Judge Griggs. John could do that. I could even ask him to try and access the casino's rewards program, which tracks how much a person gambles, but I didn't ask him to do any of it.

"I shouldn't have told you what I was working on. That was a mistake," I said, "and even if you found something, I couldn't use it. My boss would want to know how I got it, and she'd freak if she found out my boyfriend got it for me."

John smiled, his first of the morning. "Boyfriend?"

It took a second to click. I hadn't even realized I had said it, but obviously I had. "Boyfriend" was such a stupid word. We were adults. We weren't in high school anymore. It threw me off, and I forgot what we were even talking about.

"Well...yeah, I guess. Right? I mean...I'm not thinking you're seeing other people because...you're, like...here, like... all the time."

"So now you're saying we're exclusive. That's even more serious than just being boyfriend-girlfriend."

John got up and walked around the table. His expression was serious. He was evidently planning on sitting in the chair next to me but realized it was already being occupied by Mister Bones, and nobody moves Mister Bones. So instead, John awkwardly crouched down so he could be on the same level as me.

"Listen," he took my hand, "I'm glad you think I'm your boyfriend, because...I've been thinking you're my girlfriend. That's why this whole conversation this morning threw me for a loop." John kissed me on the cheek, then stood. "If you need some time to get caught up at work and focus on that, no problem. But you know, it doesn't have to be all or nothing."

"I know," I said. "That just seems to be how I think."

"Yes," John smiled. "That's definitely the impression I've gotten."

———

I spent the rest of the morning with Matthews in a conference room of a small, legal aid organization. The office was housed in an old gas station. These lawyers were nothing like the lawyers we usually dealt with. None of them had shiny cufflinks like Colton Steele or tailored suits like fancy defense attorneys. They wore jeans, tennis shoes, and T-shirts with the names of rock bands that I wasn't cool enough to know anything about. The supervisor was an immigrant woman whose office used to be where people paid for gas and bought cigarettes and lotto tickets. The others worked in the former garage.

Danny Russo was the name of the lawyer sitting with his client on the other side of the conference room table. He made me feel very old. It was like I had volunteered to be part of a training exercise for a high school mock trial team.

For three hours, we listened to immigrants from Guatemala who had crossed the border. They were transported to Missouri in the back of a windowless delivery truck and upon arrival were housed in one of a dozen pole barns scattered across Missouri, southern Illinois, and Arkansas.

The pole barns had mattresses on the floor, a wood stove, and a couple coolers for food. Six days a week, a man arrived in a van, drove them to the job site, and picked them up in the evening. Everybody was told they were working off their debt to the smugglers back home, although none of them knew exactly how much money was owed.

When the last interview of the morning was done and we were alone, Matthews turned to me. He shook his head. "It isn't wage theft. It's slavery."

"Unbelievable," I said. "How'd they even get here?"

"When Russo first reached out, he told me these were runners. They thought this was an actual gas station and were planning on stealing a car. A volunteer who was here when they came in the door happened to speak Spanish, and the next thing you know, we have a new case."

"It's righteous," I said.

Matthews looked around the space, sparsely furnished with beat-up office furniture that had likely been donated by big law firms looking for an easy tax write-off. "Very righteous, indeed," he said. "We gotta move before the trail gets cold."

I agreed, but I also knew I couldn't help right away. "I need to close out the Griggs investigation first. The memorial service is tomorrow morning, and I promised you I'd finish it by then. That's the deadline."

Matthews started to say something but stopped himself. "Fine," he said. "It'll be good to finally get it off our plate. Then we can go hard on this."

"I'm going to go back through our interview notes and everything the techs came up with tonight, and then I'll start drafting. Who knows? I may have it done early."

Matthew's expression pinched, and his head cocked to the side, skeptical. "I smell a little B.S."

"B.S.?" I laughed. "You are incapable of swearing, aren't you? You never curse."

"That's possible." Mathews began walking to the door. "Just remember to give the draft to me so I can review it before it goes to the Carrot."

"Yes, sir." I saluted, then we went our separate ways.

Neither one of us knew that after the judge's memorial service, everything would change. We'd never work together as partners again.

16

I went to a pizza-by-the-slice place near St. Louis University, scarfed it down, then headed back to the office. During the drive, I blasted Stevie Ray Vaughn, trying to tap into the ethos and energy of my father. I knew it was going to be an all-nighter, if I was going to review every-thing about the judge's suicide. I had to get myself amped, and by the time I got settled behind my desk, I was nearing the top of the roller coaster.

Multiple tabs were open on my computer. Using the bureau's template, I started working on the close-out memo. The beginning was easy, a summary of the judge's background, such as his family and education. Then I started to work on a narrative chronology of the investigation itself, such as the names of the agents involved, who was interviewed, and the evidence collected. I clicked between the close-out memo and electronic file, now reviewing each of the pieces of evidence collected.

It wasn't the first time I had looked at this stuff. I'd done it on the night of my father's funeral, and it wasn't any more exciting the second time. I felt myself fading as I clicked back and forth, summarizing what was found. My eyelids grew heavy, and I wondered whether it was really necessary to go into this much detail.

Then I got to the spreadsheet the crime scene techs had created related to the contents of Judge Griggs's desk, and I felt a little tickle in the back of my brain. The spreadsheet had the name and description of each document, as well as where it was found on or in the desk. In the far-right column was a hyperlink to the document itself. When I first reviewed it after the funeral, I hadn't found the black casino chip. At the time, my theory was drug addiction, specifically cocaine, but that was just a guess. There'd been no evidence of that. The hair follicle test, later ordered, had come back negative.

I kept working through the spreadsheet, following the links to actual documents. Most of it was mundane, but then I saw a few documents that were unfamiliar. I was sure I'd reviewed them all before, but now I wasn't. I kept clicking, reviewing, and summarizing. More and more of the documents felt entirely new to me, not that they were of any great importance, but it was strange.

I thought about that night and what I'd been through. I'd just dropped my mother off at the airport after the funeral, and I was determined to make a change. That's why I went to the office. The memory was clear now.

The Carrot had come to see me. She had told me to go home and get some rest, and I did go home. I had been so rattled by her mention of my upcoming review, I had shut down the computer and left, even though I wasn't done.

I looked at the spreadsheet on my computer screen.

How many did I not review?

The names of the documents meant little. I continued to scroll through the spreadsheet. I got to the second to the last page, and my stomach dropped. There was an electronic folder labeled "bills," and within that folder were a half-dozen financial documents, about four credit card bills, and a couple bank statements. This was what I was about to review when the Carrot had interrupted me.

The tingle grew stronger. I opened one of the credit card bills and saw it right away. A large cash advance, $15,000. Then I clicked another and saw a second cash advance. This was for over $20,000. I clicked one of the bank statements, and there was a draw on a home equity line of credit for over $50,000. To me, this corroborated everything I'd felt from the beginning.

The evidence had been there the whole time, and I'd missed it. Matthews wasn't to blame. He had been relying on me to take the lead on this one, and I had almost blown it. I thought about calling him, but what was he going to say or do in the middle of the night?

I needed to fix this myself. Somebody had to talk.

———

I WAS SHOWERED and professionally dressed when I parked in an underground ramp not too far from the law school and walked to Busch Hall. It was a beautiful building. The law school looked like it was one of the original structures built for the 1904 World's Fair—classic red stone with arches and turrets — but it was, in fact, built in the 1990s.

As I walked through its heavy oak doors, I had a briefcase, and inside were copies of the financial information I'd found in Judge Griggs's chambers. I followed the signs to a large lecture hall. Most of the seats were taken, but I found an empty chair near the back. In front, there was a podium on a stage.

I sat down and waited for the program to begin, scanning the faces of the stragglers who passed and those who were already seated, looking for Christine Griggs. I'd hoped she'd be at the door with other family members, greeting people as they arrived, but she wasn't, and I didn't see her anywhere else either.

About ten minutes later, a U.S. Marshal came through a side door. He walked up to the podium and gaveled the special session to order.

"Hear ye, hear ye, all rise. The Federal Court for the Eastern District of Missouri is now in session, the Honorable Chief Judge Cynthia Bustamante presiding."

Judge Bustamante came out of the same side door, wearing a black robe. She walked up to the podium as the marshal stepped aside.

"Good morning, everyone. My name is Cynthia Bustamante, and I welcome you to this special session of the Federal District Court, a memorial in honor of our dear friend and colleague, Judge David C. Griggs." She paused, collected herself, then continued. "I ask you to please remain standing, if you are able."

From the back, a procession of judges made their way to the front. Each wore their black robes, shoulders hung with weight unseen. They were professional decision-makers. Whatever conflict arose, regardless of whether it was a decision about guilt or innocence or a family conflict or one of business, it was their job to decide. It didn't matter if there wasn't a "right" decision or if it was picking the lesser of two bad choices, they were paid to decide.

The procession was led by the Supreme Court Justice who was the liaison for the Eighth Circuit Court of Appeals and the district courts within that circuit: Minnesota, Iowa, North Dakota, South Dakota, Nebraska, Missouri, and Arkansas. He was an ancient man. Most expected him to have died years ago, but he carried on, seemingly fueled by a bizarre quest to incorporate a reference to the Magna Carta or an obscure Federalist Paper into every decision he wrote.

Behind him were federal appellate judges, in order of

seniority, followed by federal district court judges, then members of the Missouri Supreme Court, and finally state district court judges.

It was impressive and solemn. In the program, it explained this was a tradition dating back to the 1700s, when judges throughout the British Empire donned black robes in mourning for the death of Queen Anne. Prior to that, judges wore robes of varying colors. After Queen Anne's funeral, the black robe became standard, particularly in the American colonies.

Once the judges had filed into the front rows of the lecture hall, the family progressed down the aisle. This was when I saw Christine Griggs for the first time since Matthews and I had interviewed her on her porch. As she passed, I swear she locked eyes on me. It was a cold, dead stare, as if knowing I'd come just for her.

Eventually, Chief Judge Bustamante instructed everyone to be seated so the memorial could proceed. She gave a few perfunctory remarks about Judge Griggs's integrity and work ethic, then introduced the first speaker.

"It is truly an honor to invite Senator Hoffman to provide a eulogy for Judge Griggs. Their friendship was well-known. It began as children, and it is a testament to their friendship that he was willing to fly in from Washington, D.C., to be with us today in order to participate in this memorial service."

Senator Hoffman, in his dark navy suit and red striped tie, walked onto the stage and shook Judge Bustamante's hand. "Thank you, Chief," he said, then waited for her to take a seat in one of the red padded chairs to his right. When she was settled, the senator began.

"It wasn't a difficult decision to be here to provide a eulogy for Davey. However, he was not a friend." The senator paused for drama, then smiled. "He was more than that. I considered him my brother. We talked almost every day, inseparable for years."

His descriptions of the judge and life growing up in rural Missouri were heartfelt and raw. I knew I should've been moved to tears like everyone else, but I'd inherited a healthy distrust of politicians from my father. "Power corrupts. If a politician is talkin', they're lyin'." This was another Jack-ism.

The more Senator Hoffman spoke, the more I found myself becoming more determined to find the truth. If I wasn't going to get it from the judge's wife, I decided the senator was going to be the next best option. Both would be at the reception after the memorial service.

I opened my briefcase and removed the judge's financial documents. As I studied them one last time, it was as if they vibrated in my hand, or perhaps my hand was just shaking.

———

THE RECEPTION WAS CROWDED. I saw Christine Griggs, but there was no way I could get close to her. She was surrounded by people. Everybody wanted a piece, to shake her hand, to give her a hug, or share a memory. I knew what that was like, having experienced the same awkward interactions after my father's funeral. This odd feeling of having all these people attempting to comfort you, when in reality they were the ones who were actually seeking comfort and reassurance.

This was the point where I should have left. I should have recognized and acknowledged the obvious. This was neither the time nor place to confront anyone about anything, especially the judge's widow.

In my briefcase, I had what I thought I needed to provoke a response, and maybe get some answers. I'd promised Matthews I'd close the case after the memorial, and I was fixated on that promise. It was not rational or logical, but that was my state of mind. I wanted to prove to him and myself that I could do the impossible, just like my dad. If Christine Griggs wasn't available, I'd just find the senator.

I circled the room a few times and found him in the back, shaking hands and listening patiently to a judge begging him to move a judicial appointment forward through a committee. An aide was a few feet away, half-listening to the conversation as she scanned the people in the room. Her job was to move Senator Hoffman along if she sensed a conversation had become hostile or drifted into controversial areas, while also ensuring the senator appeared to be willing to spend all the time in the world with whomever wanted to chat.

I thought about getting a glass of punch or iced tea, debating whether an informal approach would have a higher likelihood of success. I ultimately decided against it. "You don't run through a wall with a glass of punch unless you're the Kool-Aid Man" was another thing my dad would say, or maybe that was just something I thought he'd say.

Formal would be better.

I waited and watched, not more than five feet from the senator. When the aide took his elbow to lead him away, I made my move.

"Senator Hoffman?" I held out my hand. "I'm agent Amy Wirth, FBI, and I'm assigned to the Judge Griggs matter."

The senator made quick eye contact with his aide, then nodded his head with a tight grin. "FBI?"

"Yes," I said. "His suicide took place in a federal building, so we have jurisdiction."

"Over a suicide?"

The senator's eyes narrowed, skeptical. He was about to make a comment, but he appeared to think better of it. Instead, he made eye contact with his aide once more, obviously sending a telepathic message to get him the hell away from me.

He then said, "There are a lot of people here I need to talk to, but, briefly, what can I do for you?"

"Background," I said, "maybe we could go someplace a little quieter."

"I'm afraid now is not the time."

"It'll only take about five minutes."

"I'm sorry." He nodded toward his aide. "Lacey will give you her card and the two of you can set something up, but I'm on a plane to Washington, D.C., in just a few hours." He made a show of checking his watch to emphasize the point. "In fact, a car is probably waiting for me outside."

The aide took the senator's elbow, just as she had when extracting her boss from the previous conversation. It was smooth, but not quick enough.

I asked, "Did he have a gambling problem?"

The senator stopped in his tracks. His back stiffened, but he did not immediately turn. He certainly heard the question, but like all politicians he'd mastered the art of selective hearing. He continued on his way.

I was certain that would be the end of it, but then he stopped. Senator Hoffman turned, then walked back. His jaw was set. His eyes were narrow, and his face was flushed with anger. The look obviously horrified his aide, and she put her hand firmly on his shoulder. The senator did not stop. He leaned over, his face just inches from mine.

"How dare you?" His voice was a soft growl. "David Griggs was the most decent man I have ever known. In college, he wouldn't play poker. He wouldn't even put a quarter on a game of pool. He abhorred gambling in all its forms, and if you don't get out of here in ten seconds, I will personally destroy you and whatever pathetic career you have." He took a step back, plastered a fake smile on his face, and patted my back. "It's been nice chatting with you."

He then walked away. With nothing else to do, I decided to

get that glass of punch after all. I turned and ran directly into a woman. Without hesitation, I blurted out an apology, then realized the woman was Christine Griggs.

————

WE TALKED in an otherwise empty classroom. She sat across from me in a black dress, with a string of white pearls around her neck. Her hands were balled into tight fists, one clutching a tissue. She stared at me with a look of pure hatred.

"So, just to be clear," she said, "I talk to you now, and I never talk to you again. I never see you again or anyone else. This is over, correct?"

I agreed. "Mind if I record this?"

Her eyes looked at the ceiling, as if in disbelief, and in hindsight I don't blame her. Then Christine Griggs held out her hands in surrender. "Go right ahead, Agent Wirth."

I took out the digital recorder from my briefcase and set it on the table. I turned it on, then removed the papers. It was a deliberate move. I wanted her to see I had something. I wanted her to know that the judge's secrets may no longer be a secret.

"This is FBI Agent Amy Wirth, and I am speaking with Christine Griggs at Washington University." I stated the date and time of the interview and began. "We spoke earlier at your home, and I have some follow-up questions."

Christine's mood shifted back into hostile mode. "And you decided to come ask your questions about my husband here, after his memorial? Which is both intrusive and rude."

I glanced down at the recorder. Its tiny green light indicated it was capturing everything. I decided not to respond. I'd continue as if she'd said nothing.

"Your husband took antidepressants and other medications for his mental health, is that right?"

"Correct," Christine Griggs said.

"But you didn't mention that in our first interview, right? You denied it."

"I told you he had a stressful job. I was attempting to protect his privacy."

"Do you know when he started taking the medicine?"

"I'm not exactly sure," she said. "A few years ago. He was having trouble sleeping."

"We found a casino chip in his desk, and I was wondering if your husband gambled?"

"Is gambling illegal?"

"No," I said. "But the senator just told me your husband never gambled, hated gambling. As I recall, you also told us that your husband didn't gamble and there were no significant debts. So, there's an inconsistency. I was hoping you could clear it up."

Christine Griggs leaned back. With her mouth shut tight, she breathed through her nose. Then her eyes drifted down to the papers in front of me. She was clearly weighing her options.

I asked her, "Why would the senator say that, if it wasn't true?"

"I have no idea." She folded her hands in front of her. "But everybody has secrets."

"And gambling was one of your husband's secrets?"

"I'm not sure it was a secret. That seems inaccurate. He got a taste for it during a judicial conference in Las Vegas about three years ago, and then it just continued. Why he didn't tell Hoffman, I have no idea. Maybe he knew and just didn't want to tarnish my husband's reputation." She shrugged.

"Also in your husband's desk were credit card receipts and bank statements." I tapped the papers in front of me so she would know I knew. "Were you aware he'd gotten several large cash advances in the past six months?"

"I was aware but didn't know any specifics until a few days ago, when I started going over our finances with our accountant. My husband handled the money and paid the bills. He told me he'd had a run of bad luck but he'd get it back. He said, 'I always do.' And I had no reason to doubt him."

"And also tapped a home equity line for over fifty thousand dollars as well."

"Again, I didn't know that when we first spoke, but I know that now after speaking with our accountant, or I guess he's just my accountant now."

"Do you know if he borrowed money privately, like from an individual?"

"Are you asking about whether he got money from a loan shark?"

"That's one way to put it."

"I don't know," she said. "I don't know how it works."

"And was anybody threatening your husband, blackmailing him? Maybe somebody who had a case assigned to him."

"No," she said. "He loved the law. He'd never compromise. He'd rather die than—" Christine Griggs stopped herself, then said, "He would never do that. He'd tell me if it got that bad."

I studied her. Everything she'd said about her husband struck me as true, because I did the same. If somebody were to ask my parents or Matthews about whether I gambled, they'd have said I hated gambling. Yet almost every night, I had logged on to that website and gambled money I didn't have.

When I didn't ask another question right away, Christine Griggs grew impatient. "Are we done, Agent Wirth?" This time, there was a little more bite, a change of tone.

I flipped through some of the papers, an attempt to delay answering while I thought about my next move and everything I'd just heard. "Yes, Ms. Griggs, we're done. Thank you."

"Good. I need to get back to the reception." I watched her gather herself, stand, and walk out the door. I thought that Christine Griggs *was* telling the truth, but she was also *very* afraid of something.

I DROVE BACK to the office on a high. I blasted Stevie Ray Vaughn's classic blues album, "Texas Flood," in honor of my father. Everything felt more intense. Colors were brighter, sounds clearer. The whole time I was thinking, *this is what winning feels like.*

If Dr. Dan's medications were supposed to make me feel better, why didn't they ever make me feel like this? My smile was so wide, it almost hurt. I tapped my hand on the steering wheel and bounced in my seat to the music.

She admitted it, I thought, *I knew something wasn't right, and I was the only one dedicated enough to actually prove it.*

Running through walls, that's all it took. I just had to get out of my own way, no fear. I couldn't remember the last time those whispers of doubt inside my head were so silent. I wasn't a fraud. I was a real investigator, just like my dad. He knew I had what it took. I just never believed him or in myself.

From the beginning, I'd known there was more to Judge Griggs's suicide, felt it, and now it was confirmed. I had the financial documents, connection to a casino, and his wife's admission that he gambled. As I pulled into the bureau's parking lot, I decided that I'd write a close-out memo that I could be proud of. I may be closing the case, that was the deal I made with Matthews, but it didn't mean I'd hold anything back. I'd summarize all the information I'd gathered, attaching supporting documents and a full transcript of my interview with the judge's wife.

In closing the case, I'd also recommend that an Assistant U.S. Attorney review all the cases Judge Griggs presided over during the past two years. An attorney was in a better position to flag files that were inconsistent with the judge's previous decisions. Then it could be reopened if necessary. Follow the case wherever it led, consequences be damned. That's what my father would do, and that's what I was doing.

Within a few hours, I quickly finalized the memo and submitted it directly to the Carrot. In hindsight, it's obvious I was not thinking clearly. Although the financial documents and admission by Christine Griggs were important, I relied too heavily on them. My analysis was still weak. Even the conclusions and recommendations were inconsistent. I was both closing a case and recommending the investigation to continue. That didn't make sense.

Dr. Dan, had I continued going to our sessions, probably would've told me I was manic and prescribe me another pill. He'd say I was spinning, tell me I was in trouble. I'd deny it, and I'd argue with him. That's how our session would end, but he would've been right.

17

I n the morning, they were waiting for me when I arrived. Matthews was at his desk, and the Carrot sat across from him in my chair. That was how I knew this was serious. The Carrot rarely walked amongst the people, and I'd never actually seen her inside somebody's office. The doorway was as far as she would go, careful not to fraternize with the troops.

Not this time.

I looked at Matthews, but he avoided making eye contact with me. I'd brought him a celebratory coffee, fully expecting to be praised for going the extra mile on the Judge Griggs matter. I imagined we'd laugh at my audaciousness, the way Perelli laughed when telling stories of my father, and Matthews would then confess that he never had any doubt I'd figure it out. I even thought, perhaps, we could conspire to get Colton Steele assigned to review all the judge's files. It'd be sweet revenge for how Steele had treated us, bring him down a notch or two.

That was not what happened at all. There was no laughter or celebration. In fact, Matthews never said a word. He just stared at the floor as I stood along the wall with a cup of coffee in each hand, looking like a fool.

"Why don't you put those down and have a seat, Agent Wirth." It was the tone of an exasperated mother. The Carrot then got up, pointed at the now-empty chair behind my desk, and closed the office door. Then she got down to business. "I received your close-out memo related to Judge Griggs. I spoke with Agent Matthews first thing this morning, and he told me you were supposed to provide him with a draft to review prior to submission. Is that correct?"

"Yes." That was all I could say.

"I also asked Agent Matthews if he knew you were going to go to the memorial by yourself and question the judge's wife, and he stated he did not know your plans. Is that correct?"

"That's right."

"Even though you are still on probationary status, you thought it'd be a good idea to attend the judge's memorial service, then proceed to conduct an unscheduled, formal interview with the widow of a federal judge after publicly confronting a United States Senator."

I glanced over at Matthews, who still had his head down. He wanted nothing to do with this, and I didn't blame him. I turned back to the Carrot.

"I'd agreed with Agent Matthews to close-out the file following the public memorial service at the law school. So, time was of the essence."

"But you didn't tell him about the new information you discovered, about the cash advances and large withdrawals from the judge's bank accounts. Did you?" The Carrot knew the answers to these questions, but she wasn't just going to assume. She wanted confirmation.

"I didn't tell him," I said. "I was working late, reviewing the complete file before closing it, and that's when I discovered the information, then I wanted to confirm it with the judge's wife right away."

"And you did confirm it. Yet even after the memorial

service, you still didn't tell Agent Matthews what you'd learned or seek his input. You just came back to the office, finished the report, and closed the file. No consultation with your partner, and no consultation with me."

The way the Carrot described it made everything I'd done sound so foolish, but that wasn't my intention at all. I was following the case wherever it led. I was running through walls, and I was, in fact, breaking through walls. I had solved the case —consequences be damned—just like my dad would've done. Nobody thought I'd find anything, but I did. I won, and this morning was supposed to be the big celebration, but it didn't turn out that way.

The Carrot folded her thin arms across her tiny body. "Do you think you are smarter than everyone else in this office, Agent Wirth?"

The question caught me off-guard. "Excuse me?"

"This office is filled with many agents, very experienced investigators." She looked at Matthews, then back at me. "You may have been a city cop for a while, maybe even done some great things during your time at the St. Louis Police Department, although I've heard your time there was a mixed bag...yet for some reason you consulted with nobody before causing a scene at a public memorial and closing out a high-profile investigation."

"I don't think I caused a scene...I guess I don't understand the—"

"Okay, I'll go a little bit more basic for you. In a situation like this, we have to be both diplomatic and thorough. In your memo, you identified loose ends, making suggestions perhaps the judge's legal decisions may have been compromised. You suggested there may be extortion or his family is at risk. Yet you closed the case. Does that make any sense to you?"

"I told..."

"You told Agent Matthews you would close the file after the

memorial. I know that, but the deadline was arbitrary, created when no further investigation appeared to be needed. Now I have a United States Senator who wants you fired and I have an official document that recommends closing a case that maybe shouldn't be closed without further investigation."

I said nothing, because there was nothing I could say, and the Carrot continued her lecture. "A close-out memo is not an opportunity for an agent to engage in magical thinking or posit all the various theories of a case."

"I didn't really think about—"

"No," the Carrot said. "You didn't think about a lot of things. A good agent closes a file when there is nothing further to be done. Yet you state in the memo that you were not done at all, and perhaps you are at the beginning."

"I suggested—"

The Carrot held out her hand. "Based on this conversation, it is clear to me Agent Matthews had nothing to do with it, which is not surprising. As for you, I'm assigning you to the gun task force as of right now. This is a full-time assignment. Agent Matthews will simply have to manage on his own until I figure out the appropriate staffing." Her eyes narrowed. Then in a flat, sarcastic tone, she said, "The task force is really a perfect place for all of your energy and talent, Agent Wirth, and my hope is that I don't hear anything more from you until we meet at your probationary review." She opened the door, and as she walked away, the Carrot said, "I'll send you an email with all the details."

When she was gone, I slumped in my seat. I felt like I got sucker-punched. "What just happened?"

There was silence, then Matthews said, "You got deported to Siberia, which means even more work for me." He looked at the growing stack of files on the corner of his desk, now taller than I had ever seen it. "Not cool."

"I'm sorry," I said. "I really was going to let the thing with

Judge Griggs go, but I wanted to make one more run at it and then..."

"You went off on your own, doing your own thing, then submitting a report to the Carrot without running it past me, making it look like I'm either lazy or just out of the loop. I specifically asked you to provide me with a draft before submitting it to the Carrot, and you agreed."

"That's not it. I just—"

"Wanted all the glory? Wanted to prove me wrong? Wanted to show this old dog some new tricks?" Matthews still had difficulty looking me in the eye. I'd hurt him. He was the one who'd vouched for me. He was the one who got me the job, rescuing me from the dysfunction of the St. Louis Police Department.

"I should've talked to you first before submitting it," I said. "I'm sorry."

"You ought to be."

I tilted my head back and stared at the ceiling as my phone vibrated in my pocket, alerting me to a new incoming email. I looked at the screen. It was from the Carrot. As promised, she sent me an email, likely written in advance of the morning's ambush. The email contained all the details related to my new assignment, concluding with a directive.

"The task force meets in five minutes in Room B102. I expect you to attend."

EVELYN

She sat on her bench in the park. Today, she had their favorite. The birds loved French fries. Evelyn knew it wasn't good for them, wasn't healthy, but they deserved a treat as one after another relayed his movements as the man made his rounds.

Evelyn knew he was always aware of his surroundings, always on high alert. He handed out his small plastic bags to those in need. They were people in pain, and he perversely considered this part of his work to be quite righteous, most of the time.

The man wasn't delusional, of course. He was not on a humanitarian mission. He was hunting, just as she and Cain hunted him. Such facts could not be sugar-coated. He was like the men in orange who left piles of corn at a particular spot in the woods for months so, come the fall, the strongest bucks may be killed for their beautiful racks, lulled into complacency by the easy fix.

"Give to the one who asks of you, and do not turn away from the one who wants to borrow from you," the birds told her that the man muttered this as he went about his chores. "He comforts us in our affliction so that we will be able to comfort those who are afflicted."

Evelyn knew he liked that word: affliction. It was a good word, an ancient word. People didn't talk like that much anymore, but they should, because it's honest. The human race was afflicted, every one of us.

She tossed out another French fry, quickly eaten, as they informed her that he was now in a filthy warehouse. It smelled of urine and feces and rotten food. Its corners were piled high with garbage, and on the floor, the man passed a half-dozen men and women; some seemingly comatose on thin mattresses, others laughing, some weeping.

In the far corner, he went to one. She was dimly lit by a battery-operated lantern. The birds told of a woman's face that brightened with a toothless grin.

"You're late." The woman opened a pack of Ramen. Water neared a boil on the green camping stove near her feet. "Worried you weren't coming."

"I said I would be here, and here I am."

She dumped the block of dried noodles into the water, watched it for a second, then looked back at the man, or more specifically at his backpack. She licked her lips in anticipation of what was inside.

"Is he here?"

She nodded. "Second floor, dark green sleeping bag."

"Alone?"

"The kid is always alone." She picked up a fork and stirred the noodles as the water returned to a full boil. "He's a screamer. Nobody wants to listen to that all night. You'll be doing us a favor."

"Thank you."

Then the birds told Evelyn he unzipped his backpack and removed one of the plastic bags. It contained two pills. He handed the small bag to her.

"Have a peaceful night, ma'am."

She took the bag. "I will."

Then the man walked to the steps. He didn't need a light, even though it was dark, according to the birds. Evelyn thought his senses kept getting better, all of them: sight, smell, taste, and hearing.

The birds told Evelyn the kid was arguing with the voices in his mind as spirits circled around him. That's what Evelyn expected. The kid was one of the gifted. He was part of the line, both common and rare. He was an oyster with a pearl inside, and the man coming for him intended to take that pearl.

He knelt next to the boy and tried to calm him. His whispers, however, were ignored. His voice was just one of many, and not nearly loud enough. The intervention would need to be more aggressive.

The birds then told her that the man stood. He looked down at the boy with pity, then kicked him in the thigh. The kick was hard, but not too hard. It didn't need much force. If the toe of his boot hit that sweet spot in the middle, right between the knee and hip, the pain would be immediate.

And it was.

The kid howled. He rolled around on the floor, clutching his leg. Then the man pinned him to the floor. The kid bucked his body back and forth, his head shaking like a baby dodging another spoonful of prunes, but then the man laid his hand near the kid's heart, and he went still as the pills were eventually swallowed.

"Good boy," the man whispered. "It'll just take a minute, now enjoy the ride."

And he was right. A few seconds later, the kid's body settled into a calm. The kid's eyes rolled into the back of his head, and his breathing slowed.

Evelyn knew what would happen next. It had happened before. This was it. These were the final moments of life. The man would straddle the kid, put his hands together, and push the air out of the kid's body, hard and deep, smothering the boy. Leaning in close, so he could collect every ounce of the kid's final breath. With each one, his abilities grew; his senses more refined, sharper. It would never plateau, Evelyn thought, if he wasn't stopped, the man would surely become a God.

18

The task force meeting was already in progress when I arrived. A bald, overweight man sat at the head of the table and stopped mid-sentence. A flash of pity crossed his face before he forced a smile and began the introductions.

To the group, he said, "I should've warned you all at the outset of this confab that we were going to have a new member of our team." To me, he gestured toward one of the empty chairs. "Have a seat."

As I settled, the man said, "My name is Robert Cook, but folks call me Bob. I'll let everybody here tell you their own origin story as to how they were personally selected to serve on this prestigious and career-defining task force in whatever way they deem appropriate, but for now it's important you know that every person around this table shares one thing in common—we all hate this task force, and we all hate this work."

I looked at the others, and they all nodded their heads in agreement. It wasn't a joke. They were sullen, not smiling.

Cook continued. "What we do is tedious and mind-numbing, and I think I get dumber every day I come down here." His features tightened, but his tone remained level, as if controlling the rage and emotion within. "I've been doing this for over a year," Cook said, "and I'm now ninety-three days from my max pension. The Carrot, my doctor, and my wife all agree it's best if I spend my final months at the bureau behind a desk, which is insulting. I am, however, not going to leave until I squeeze every last penny out of the government. It's a matter of principle, and it's also a matter of spite." Then Cook pointed at me. "Any questions?"

"No."

"Good," Cook said. "You're already off to a great start. I like people who don't bother me with questions." He then pointed at a very attractive woman with a sharp nose wearing a $1,500 suit. "This is Agent Tory Rebekah, who's called Becks."

Then Cook nodded toward the man in the next chair. "That's Agent Mohammed Krashnae, most people call him Crash. He's our in-house computer guy."

Crash bowed his head slightly. "Just doing my part to fulfill all requisite stereotypes. If you're playing along at home, you may now check the box for 'Generic Indian Computer Guy.'"

I laughed, but nobody else did. They'd likely heard the joke before.

Next, Cook pointed at two people sitting directly across from me. "And finally, those knuckleheads are the dynamic duo, Agents Christian Bats and Robyn Faust." Cook paused, waiting for my reaction, but I wasn't sure what, how, or why I would react in any way to his introduction.

Sensing my confusion, Cook said, "Don't you get it, Agent Wirth? Bats and Robyn. Batman and Robin. The dynamic duo." He waited for me to acknowledge the joke, which I did with a very slight nod and smile, then he continued.

"Nice," Cook said. "You've got good instincts. I really like how you're not saying too much. Seriously, the less people speak, the quicker these meetings will be over, and we can go back to our miserable jobs and miserable lives."

He looked at the agenda and pressed on. For the next forty minutes, each of the task force members summarized the cases they were working on, which could be categorized as either initials or hits. Initials were guns seized from various crime scenes. Once the guns were seized, they were taken to a lab on the outskirts of the city and fired in a water tank that looked like a large metal coffin. The water slowed the bullet, which was then caught in a net and placed inside a machine that created a 3-D map of the unique signatures left by the firing pin on the shell casing when the gun was shot.

The digital map was then transmitted to Alabama, where an analyst from the Bureau of Alcohol, Tobacco, and Firearms determined if the unique signatures matched any bullet casings recovered from other crime scenes anywhere else in the country. If there was a match, it was considered a "hit," and members of the task force followed up with the jurisdictions where the gun had previously been used to commit an offense in order to gather additional information.

When the meeting was over, everybody left except for me and Bob Cook. "This doesn't sound so bad," I said. "I mean, the initial part is pretty tedious, but it sounds like following up on the hits could lead to some larger-scale networks."

"You're right. Investigating the larger-scale networks is interesting," Cook said. "It can and does force us to look at the whole criminal ecosystem, rather than just an individual drive-by, drug deal, or bank robbery, but we don't do that investigation. It gets assigned to other agents upstairs."

"None?"

"Zero. Once we get the paperwork and organize the file, it's passed along. This is just administrative, pushing files around."

"Why?"

"Because the Carrot has designated you all as a bunch of

screw-ups, and she wants to force you out." Bob held out his hands, abdicating any responsibility or role in making such a designation. "Not my call. I just run the show for now. Soon, I'll say goodbye and immediately fly to Mexico for a margarita on a beach, likely never to return."

I sat, thinking about my new day-to-day. Then, "Does anybody ever make it out of the basement?"

"There are some who make it back to the game, but it's rare; very rare. My advice is that you don't get your hopes up."

"That's it?" I said. "That's your advice?"

"Pretty much." Cook shrugged. "In about four to six months, you could make an appointment to see the Carrot, and a meeting may or may not occur."

"And if I do get a meeting?"

Cook was now gathering the papers in front of him, and once collected, he looked back at me. His eyes were tired. His skin looked pale yellow under the fluorescent tubes that lit the room. Then he said, "The successful ones beg for forgiveness, usually they cry."

———

I WENT BACK UPSTAIRS to my office, or what could be more accurately described as my former office. Matthews was at his desk. I stepped in, tentatively.

"Hey, am I still allowed in here?" I pointed at my desk. "Just need to collect my things."

Matthews glanced up from his computer, then continued to type. "I'm not stopping you."

I walked over to my desk. There was an open cardboard box in the corner, which used to be filled with reams of paper, but only a few remained. I emptied the box, then went through my desk drawers and filled it.

Matthews said nothing.

When the drawers were clear, I started gathering the various computer cords and chargers. Again, Matthews continued the silent treatment. I didn't blame him, but I also couldn't let it be. I didn't want to walk out the door without a little closure.

"Can we talk for a minute? Real talk?" I sat down.

Matthews stopped typing, pushed back from his desk, and folded his arms across his chest. "Why can't you just let me be? I'm mad and disappointed and sad. That's just the way it is. I don't feel like talking it out."

"You're right," I said. "I just hope you don't feel that way forever, because I really like you and you're as close to a friend as I've got. The job can disappear, it almost certainly will, but I hope we can be okay."

Mathews took a deep breath and blew it out, then unfolded his arms and said, "You and me will be okay...eventually." He gave me the slightest of smiles. "Just give me some space. I figure we can have coffee again, about the time I work through all those blue tag files you dumped back on me."

"I could still help with those."

"No, absolutely not," Matthews said. "The Carrot was clear, and I, frankly, don't want to cross her and get myself assigned to the gun tracing task force."

"I don't blame you for that." I got up from my chair, swung the strap of my computer case over my shoulder, and picked up the box of my personal items. "I'm sorry to leave you high and dry."

"Apology *not* accepted, Agent Wirth." His grin was wide, clearly playing with me. "I get at least a couple weeks to be pissed at you and curse your name. Then you can try to apologize, again."

"You don't ever curse, remember?"

"I do now," Matthews said, "You've been a bad influence on

me. If I hear you quote your father one more time, I think I'm gonna jump out that window."

"Okay." I took a couple steps to the door, then asked, "Ever heard of an agent named Bob Cook?"

"Of course," Matthews said, "that guy was a legend. He was the best agent here, probably one of the best agents in the country for a long time. He even taught at Quantico. A couple years back, he had some big health issues, major heart problems, quadruple bypass surgery or something. Usually that'd be a mandatory retirement, but he had so much pull in D.C. that he stayed in. I think he was moved to the Tulsa office or something."

"Well, he's not in Tulsa. He's the agent-in-charge of the gun tracing task force."

"For real?"

"For real."

———

I LOADED everything into my car and drove down to the Expedition. John was working the day shift at the casino and off at six. When I arrived, he was already at the bar with a gin and tonic, waiting for me. He pointed at the tumbler with a wedge of lime on the rim.

"Thought you might need this."

"You're the best." I kissed his cheek and sat down.

It looked at first as if John was about to crack a joke in response, but he didn't. His eyes softened, and he took my hand. "So, I guess everything's cleared up at work and we're good?"

"Not exactly." I took the lime, squeezed it into the drink, then set it aside. "We—meaning you and I— are definitely good, but work is pretty bad."

"But on the phone this morning, you told me you solved the case? I mean, that's great."

"I did solve it, sort of, I figured it out. The judge was a gambler, just like me. He had gambling debts, just like me, and I think he might've been compromised in some way. His wife is afraid, I can feel it. She's hiding something."

"So what's the problem?"

"I didn't solve it the right way," I said. "My boss didn't like the way I wrote my report, and I was supposed to have it checked before submission. The FBI is a pretty formal place, and I've never had much respect for protocols and people in authority."

"Sounds like you're just like your dad," he squeezed my hand. "And he sounds like he was a great man."

"He was." I closed my eyes. A lump formed in my throat, and I willed myself not to cry. "I'm his legacy, but I still find myself coming up short. It's like I need to try even harder."

WE MADE love at my apartment while the Mexican take-out went cold on the kitchen table. Neither one of us seemed to care. We pulled and grabbed and kissed with an underlying panic. It was as if we both knew this was a threshold moment. Our relationship was changing.

I'd been down this path before. As I ran my fingers down his chest and caressed his cheek, I couldn't help thinking this was more likely the beginning of the end, rather than the start of something deeper.

Why was that? Why was I always so negative? Why couldn't I accept that somebody might want me, might love me forever?

John turned. He propped himself up on one arm. A feeling of dread formed in the pit of my stomach. Surely, this was going to be "the speech," confirmation of my fears. It goes by many names: "It's not you, it's me;" "Let's take it slow;" "I really like you, but I don't want you to get the wrong idea;" etc. The tone and pace may be slightly different, but any variation of the speech accomplished the same goal, which was separation.

As John began to speak, I braced myself.

He said, "As we drove over here, I was thinking about what happened to you at work."

"Work?" My eyes narrowed, a little confused, quickly recalibrating the possibilities in my head. "What about work?"

"I don't know. Maybe it's a good thing. Maybe this gun task force might be a blessing in disguise, you know? Like, maybe it'll give you more time to prepare for whatever happens after that probationary thing... review meeting?" As he continued, I thought this was the most unique way a man had ever broken up with me. Ten points for originality. Then John said, "And it would give you a chance for some closure."

"Closure for what?"

"With your dad." John sat up, pulled me close, and put his arm around me. "Seems like the task force is less intense than your other work, so you'll have more time to process your grief, and maybe even work on his case. Figure out...you know? Like, what really happened to that girl who died. Maybe not solve it, but at least get a better understanding about why it was so important to your father."

"I'm supposed to do this while I'm tracing guns?"

John shook his head. "You don't get it, do you?" He laughed a little and tried again. "You see, I was not always the absolutely perfect and flawless person you know today. I've flunked classes and lost many jobs in my past, so you can take it from me that you're now in the sweet spot."

"The sweet spot?"

"Yes, the sweet spot is this glorious period of time between the point when you realize you're going to get fired and the point of your actual termination, meaning you can do whatever you want and collect a paycheck. Do you understand? It doesn't matter, because they can't fire you twice. Nothing you do matters, so you might as well do stuff that will make you happy."

I smiled and kissed him on the cheek. Then three words unexpectedly came out of my mouth.

"I love you."

My eyes widened in surprise, and I began to mumble some sort of apology, trying to take it back, but John stopped me.

He kissed me on the cheek, then said, "I love you, too."

19

T he next day, I arrived at the bureau feeling lighter than I ever had. Perhaps it was the act of falling in love, but I think it had more to do with being in that "sweet spot" John had described. I was going to be fired, and there was nothing I could do about it. Whatever pressure I'd put upon myself was gone, and I was no longer torn between what others expected of me and what I expected of myself.

I was free to do whatever I wanted. I was free to be my father's legacy.

Before heading down to the basement, I dropped in on Matthews. "Hey," I said. "I come in peace and have brought you some goodies." I put a coffee down on the desk in front of him, then opened a box of doughnuts from Donut Drive-In.

Matthews looked at me, then the coffee. "You think you can get back into my good graces through bribery?"

I nodded. "Pretty sure that's the way to do it," I reached into the box and removed a Chocolate Long-John, "or at least a pretty good way to start."

"Well, thanks for respecting my space." His tone was sarcastic. "I think that promise lasted about twelve hours." Matthews took an Apple Fritter, which I knew he would. He took a bite, then added, "but it's the Carrot you need to bribe, not me."

"I've been thinking about that, and maybe it's all for the best, you know? I didn't really fit in as a city cop, and I don't really fit in here. That's just the truth. She's going to fire me. I don't think that's a secret."

His expression tightened. "If you're giving up, that's a mistake," Matthews said. "You just have to do whatever the Carrot wants, to get back in her good graces. You've got all the skills to be a great agent."

I wasn't going to argue with him. I knew how much Matthews had invested in me, but I was already making different plans. I still had walls to run through, and playing nice with the Carrot didn't fit that plan.

I walked over to Matthews, patted him on the shoulder, and gave it a squeeze. "You're the best partner I ever had, but now I'm going down to the basement to do my duty."

Matthews smiled. "Good luck."

I picked the box of doughnuts off his desk and walked toward the door, stopping and turning back just as I was about to step out. "Thanks for everything, Matthews," I said. It felt a lot like a final goodbye.

––––––––

THE GUN TASK force occupied four rooms in the basement. All of them were windowless, most had exposed pipes criss-crossing the ceiling. Each was wrapped in some type of foam or insulation. I was pretty sure it was asbestos but tried hard not to think about it.

Bob Cook had his own office at the end of the hall. Next to his office was the conference room where we'd all met the day before. Then there was a secure storage room, and next to that was "the pen."

The pen was the office for the rest of us, an open space with no cubicles or other dividers. There were three mismatched desks with computers along one wall, dented file cabinets and a map of the United States along the other, and four plastic tables with plastic chairs in the center of the room.

Nobody else was there except for Crash. He was in the far corner, surrounded by computer screens. His back was to me, with a headset on. I walked over to him with my box of doughnuts. I was, in a way, buying friendship with copious amounts of sugar, but I didn't care.

When I tapped his shoulder, Crash visibly jumped. "Whoa." He turned, then looked at me, eyes wide. "What are you doing here?"

"I'm here to work."

"Well, that's different." Crash laughed. "Usually I'm the only one, but that's just because my partner, Benson, works from home. I love him, but he drives me crazy." Then he pointed at his screen, which appeared to be some type of multiplayer war game. "Plus, the Internet speed here is wicked fast. I love it."

"What about, like, tracing guns?"

"We do that sometimes, but you gotta take a break, gotta take care of your mental health, you know? Not burn yourself out."

"You're taking a break at nine-fifteen in the morning?"

"No, not a break exactly," Crash said. "I'd say I'm just playing Zombie Wars to get my brain warmed up. Then I'll delve right in, for sure."

"What about the others?"

"The dynamic duo roll in about eleven a.m. and then work until four-thirty sometimes. Toward the end of the month, though, watch out. They're here, like, twenty-four-seven, bro, crammin' and jammin'. It's crazy."

"What about the other one? The woman?"

"Becks?" Crash shook his head. "She's a ghost. Only see her

at the meetings. That's it. She's been here a couple months. Never had a conversation. Never heard her say more than a couple words. Don't know what's up with that."

I turned, looked around the room, then back to Crash. "So this is it?"

"Yep." He then pointed at the box of doughnuts in my hand. "Did you bring those to share?"

I nodded.

"Nice, very team-oriented. I like it. You are now my favorite colleague. Congratulations. I'm sure it's an incredible honor for you." Crash tapped something on his keyboard, then picked up a tall silver can with a neon skull and "ENERGY DRINK" emblazoned on the side. "Let's eat."

He clapped his hands, spun his large, padded chair around, popped up, and walked over to one of the plastic tables in the middle of the room. I followed with the box of doughnuts and set it down on the table in front of Crash.

"This is so excellent." He had the box open and half a doughnut stuffed in his mouth before I'd even sat down. "So, like, what's your name again?" He stuffed the remainder in his mouth and looked for another.

"Amy," I said. "Amy Wirth."

"Wirth...like Mrs. Butterworth."

"No," I said, having flashbacks of junior high school. "Just Wirth, no butter." I pointed at the doughnuts. "And if you call me 'Mrs. Butterworth' or try to make that my nickname, I will never bring doughnuts to work again, understood?"

"Cool beans." Crash took a sip from his can, then picked a classic glazed from the box. "You seem like a polite and professional person, so I'll answer some of the questions I know you've got rattling around in that big brain of yours."

He took a bite. "First, I've been in the basement for about two years due to a malware attack on the FBI, which may or may not have been my fault. I won't get into the details, but let's just say downloading pirated movies off the Internet can be risky."

Crash took another bite. "Second, Bob is a total badass, and you gotta respect that. I say this as somebody who hacked his personnel file and knows way too much about the dude. Bottom line is that as long as we meet the quota every month, he's cool. Doesn't matter whether you work a little every day or pull a Dynamic Duo at the end of the month. He just wants the work done. That's it. He's not about us punching the clock or desk time."

"Am I ever going to see him?"

"He'll probably give you a call sometime this morning, for a little more formal orientation. After that, just make your quota, go to that monthly meeting, and collect your check. That's it."

"Is he here now? Like, can I just drop in?"

"Not a bad idea." Crash nodded, then finished off his second donut. "Lastly, I've seen about a half-dozen people come and go during my time. None of them made it back to the show. All of them quit or got terminated."

He pointed at me. "I'm not saying you couldn't be the one to break the streak—especially if you keep bringing me a box of these doughnuts every day— but it's best to know the odds are not in your favor."

"I already know that." I picked a chocolate with sprinkles out of the box. "I think I've come to terms with my fate."

Crash nodded his approval. "Truth. Acceptance is the only way to go, man. People who fight it, yo, I've seen them go crazy down here. They get all angry and stuff, and that bad energy really throws me off. Throws everybody off."

"Well, I don't want to do that."

"Good," Crash said. "That's really good. I think I like you, Mrs. Butterworth."

My head cocked to the side, then I pointed at the dough-nuts. "What did I say about that nickname?"

"Oh, man, sorry about that; just sorta rolls off the old tongue." Crash put his hand on his heart. "I apologize, Agent Wirth. It'll never happen again. I promise."

———

Bob Cook was in his office. It wasn't what I had expected. Most agents, particularly senior agents with a pedigree like his, have an ego wall filled with certificates and commendations, along with photographs of them shaking hands with powerful people. The walls in Cook's office were bare.

He was at his desk. Like Matthews, Cook was a clean freak. The top of his desk was free of clutter. It looked as if it was wiped down at the end of every day. In front of him was a single notepad, pen, and stack of files.

Cook looked up at me, then at the box in my hand. "Those doughnuts?"

"They are," I said. "Brought them in for everybody, but..."

"Only Crash was here." He gestured to one of the two chairs in front of his desk. "Have a seat, and if you don't mind, I'll take one of those doughnuts." He paused. "Just don't tell my wife."

As he said it, I thought of Matthews at the Waffle House every time he ordered the biscuits and gravy and wondered if one day John might be instructing his fellow teachers to keep secrets from me about what he eats. I opened the lid, and Cook picked a glazed pinwheel out of the box.

"Thank you." His eyes sparkled as he took a bite. "I do feel guilty about it, though. My wife is trying to keep me alive, and this is not going to help the diabetes or heart or kidneys." He took a second bite, this time savoring it a little more. "I stick with the plan, already lost some weight, and my numbers have improved, but damn if this doesn't taste good."

"Even Tom Cruise gets a cheat day."

"Exactly," Cook said. "Even Tom Cruise gets a cheat day."

He finished the doughnut, washing it down with a slug of coffee. "So here's the deal, which will likely come as no surprise if you've already talked with Crash." He pointed at the stack of files on his desk. "Each month, I assign you a certain number of new firearms to trace, then I also have expectations related to the number of hits we refer upstairs. It's not a set quota. I assign a different number to each agent, and each month the number is different. Sometimes it's high, and sometimes it's low, but it's always realistic. It's not the same number, because I don't want the Carrot sticking her nose too much in our business. Inevitably, somebody like her would say, 'the quota is twenty, let's do twenty-five this month.' I don't want that. I want to keep it random, and," Cook paused and looked at me hard, ensuring he had my full attention, "if you tell someone outside this unit that this is what we're doing, I will kill you, and, Agent Wirth, I also assure you I will never be caught and your body will never be found."

Given Cook's background, I knew this wasn't a joke. "Understood."

"Excellent," Cook said. "I will email you everything you need by the end of the day, and tomorrow you can get started. This will include step-by-step instructions— although it's not that complicated— and links to the electronic files assigned to you. If you have any questions, don't hesitate. I will be here every day from eight-thirty a.m. to four-thirty p.m. until my retirement."

"What do I do now?"

Cook leaned back. "Whatever you want, and the same goes for tomorrow. You can work wherever you want and whenever you want, just come to the monthly meeting and hit your number. That's it." He nodded, and as I was getting up from the chair, Cook said, "I read your file, Agent Wirth."

"You did?"

"I did," Cook said. "I read all the files of the people who the

Carrot sends down here, and I have to say, I really like your style."

"Thanks."

"No problem, I mean it." Cook, then, pointed at the box of doughnuts in my hand. "Can I have another one of those?"

20

———

Cook had told me I could do whatever I wanted for the rest of the day, and I took him up on that invitation. Although it was unlikely he'd approve of using the FBI's proprietary search engines to find Kasi Barnes's mother, I reminded myself that I was in the sweet spot. I was getting fired anyway, so why not? My dad wouldn't stop. He'd find what he was looking for by any means necessary, and I decided I needed to do the same while I still had unrestricted access to government databases. Once I was just an unemployed single woman living on Cherokee Street with no title, badge, or gun, investigating would get much harder.

As Crash played Zombie Wars in the corner, I claimed one of the workstations, docking my laptop and logging on. Although nowhere near the sophistication and breadth of the National Security Agency or CIA, the FBI's databases were certainly better and faster than anything available to the general public, as well as the vast majority of local police departments.

I started with the driver's license database. I figured that it wasn't going to be that easy, but I had to try. I punched in her name, and the search pulled up thousands of women named Heather Barnes from around the country. There were close to over fifty in Missouri, over a hundred in Illinois, thirty in Kansas, and about twenty-five in Tennessee.

I narrowed the search to just the City of St. Louis, and I got nothing. Then I typed in the name of some of the larger suburbs in Southern Illinois, and in the St. Louis area, and again I never got a hit. I needed another way to narrow it down.

That's when I clicked out of the license database and pulled up a database with vital records. This database consisted of birth and death certificates from a patchwork of agencies and departments across the United States. I maximized it on one screen, then opened the Kasi Barnes file on the other. I worked my way through several drop-down menus, narrowing the state, county, and years, figuring I might be able to find something on Kasi's birth certificate.

I clicked the search button, and the record popped up. I felt my pulse quicken as I read it. Kasi Barnes was roughly the same age as me, born in a hospital that had been closed more than a decade ago in the central corridor of the city. Her mother was Heather Barnes, which I knew from the police reports, but now I had her middle name, "Lynn," and I also had her date of birth. I wrote both down in my notebook, and I also noted the address where she lived at the time of Kasi's birth.

In the space for "father," nobody was listed. If a woman isn't married, there's no requirement that she divulge the father. It also means the mother likely had never applied for welfare or any form of government assistance. If she'd have done that, Social Services would've conducted a search to locate the father. DNA from potential fathers would be tested, and if there was a match, he'd be adjudicated through the courts, added to the birth certificate, and required to pay child support. That apparently didn't happen.

I went back to the drivers license database and ran a new

search that included the mother's middle name and date of birth. There was a brief pause as an hourglass spun. I felt myself holding my breath, then I got my answer, or at least an answer.

There were "Zero Matches." In the entire country, there was nobody named Heather Lynn Barnes who had that birthday. I stared at the screen in disbelief. That just wasn't possible. I tried again and had the same result, then a third time, and still nothing.

I pulled up another database. This one was linked to historic and current property tax records, the Department of Revenue, voter registration, and utility companies. I included both Missouri and the adjacent states. Again, the search yielded no results.

I removed the specific date of birth and instead just searched for a Heather Lynn Barnes born within a date range of beginning the year before and after the date of birth listed on the certificate. It took a half-dozen attempts, but I managed to narrow the search to people living in the St. Louis area as best I could. This time, the list shrunk to eight.

Much better, I thought as I sent the list of addresses and phone numbers to the shared printer. I knew my chances were low, but I was anxious to get out and knock on some doors. At least I could feel like I was doing something.

———

MY FIRST STOP was a little two-bedroom house in Richmond Heights. Although I wouldn't be an FBI agent for long, I was still hesitant to flash my badge and falsely tell somebody I was investigating a federal case. If, however, I allowed people to assume those facts—without ever expressly saying it— that couldn't be my fault, theoretically.

For that reason, I removed my coat when I got out of the car and fastened my FBI credentials to my belt. The photo ID along with the silver badge would be hard to miss, and it'd hopefully prevent people from directly asking to see my ID or asking too many questions.

As I walked up to the door, I rehearsed the lines in my head. Then it was time. I rang the doorbell, and a few minutes later a large woman with even larger, frizzy blonde hair opened the door. The woman's eyes were immediately drawn to the shiny badge on my hip.

"Can I help you?"

"Perhaps," I said. "I'm looking for any relatives of a young woman who passed away quite some time ago. Her name is Kasi Barnes."

"Kasi Barnes?" Her eyes shifted back and forth, then she shook her head. "Not that I'm aware of," she said. "How long ago did you say she died?"

"About thirteen years ago," I said. "She was eighteen years old."

The woman's eyes widened. "Oh, my," she said. "That's awful, but I don't know any Kasi Barnes. I'm sorry I can't help."

"Not a problem." I took a step back with a nod. "And you have no relatives by that name?

"No," she said.

"You are Heather Lynn Barnes, correct?"

"That's me, but I don't know a Kasi Barnes."

"Very well," I said. "Thank you for your time."

I turned without saying any further goodbyes or providing the woman with an opportunity to ask for my business card.

I got in my car and drove away. One down, seven to go.

———

As I MERGED onto the highway, I checked the time and figured I had plenty. There were two more people named Heather

Barnes on my list who didn't live that far away, and I had no other obligations. I didn't have to worry about the stack of Blue Tag files or disappointing Matthews. Like Mick Jagger, I was free to do what I want.

I drove to Bridgeton. This Heather Barnes lived in a subdivision with no sidewalks, just narrow, twisty roads and cul-de-sacs. The sound of airplanes landing and taking off was constant. The homes had a temporary feel, like people weren't from Bridgeton or intending to stay long enough to claim the city as their own.

With my identification and badge still attached to my belt, I walked up to the house and knocked on the door. A stout man in a white t-shirt opened it a crack. The chain remained in place. There was silence as he studied me.

Then he said, "What did Juanita do now?"

"I'm sorry, did you say Juanita?" I shook my head. "No, I'm not here about that. I was hoping to talk with Heather Barnes."

"She moved out months ago... gone to Texas. Says Missouri is getting too liberal."

I smiled. "That's the first time I've heard that complaint."

The man shrugged. "Is what it is." He continued to make no attempt to remove the chain or encourage further conversation.

"Do you know if she ever had a daughter named Kasi?"

"No," he said. "Only boys, but they be gettin' all grown now."

"This daughter would have passed away about thirteen years ago."

The man continued to shake his head as I spoke, mumbling, "No. No. No." Then, "Never said nothing about that to me."

The door started to close, but I persisted. "Did you know her back then? Ten, fifteen years ago?"

"Nah," he said, "but something like that...I'd know." He

began to close the door but stopped just before it was completely shut. He reopened it less than an inch.

I could see only part of his bloodshot eye. Curiosity must have gotten the better of him. Then, "She in trouble?"

"Not at all," I said. "Thank you for your time."

———

THE THIRD LIVED in a new subdivision in O'Fallon. As I drove past the various signs advertising the latest developments, I couldn't help wondering who these people were and where they all worked. Missouri was not California. It was not a place filled with tech millionaires and Fortune 500 companies. Yet somebody was buying these homes with prices "starting at" amounts I could not fathom ever being able to afford.

In the driveway, I took a deep breath and reminded myself of my father's mantra to "break down walls." Then I walked up to the door and rang the bell. A woman in a nice blue sweatsuit answered. She immediately noticed the badge on my belt and promptly confirmed that she was Heather Lynn Barnes.

I felt excited. There was something about her that made me think she may be the one. It felt right. It was like she had been expecting a visit like this.

"I hate to bother you, but I'm looking for people who were related to Kasi Barnes. She passed away quite some time ago."

There was silence, then a shake of the head. "I'm sorry. I don't know anybody by that name."

"How about a distant relative?"

"No," she said. "My husband may know. I'm not really a Barnes, I'm actually a Kretzmann. Barnes is my husband's name. If you leave your card, I can ask him if it might be a cousin or something."

I didn't leave a card. "No, that's okay. I'm sorry to bother you, ma'am. Have a great day." Disappointed, I turned and walked back to my car. It was another dead end.

However, as I got inside, I realized this might not be the end. This Heather Barnes was not Kasi's mother, but she revealed a major flaw in my search. It was so basic, it was embarrassing.

People got married, and when they get married, they often changed their name.

Kretzmann changed her name to Barnes. So, how many women with the last name Barnes changed their name to something else? I turned the key and started the engine. I wasn't going to visit or call any of the other names on my list that had the wrong birthdate. I needed to go back to the office and conduct a new search, this time focusing on marriage records and name changes.

EVELYN

The scones were freshly baked and filled the cottage with the smell of lemons. Cain, the little man, sat at the table across from Evelyn. He ate one after another as they drank tea and discussed what, if anything, they should do.

"We should tell her," Cain said. "I'm tired of the secrecy. The line is growing stronger, and people are beginning to notice. It's going to accelerate."

"I'm not completely ignorant," Evelyn said. "I've seen the articles in the newspapers. I've heard about the glacier and the impact it would have, but I have doubts."

"Any day, it could fall," Cain says. "And then how fast will it come? How powerful will the line become?"

Evelyn shook her head. "Nobody knows, and people have been predicting such things for millennia." She paused and sipped her tea, thinking. "I'm not even sure it'll fall this year. I'm skeptical of these people who claim to predict the unpredictable."

"They are scientists, Evelyn, not tarot card readers."

"I know that," Evelyn snapped, "but nature is a mystery, and there are so many variables. I'm not saying it won't fall. I'm not in denial. Surely it will, and other disasters and wars will follow, but we mustn't act prematurely or overestimate our own abilities to change the future."

Cain thought about this. His eyes narrowed, then, the realization. "He came back, didn't he?"

"Who?"

"Pike," Cain said. "He was here. I can feel it now. What did he say?"

"He knew about us. He knew about what you did in the casino. Our attempt to give our friend a little confidence boost, and he warned me to stop."

This obviously rattled Cain, because his own self-assuredness was gone. "What did they do to him?"

Evelyn looked away. "They took his hand."

Cain's face hardened. "They can't do that to us," he said. "They have no right. We are of the same line."

"Are we?" Evelyn asked. "I'm not so sure. In fact, after Pike left, I wondered why they didn't just kill him. Certainly, his death would inure to their benefit, a further consolidation. Then I realized a weakened Pike is a wonderful message to us all, nobody is untouchable. If they can do that to him, nothing stops them from doing it to all of us who resist the hastening."

Cain looked through the window and up at Amy's apartment. "I'm not stopping."

"And neither am I, but there may come a time when we should... pause."

Cain turned back to Evelyn. "Never...and I don't believe for a second that Pike would want that either."

"Fair enough, but we must be careful...and we must also trust that she can do it without us. That is for the best."

21

I had a leisurely breakfast with John, then got into the office at about ten. I wasn't in a hurry. I thought searching for people who had changed their last name would be easy. I figured it'd be two databases. There would be one maintained by the court, which I'd narrow by case type and last name of the party. The other one would be maintained by the state, similar to the databases of birth and death records.

The problem, I quickly learned, was that there weren't two databases. There were, instead, hundreds, if not thousands. An orderly and centralized system did not exist, and the FBI hadn't prioritized creating one for itself. It was relatively easy to find out when somebody was born or had died, but name changes weren't that simple.

The census people had information, which I could probably get with a phone call, but I didn't want to risk that. They would ask questions. Money was not power amongst the different and warring fiefdoms of the United States government. Information was valued. Whoever controlled the information had the power, and another agency wasn't going to give it away for free. They'd ask questions, for sure, and I wasn't going to go to jail for this. I'd done some additional research about conducting an unauthorized investigation on bureau time, and it was not encouraging.

So, I stuck with what was easy and what I thought was untraceable. I accessed the offices for the Missouri and Illinois Secretary of State. They had some records, but not all, and usually the search was limited to a particular year. I had no idea when Heather Barnes may have gotten married or simply changed her name if she had done either. The other problem was that not everything was online. Some information would require me to go to a terminal in the county where the marriage ceremony or name change occurred.

For the past week, I had alternated between searching name change records and tracking guns. It's unclear which of those two tasks were the most painful. At least with the guns, I had something to show for my effort. The name change searches were just an exercise in futility.

"NO RESULTS FOUND"

My fingers rested on the keyboard as I stared at the screen, then I emitted a groan as I laid my head down on the table and closed my eyes. Crash, who was usually focused on Zombie Wars, noticed.

"You okay, Mrs. Butterworth?"

I did not lift my head off the table. "Don't call me that," I said and issued my warning, "Do not make me hurt you."

"I believe when the deal was struck, there was an implication that you were going to continue bringing in donuts, but since you haven't been bringing donuts lately, I thought...whatever, you know? I like it. So, I'm just gonna call you Mrs. Butterworth, okay?"

I said nothing. Head still down.

"So, what's the side hustle, Mrs. Butterworth? What's causing you grief?"

This got my attention. I lifted my head off the table and

turned to look at him. Crash had a big smile on his face. I tried to appear innocent and confused by his question. "What are you talking about?"

"I've been seeing all the stuff you've been doing over there," Crash said. "I got curious, so I hacked into your account to see what you've been up to."

"It's personal," I said.

"Obviously," Crash said. "Are you stalking some old girlfriend or boyfriend?"

"No, nothing like that." I kept hoping Crash would just turn around and go back to playing Zombie Wars. "It's nothing that exciting."

He laughed. Crash obviously sensed my discomfort and was thoroughly enjoying this interrogation. "Oh, don't do me like that, Mrs. Butterworth," Crash said. "Pray tell, little lady, pray tell, or I just might have to walk down the hall and talk to Bob about this. The guy is cool about not being in the office, but this might be deemed a violation of his trust. I've heard he's cut a few throats over less, and I don't mean that figuratively; like, I actually think he's taken a knife and slit somebody's throat and probably dumped their body in a swamp."

I didn't have any options. Even if he was kidding, I could not allow Crash to talk to Bob or anybody else. Although I was going to get fired and had come to terms with that, I needed more time. I also still needed the paycheck.

"Fine," I said, "but this stays between us."

"Excellent. Secrets are a wonderful foundation for friendships." Crash then opened a small cooler near his desk. "You want an energy drink?"

———

I TOLD Crash about my father and his dying wish, then I described what I'd done to find Kasi's mother so far. He sat patiently, listening. Crash didn't say anything. He let me go uninterrupted, and as I prattled on, his bemused expression blossomed into a full smile.

I stopped. "What is it? What's so funny?"

"Nothing," Crash said. "It's cute."

"What's cute?"

"I don't know," he said. "The bias of federal agents always amazes me. You're all cut from the same cloth, so simple and predictable."

"Excuse me?" My eyebrow raised as I crossed my arms. "I hate to break it to you, Crash, but *you* are a federal agent."

"Technically, yes, but it's only a matter of time before they dump me, which will be a relief. It was never a good fit." Crash looked around the room, then spread his arms wide. "Which is why I'm the 'King of the Basement' and not doing actual law enforcement, like the suits upstairs."

"Okay, so spill it," I said, "Tell me what I need to do."

"You first need to recognize that the government is not the best source of information about people or where you can locate people. That's your bias." Crash turned his chair and started typing on his computer. "I'm not saying these government databases are worthless, but it's macro, when you need micro."

The screens in front of Crash began to change, raw code blinked into images, then back to code. "When the National Security Agency wants to find somebody, they don't go to a government database." He hit enter, and the screens flashed again. "They buy it from aggregators, who compile information from all the websites you visit, things you buy with your credit card, where you shop, and all the GPS information on your phone or maybe from the computer in your vehicle, if it's connected. That's where the NSA goes, then they sift it all with A.I."

I leaned closer to get a better look at what he was doing. "How long will it take?"

Crash looked back at me. "About half a second." He pressed enter, and up popped an image of what I soon learned was Heather Lynn Barnes, born in St. Louis with the same birthdate as the mother on Kasi's birth certificate. "There she is." Crash double clicked a button, and the printer next to his desk came to life.

The amount of data and random bits of information Crash was able to obtain about Heather Barnes in such a short amount of time was astonishing. Five years after Kasi's death, she married and changed her last name to Quillan. So, at least I was right about that theory and hadn't wasted my time with the other women with the same name as Heather Barnes but different birthdates.

The credit bureaus had a list of every place she'd lived going back to her first bank account as a kid. From her credit card transactions, there was a list of every plane ticket, rental car, and hotel she'd ever stayed at. There was data about cars she'd owned and the number of miles driven per month and per year.

The reports listed when she was paid and when she'd be most likely to make a large purchase, preferred clothing brands and sizes, favorite household cleaning products, and restaurants regularly visited. In short, it had everything I needed except for her current address, but that wasn't Crash's fault. It also wasn't a problem with his search or the database.

Kasi's mom was dead.

IT WAS a hit and run accident that had occurred six years ago at approximately 5:30 a.m. on an overcast December morning. Heather Barnes, now named Heather Quillan, was walking her dog along a dimly lit, country road. It was a routine, something she did every morning before going to work as a nurse at a hospital in Columbia.

There were no witnesses. There were no traffic cameras on light posts, and it was long before the proliferation of wireless cameras installed on the outside of houses. She may not have even been found, except an old man driving a truck spotted the dog at the side of the road.

He got out and checked the dog's tags, figuring the black lab had gotten loose and needed to be returned to its owner. That's when he saw Kasi's mother in the ditch.

It wasn't as if the police had failed to investigate. There simply wasn't anything to investigate. Jake Quillan, Heather's new husband, offered a small reward for information, but nothing ever came of it.

As Crash and I sat on the patio of Vito's Pizzeria and took advantage of its happy hour appetizers, we discussed my next move. "You could call the husband," Crash said. "She might've said something to him, or he might still have some of Kasi's stuff."

"That's not a bad idea." I pushed a few of the toasted ravioli from the platter onto my plate. "I'll put that on my list, but Kasi's stuff is probably long gone. When her mom moved from here to Columbia, my guess is, things were left behind. When the mother died, I doubt her new husband kept mementos of a child he never knew."

"You're probably right, but you should try." Crash poured the rest of his bottle of Side Project imperial stout into his glass. "What about the file? Just give me some other names, and I'll run them through the sifter and see what spits out."

I thought about that. The file was filled with various police reports and medical records. There weren't, however, many interviews. Besides Kasi's mother, who I now knew was dead, I couldn't remember reading about another interview.

My dad would've certainly gotten a list of all of Kasi's friends, either from her mother or teachers or counselors. My dad was thorough. He ran through walls. That's just basic investigation, but there was nothing like that in the file. It was odd.

"I'll check for something," I said. "Hopefully, I can bring you another name tomorrow."

———

JOHN SAT at the kitchen table with a pile of child psychology books, studying for an exam. Mister Bones sat in front of the muted television, sleeping as the Cardinals played the Cubs. I was on the couch with my laptop. I'd scroll through the file, watch a little of the game, then scroll through a little more. By the seventh inning, I'd found nothing.

I wanted to find an interview with the last person who'd seen Kasi alive or an interview with her best friend, maybe somebody she was dating. None of the reports contained any of that information.

I wondered if my father just didn't do it, and that may have been the reason why he wanted to come back and restart the investigation. I always believed that he was thorough, because that was what he'd preached to me. It was the high standard every case deserved. A twist on the old theater saying about there being no small parts, except as related to police work: "There are no small cases, just cops with big egos."

But reality was something different. My experience as a cop was that there were, in fact, small cases that don't warrant the resources.

Isn't that essentially what Matthews and the Carrot said about Judge Griggs? A suicide is just a suicide?

Maybe an overdose was just an overdose. Except Judge Griggs was not just a suicide; there was something more. I'd found it, and his wife was afraid. More digging needed to be done, just like more digging needed to be done about Kasi Barnes.

I looked at the television. The game still hadn't restarted after the seventh inning stretch. It was one commercial after another. I clicked back to the beginning of the electronic file that Perelli had given to me. Going to the crypt to retrieve the file now felt like ages ago.

I pressed on. The first six pages were called "chronos," short for chronology. It was a timeline of what the investigators had done, where they went, and who they talked to. I glanced at the television, still in the commercials. I watched a guy in a red shirt talk about home and life insurance, then I got back to work.

I clicked through the pages again, tracking the progression of the investigation. Then I found what I'd been looking for as the television showed a black truck climbing a mountain somewhere out west. The report stated that my dad had gone to Kasi's high school and talked to her school counselor. The line was a single sentence buried in the middle of a report, easy for me to have missed my first time through.

If it was true, which I had no doubt it was, then there should've been another report in the file, but there was nothing that summarized an interview with a school counselor or any activities at Kasi's school.

Now a promo for the nightly news appeared on the television. An anchor stood in front of the camera. The set, including the anchor desk, was behind him. Although the sound was off, it was obvious the anchor was giving a run-down of the day's "top stories." Then the weatherman appeared. He stood in front of an image with rain, then the image changed to the Doomsday glacier. Apparently, it remained on the edge of collapse but hadn't quite yet.

Mister Bones yawned, bored with everything. Then I

noticed the pigeon on the windowsill. It appeared to be watching me, and I wondered how long it had been there.

I flicked my hand. "Shoo."

The pigeon bobbed its head a couple times and flew away as I typed the name of Kasi's high school into the computer and mapped the best route on how to get there.

22

Kasi Barnes had gone to St. Mary's High School, which wasn't too far from where I lived. It was a Catholic School founded in the 1930s, sitting on a large leafy campus not too far from Carondelet Park. I pulled the car into the lot, got out, and walked down the path toward the main building. Just as the weatherman had predicted the night before, rain was imminent. The sky was gray, and the air was heavy.

I hustled through the quad, feeling a drop of water, and then another, seconds later. By the time I got under the awning at the entrance to the high school, the rain was coming down hard.

I pressed a button on the intercom, introduced myself, then was buzzed inside. A nun sat at a table near the door, watching who came and went.

In a tone clipped and irritated, she said, "You need to check in at the office."

I knew that, because every school in the country now required a visitor to check in at the office, but nodded politely anyway. Even though I was the one with the gun and badge, the woman scared me.

In the office, I introduced myself to another old nun and explained why I had come. She tut-tutted at the mention of Kasi Barnes's name.

"That was a sad one," she said, "but not entirely unexpected."

"In what way?"

She opened her mouth, as if ready to explain, but stopped. Her lips pursed, almost a wince, obviously regretting that she'd said anything at all. "Let me introduce you to Father Michael; he's really the person you should be speaking with, not me."

The nun stood, then motioned for me to follow her. As we walked past a large window, sheets of water pounded the sidewalks that crisscrossed the school's campus. The rain pooled under a nearby tree.

The nun knocked on a door frame, and a man called for us to come inside. I had expected to see somebody bald, grizzled, and hunched over a Bible. I was wrong. Father Michael was younger than I was. He had a thick head of black hair and piercing green eyes.

"Whom have you brought to me this time, Sister Charlotte?" He popped out of his chair and bounded around his desk to greet me. "I'm Father Michael Hague, but the kids around here call me Father Mike, whether I like it or not."

We shook hands. "I'm Amy Wirth."

He looked at the badge attached to my belt, and the smile faded. "FBI, meaning you are not a parent of a potential student seeking a tour of our fine school." He tilted his head, appraising me. "Too bad." He turned, walked back to his desk, and sat down. "Because that means the reason you are here is not a joyous one, nor will it help me in my conversations with the diocese about our budget and enrollment." To the nun, "Sister Charlotte, would you like to stay for this conversation?"

Sister Charlotte got the not-so-subtle hint. She shook her head and left.

Once gone, Father Michael and I continued.

I told him, "I'm here about a former student who died quite some time ago."

"How long?"

"About fifteen years," I said. "One of the investigators spoke with a counselor at the school, and I wanted to follow up."

Father Michael shook his head. "That was well before my arrival. This is only my third year, and I'm afraid we've already cycled through two counselors. I don't know who would've been our counselor back then." He looked past me, a little knowing twinkle in his eye. "Sister Charlotte, who was the counselor here about fifteen years ago?"

There was a long pause.

Father Michael smirked as he called out again to the eaves-dropper. "I know you're right there, Sister, on the other side of the door, and Agent Wirth knows it as well, so reveal yourself and help me out. It's the least you could do."

An embarrassed Sister Charlotte came into the doorway. Her cheeks blushed, and she shifted her weight from one foot to the other. "Yes, Father, I believe that was Sister Peck, Helen Peck."

"Is she alive?"

"Yes," Sister Charlotte said, "but memory care. I doubt she could remember any former student, but you never know. The older memories are the last to go."

"Do you know where she's at?"

"Dutchtown Garden," Sister Charlotte said.

I wrote down the name, then decided to put Sister Char-lotte on the spot again. "What do you remember of Kasi Barnes?"

The nun looked at Father Michael, obviously hoping for some direction. There were a lot of privacy laws about educational records, communications with therapists, and counseling given by church leaders to their members. Any one of them could theoretically apply, but Kasi Barnes was dead, and so was her mother. Who was left to complain?

"Without violating confidence," Father Michael said, "you can talk about what you saw and heard in the hallways here. Gossip may be sinful, but not confidential."

Sister Charlotte put on a show of being conflicted and eventually let loose with what she'd had on her mind since we first met. "She was a wild child. Everybody knew it," she said. "We knew that coming in. That's how she ended up here. The girl's mother was worried and wanted her out of Roosevelt. She was getting into big trouble there, and the mother thought the change of scenery would do her some good."

"How long was she here?"

"Came in halfway through the first semester of her senior year. She got her diploma from us, but I think it was more of a social promotion than something earned. I'm not sure she even attended the graduation ceremony. We're a pretty reserved place, you have to understand, and Kasi Barnes was far from that. When she died so soon after graduation, it was shocking. So, that's why I remember her."

"Any friends?"

"Just boyfriends," Sister Charlotte said. "Lot's of rumors about what she'd do for the boys and what she'd get in exchange. I think she enjoyed scaring the other girls."

"Drugs?"

"Anything and everything, at least that was the talk. I'd take it with a grain of salt, likely exaggerated chatter."

"You don't believe it?"

Sister Charlotte paused, then went a little philosophical. "I believe at the core of any gossip, there is often likely a seed of truth."

"Did she have a best friend?"

"That I don't know."

"Would the counselor, Sister Peck, know?"

"I doubt—"

There was a clap of thunder from outside, and a burst of rain blew onto the priest's window. It was the last big burst before the storm moved on.

Sister Charlotte continued. "Back then, our counselors were more about discussing possible occupations and college, not about emotions and mental health. I'm not saying there couldn't have been a conversation like that, but it's doubtful. Kasi Barnes didn't strike me as a girl who would open herself up like that, especially to a nun. She wasn't here long enough to develop much trust with anyone, not that she tried."

I thanked both of them and thought about my next move as I walked back to my car. The air was now filled with just some light sprinkles and drops falling from the leaves. The storm had mostly passed, and the dark clouds had begun to break apart.

I thought again about the file and absence of any report by my father about his conversation with the counselor. Perhaps he had made a conscious choice not to write it down, especially if the counselor had relayed the same rumors Sister Charlotte had just told me.

Maybe my father didn't want to turn those rumors into fact by recording them in the official police file, permanently tarnishing the reputation of a young, troubled girl. I could imagine my dad doing something like that, making that decision. He wasn't afraid to run through walls or follow a case wherever it led, but he also wasn't a cruel man either.

I drove north on South Grand, figuring I should head into the office. I wanted to check in with Crash and see if Bob had some more guns for me to trace, but instead I found myself at Roosevelt High School.

The sun was now fully revealed, clouds pushed further to

the edges of the sky. Whatever dust and pollen had been in the air was gone, and everything felt fresh and clean.

Roosevelt was a beautiful, historic public high school. Built in 1922, it was designed by the famous architect R.M. Milligan. The building resembled a castle, red brick with four round copper turrets in the middle tower.

Given what had just happened at St. Mary's, I had little hope anybody at Roosevelt would have useful information. I didn't need another person to tell me Kasi Barnes was bad. I needed to know who she hung around with, a friend who likely knew the person who supplied the drugs that killed her.

Acquiring that type of information necessitated a different approach.

———

I SAT at a large wooden table in the high school's library. In front of me, I had what I wanted: old yearbooks. As expected, nobody at Roosevelt knew or remembered Kasi Barnes at Roosevelt High School, but the principal was more than happy to give me copies of all the yearbooks published during the years Kasi attended.

Starting with her first year, I found Kasi Barnes in the index and looked at the pages in the yearbook where she's mentioned or her photograph appeared. I took notes as I worked through each reference, and what I saw amazed me. As a freshman, Kasi's portrait was that of a young woman unsullied, innocent. Her smile was broad and contagious. She wasn't the least bit self-conscious about her braces. Her cheeks were still rounded like a little girl, a prominent dimple on the left.

She was a joiner, too. In the fall, she was on the Roosevelt volleyball team. In the winter Kasi played basketball, and in the spring she ran track. She also sang in the choir and competed in a speech competition. This was very different than the person Sister Charlotte had described.

The next year, she was a sophomore. The braces were gone on picture day, but her brightness had dimmed. She was still on the volleyball team and sang in the choir, but no sports in the winter or spring, and no speech either. There was a photograph of the choir during the final concert of the year.

Kasi stood in the front row. Her shoulders slouched, dark mascara was on her eyes, and her bangs were kept long. It was as if she was hiding, embarrassed of herself.

For her junior year, there was no smile on picture day. The makeup was heavy. The few remnants of the little girl were gone. Her cheeks no longer rounded, now sunken and sallow. Kasi played no sports. She did not sing in any choir. Her interests were obviously elsewhere, darker.

In reviewing the yearbooks, I'd hoped to see a pattern in the photos. I wrote down the name of every person on those teams, in the choir, or who had participated in the speech competition. I wanted to see if there was someone who did the same things Kasi did or who was always standing next to Kasi in those group shots.

I thought this might be the key to unlock her past and lead to others whom, through the passage of time, might be willing to talk about what happened. I never found that pattern, but luckily there was something better.

It was a random photo taken during Kasi's last year at Roosevelt before her mother made her transfer to St. Mary's. It was not a posed shot. Kasi, it seemed, was not even aware a student with a camera was taking a picture.

She was in the lunchroom, partially turned away from the photographer. Kasi's mouth was open. Her head tilted back, laughing at something the young woman across the table from her had apparently said.

It was a beautiful picture. Kasi had, in that moment, a little of the sparkle I'd seen in the photographs contained in the first yearbook I'd reviewed. Although she'd changed a lot in three short years, the photo revealed that she was still very much alive, and the caption below provided the information I needed.

———

"Tell me the name again?" Crash turned around in his chair and readied himself to type.

"Jenae Malmo," I said as I slid a chair from one of the plastic tables in the middle of the room over to Crash's workstation.

He typed the name and surrounded it with computer code I didn't understand. Then Crash said, "Got a birthday?"

"No. I figure she was born the same year as Kasi."

Crash thought about this. Then he shrugged his shoulders. "Might work. We can try." He began to type. His fingers were a blur, and soon the various monitors came alive.

I didn't really understand it, and I wasn't going to ask Crash for a tutorial. All I knew was that he was performing the same type of magic trick he'd done with Heather Barnes. He linked various commercial databases that were filled with millions of pieces of information and ran them through some type of program.

We sat for about a minute, then the activity on the screens subsided. "Let's see what we got." Crash clicked through a half-dozen screens, briefly studying each. "I think we got a little something to get started."

He pressed a button. The printer beeped, then began to hum as paper rolled into the tray. Crash took each one, glanced at it, then handed the paper to me as if I would understand. These were not pretty reports. It was raw data, sometimes the information was in a column, and sometimes it was just long lines of numbers, symbols, and letters. At the bottom were several columns, with what appeared to be times of day and addresses. When everything was done printing, I read through it all again, then handed it back to Crash.

He smiled as he took it from me. "Did you see it?"

I shook my head.

"They were roommates," he said. "Kasi and Jenae were living together when Kasi overdosed."

"How do you know that?"

"It wasn't in the credit reports," Crash said. "When I did this with the mom, I got a nice list of everywhere she lived, because she lived a more traditional life, you know? But with Kasi, she didn't live that kind of life. While you were visiting high schools this morning, I was working on Kasi, digging deeper and piecing it all together. It wasn't easy, by the way, because big data wasn't all that big back then. I had a lot less to work with than with the mother."

Crash bent over, opened his personal mini fridge, and retrieved another can of energy drink. "She was older than the other seniors at her high school, turned eighteen about halfway through, and got some credit cards, maxed them out, defaulted, and that was the end of that. The only address on file with the credit bureaus was the mother's address, and that doesn't help us."

"The police reports said she was on her own. Her mom had pretty much kicked her out when she overdosed."

"Exactly." Crash opened the can, then downed half of the blue liquid inside. "After graduation, or maybe even a little before graduation, it appears from the data she was moving around a lot. I could tell by the addresses of where she was using her card. There would be a cluster in a particular neighborhood for a week or two, then a cluster someplace else. It kept moving. That means no lease, nothing, but we got lucky."

He turned and began looking for something, then he picked

up a folder, which I assume was the research he had done that morning. He plucked a piece of paper out of the pile and showed it to me.

"Look at that."

Crash pointed, but it meant nothing. So, he explained. "Kasi bought a cell phone with one of those credit cards. So, when you gave me Jenae Malmo's name, I had something really good to work with. The program combed through Kasi Barnes's cell history and pulled out regular calls, compiling a list of incoming and outgoing calls. Then after you gave me the name, I did the same thing for Jenae Malmo, and of course Kasi and Jenae were on one another's list. As you thought, they were making frequent calls to one another around the time of the overdose."

Crash finished the can of energy drink, crushed it, and tossed the can onto the top of an overflowing recycle bin. "Since I had the program and the queries all set up, it went faster with Jenae, except I added some special sauce when I got your phone call as you were driving over here."

"What was that?"

"I got the computer to focus on the nighttime GPS data based on the cell towers used."

"Why nighttime?"

"Because the cell phone is always working. It's refreshing and updating, always connected to the network, even though no calls are being made. This nighttime data tells us specifically where Kasi and Janae were sleeping at night, and whether they were sleeping in the same place—boom, baby, boom—lo and behold, we just got a lot of hits, meaning they were definitely friends and they were crashing together most nights, just like you thought."

I felt myself getting excited, but I should've known it wasn't going to be that easy.

23

Crash sensed my disappointment and tried to cheer me up. "The good news is that I'm pretty sure Jenae Malmo is not dead."

"Pretty sure?"

"Like, yeah, pretty sure," Crash said. "Like, ninety-nine-point-nine percent sure she's not dead."

"I don't get it," I said. "You can tell me what kind of shampoo she buys and when she buys it, but you can't guarantee that Jenae Malmo is alive."

"I'm just being straight with you." Crash pointed at one of the screens. "Look at this. You see that?"

I leaned in. It was a blue dot on a map of downtown St. Louis. "So?"

"So, that blue dot is Jenae, and it's from a cell tower ping off a tower on Sixth and Lucas at three-forty-six a.m. about two months ago. That's it. I got no more pings off any more towers after that. The trail goes cold."

"It never went cold like this before?"

"It does, but then the thread picks up with a new cell phone or police record or medical record or something that puts a person back on the grid." Crash typed in new search parameters, pressed a button, and the blue dot disappeared. "Now we got nothing, see?"

"But that doesn't mean she's dead?"

"Right," Crash said, "but it doesn't guarantee she's alive either. We got no jail records, medical records, or anything else that explains where she went. She's got some pending court cases, and she's on warrant. Could be she's in an abandoned house over on the North Side and high as a kite, or it could be her body is in the river, or maybe someone took her up to Chicago. Who knows these things?"

"Can you keep monitoring it?"

"I can, and I will," Crash said, "but unless you get other names, we're sort of stuck for now."

I walked over to my bag and pulled out my notepad. "Here's a list of other people she went to high school with. Maybe when you run the cell phone records search and the GPS thing again with these, you might get a hit."

Crash took the list from me and looked at it. "How likely do you think that is?"

"If I'm being honest," I said, "not very likely."

"But I'll do it anyway." Crash turned back to his computer and started typing.

"Thanks," I said. "I owe you."

"No biggie." Crash turned and smiled. "I was bored. Gives me something to do until they bring down the axe. You going home?"

"No, not home. I've got some people to talk to."

IT TOOK ABOUT twenty minutes to drive across town to Pooh's Corner, the legendary dive bar on Virginia Avenue. Even though the beer was cold and cheap, it wasn't my first choice to have an after-work drink. This was a blue bar. Hanging around a bunch of drunk, off-duty cops made me nervous. I'd already endured years of harassment from them, but I had to go because I knew this was where I'd find Frank Perelli, and we needed to talk.

I parked my car and entered the dark, narrow bar. A couple guys looked up from their beer as I came through the door. Their eyes were glazed, and they were checking me out. If they recognized me, I couldn't tell, but if one tried to pinch my ass or made a stray comment, it wasn't hard to imagine things could turn ugly.

Perelli was in a corner booth, all alone. I slid onto the bench across from him. "How's it going?"

He looked up from his folded newspaper. His eyes didn't look much different than the two cops at the bar. Perelli had been working on a crossword puzzle. "Amy," he smiled, "what are you doing here?" His speech was slow and slurred. Perelli turned to the bartender, made eye contact, and held two fingers in the air. He then turned his attention back to me. "It's the old case, isn't it?"

There was no reason to deny it. "I've been working through the file."

"I bet you have, because you're just like your old man. Can't let it go."

"I've got a person who could be helpful, Frank. I figure she might've stayed quiet at the time you and my dad were investigating—like, afraid she might get in trouble—but now with so much time having passed, she might be willing to talk."

"Boyfriend?" Perelli asked as the bartender delivered two glasses of beer, putting one in front of each of us, then left. "That was a long time ago, but I don't seem to remember no boyfriend."

"It's not," I said. "Her name is Jenae Malmo. I figured out

they went to high school together at Roosevelt and lived together around the time Kasi Barnes overdosed."

"So she's a lesbian now?" The slur seemed to be getting worse.

"I don't know, Frank. What does it matter?"

"And this girl is gonna do what?"

"Identify Kasi's dealer," I said. "She has to know who it was."

Perelli considered this as he pushed his empty glass aside and started on the fresh one. "So go talk to her," he said. "Don't need me for that. I'm off the streets, remember? I'm a lazy, washed-up has-been." Then Perelli pointed at me. "Don't think I don't know what your pops said behind my back." He took a drink. "Maybe he was right."

I wasn't going to get sucked into Frank Perelli's pity party. "I can't find her. That's the problem. She disappeared about three months ago, and she's not in jail, the hospital, or the morgue."

"And you want me to call in some favors for you?"

"Not for me," I said. "For my dad. For your partner. This was the last thing he talked about with me. He wanted to figure it out. That was his dying wish."

"I don't like it." Perelli looked around Pooh's Corner, just to check on who might be listening to what's being said. The small bar was now starting to fill up, not quite as private as before. "I just have a bad feeling, kiddo. I'm not trying to be mean or nothing."

I begged him. "Come on, Frank. Help me out. You know people, and they'll listen to you because they like you. Tell them it's for my dad."

"Why don't you have the feebies do it? You guys have all the resources."

"Not these kinds of resources. The FBI doesn't have the contacts on the street like you do. The beat cops know almost every junkie by name and where they're squatting. This is easy for you guys, low hanging fruit."

Perelli grunted, then scratched the back of his neck. "Fine," he said. "I'll do it, but you need to keep me in the loop. I don't want you getting hurt, and if you need me, I'll be there."

"I promise."

———

ALTHOUGH PERELLI SAID he'd put the word out for me, I wasn't so sure. Outside Pooh's Corner, in my car, I dug through my briefcase. On the bottom there was a stack of old business cards, which I kept together with a black metal clip. I sifted through them and found the card for David Schmidt, who everybody called Schmitty.

He was now the Chief of Police for the City of St. Louis, following the disastrous tenure of Barry from Gary. Chief Barry was a self-promoting reformer who wore out his welcome fairly quickly after failing to enact any substantive reforms. It also didn't help that the downtown streets had become increasingly lawless after midnight, sometimes resembling scenes from the *Fast and Furious* movies.

Schmitty loved my dad, and he was the one who had introduced me to Matthews as I was looking to escape the department. He was a deputy commissioner then, and I hoped he'd still have it in his heart to help me out one more time.

On the back of his business card, Schmitty had written his cell phone number. I dialed it. The phone rang, but he didn't answer. I thought about just hanging up and trying later, but I felt the clock was ticking. There was nothing preventing the Carrot from getting rid of me before my probation review meeting.

So, I left a message. "Hey Chief, it's me, Amy Wirth. Thanks for coming to my dad's funeral...um, before my dad died, he wanted me to work a little on a cold case. I think I've identified a potential witness, but I need some help locating her. That's why I called. Maybe we could meet and talk?" I ended the message by leaving my cell phone number and disconnected.

Then I called John. I gave him an update and told him I was on my way home. At the end, I said, "Draw me a warm bubble bath." I said it as a joke, but when I got back to the apartment, he'd done exactly that.

24

———————

I spent the next several days tracing guns, and the following week I met Schmitty for lunch at McGurks. It was a sprawling Irish pub in the Soulard neighborhood. Comprised of a series of small rooms, nooks, and booths with high, dark wood dividing one from the other, it was a perfect place to have a private conversation, especially in the middle of the day. In the evening, the bar and patio would be packed as a band played the small stage in the front.

When I arrived, a waitress pointed to my left, and I found Schmitty waiting for me in the writer's room. The walls were covered in large black and white photographs and etchings of the great Irish literary figures. Schmitty's back was to the wall, so he could see who came and went. He was a careful man who valued discretion.

For years, Schmitty was the power behind the throne. As police chiefs came and went, he survived and somehow became a trusted advisor to everyone. He knew all the secrets and had an uncanny ability to know when to share a bit of information, and when to be quiet.

"How's it going, Chief?"

He stood to greet me. "It can always be worse." We shook hands, and as we sat down, he said, "How about we stick with just Schmitty? That Chief stuff gets old. Every time somebody calls me that, it just reminds me there's no longer anybody higher up the food chain to pass the buck."

"The burden of leadership."

"True." He raised his pint of Guinness to his health. "Slainte." Then he drank. "So sorry about your dad. He was a great man, and a great cop."

"It's been tough."

A middle-aged waitress entered the room and took our orders. We watched her disappear, leaving us alone again, and Schmitty picked up where he left off. "It was a beautiful memorial service, by the way. I wanted to go to the wake so bad. I'd even taken the rest of the day off so I could see old friends and drink as much as I wanted, but I got called down to the mayor's office instead. She wanted to talk about carjackings."

Schmitty shook his head. "I told her we need to lock up the teens who are doing this and get more cops on patrol. I told her we had to reopen the curfew center, so the ones who are just hanging out on the corners smoking weed can be brought someplace where we can connect them with mentors and services. She says that's a hard no. Says a curfew center is just gussied up jail, and around and around we go. I wondered why she even called me down there; the mayor knows what we need and what I'll say, but she keeps asking, thinking there's going to be another answer."

With heavy sarcasm, I said, "So what you're telling me is that the new job is a dream come true?"

"That's about right." Schmitty laughed. "Most days I feel like the dog that finally caught the car, but it ain't all bad. Helps that I know this is the last stop on the train before retirement." He drank. "You know, I never understood these traveling police chiefs who go from one city to the next. Guys who have no relationship with people who have boots on the ground, a city's culture, or its history. They got none of that, but they make the promises and know all the buzz words and always fail spectacularly."

"Like Barry from Gary."

"Exactly."

We talked shop a little more as we waited on our order. I told Schmitty about Judge Griggs and the gun tracing task force. He listened patiently, but I got the impression he knew it all. Maybe he'd talked to Matthews beforehand, maybe even the Carrot.

Our food arrived, and about halfway through the basket of fish and chips, Schmitty got to the point. "I love seeing you, Amy, but what's really going on with this old case you mentioned in your message? I don't get it."

"It's my dad," I said.

"What about your dad?"

"Finding who killed this girl, who sold her the drugs she overdosed on. I'm doing it for him." I gave Schmitty a brief summary of the work I'd done on the case, leaving out the parts about Crash hacking phone records and credit reports. This seemed to pique Schmitty's interest.

"And your dad asked you to do this?"

"It was his dying wish," I said.

"Just an overdose case?" Schmitty was skeptical.

"I don't understand it either, but I feel like I can't let him down, and I figured you guys sort of came up through the department together, right?"

"We did indeed come up together," Schmitty said. "I was a little younger, and much more stupid, but your pops was like my unofficial mentor." Schmitty seemed to drift away, remembering a simpler time, then he came back with a chuckle. "Luckily, I didn't listen to half of the advice he gave me back then. Otherwise, I'd probably be in the crypt with Perelli."

"So you'll do it?"

"Put the word out to find this witness?"

"That's right." I reached into my bag and pulled out a sheet of paper and put it on the table. "Here's the name, description, and last known place where she was staying. She disappeared about three months ago, and she's on warrant."

Schmitty picked up the paper and studied it. "Jenae Malmo," he said. "A junkie."

I nodded. "Most definitely."

"Okay, and what do we do if we find her?"

"Call," I said. "I got a burner phone just for this. If anybody has information, I don't care who it is, whether it's a cop or anybody, just have them call the number at any time. I'll answer." Then I took the piece of paper back from Schmitty and wrote the number on the bottom of the page. "I have to find this girl."

"We will," he said, "unless she's dead."

EVELYN

This time, she sat on the top of the Cahokia Mound, while her birds followed the man as she had directed, safely and at a distance. They were careful not to circle like buzzards or otherwise draw attention. This was not difficult.

Unlike her parrot, they had no bright feathers, nothing exotic. On ledges and rooftops, the birds disappeared into the background as the man went about his business. They watched as he visited alleys and parks, distributing his candy.

They had seen it all before, many times, relaying the route to her. The birds wanted to go home. They were tired, but she told them today was different than the others. She knew there was to be one more stop. The old woman had a vision, and Evelyn's visions were true. The birds must continue as the man came closer and closer to her.

The birds followed him as he drove down Front Street, then to Trendley Avenue. There was a large park located there, on the Illinois side, with a commanding view of the entire St. Louis skyline. She could see the park clearly from where she sat.

It was a grassy island, named Martin Memorial Park. It was truly a sanctuary, an alternate universe disconnected from the poverty and boarded buildings that dominated the rest of East St. Louis. The birds flew high above the man as he parked and walked over to an ellipse. There was a woman waiting near a shallow pool with a fountain in the center. It was called the Gateway Geyser because it shot water 630 feet in the air every ten minutes or so.

When the man sat down next to the woman, the birds flew closer so they could relay the conversation to the old woman, their mother.

"You got it?" She did not look at the man. Her right leg bounced. One hand cupped tightly with the other, while she stared at the water.

"Maybe." The man's eyes narrowed, examining her. "Depends on whether you got something for me."

"I got it," she said. "I always have it."

"And I suppose you want the discount?"

She said nothing, but the man already knew the answer. A little smile, then he nodded. "Then let's take a walk for a bit more privacy."

He stood and followed the path toward a copse of trees a few hundred yards away. She hesitated, but her addiction seemed to override her pride, because she eventually followed. If that's what it took to get her fix, then that's what she would do.

The young woman got down on her knees before the man and unzipped his pants. She took a jagged breath as he reached down and groped her breasts. Then she closed her eyes and began the job. That's all it was, she thought, dirty work. It wasn't her first. It was something she knew would be quick.

But this time was different. Before she finished, he pushed her head away. Then the man kicked her in the stomach. The young woman rolled back, cursing him. Then he kicked her again.

"What the hell are you doing?"

The man put his hands on his hips, a look of disappointment on his face. "I just can't," he said. "You're just too disgusting. I mean, have you looked at yourself in the mirror lately?" He began walking back to his car.

The young woman struggled to get back onto her feet. "We had a deal?"

The man waved her away and kept walking. She hustled after him, panic now in her eyes. "I need it," she said. "I'll do anything you want. Anything."

"No."

The man continued to walk with her following behind, like a small child. She kept begging, but he ignored her.

At the car, her panic piqued. It was written all over her face. This was not a game. He was really leaving. She watched with dismay as he got in his car and started the engine.

"Please." Her hands banged on the window. "Don't go."

The man put the car into reverse and backed up a few feet, then stopped. He rolled down his window. "Anything?"

"Anything," she said.

The man examined her from head to toe. "Fine, get in the back. You have work to do."

25

———

I
t took another week for the phone to ring. I was in the basement of the bureau, filling out paperwork for another ballistics test, when I got the call. The ringer was set so loud that both Crash and I jumped in surprise.

I tapped the green button. "Hello?"

There was no response, just background noise. It sounded like whoever was on the other end was making the call from the side of a highway, a light-rail platform, or something like that.

I tried again. "Hello? I can't really hear you." I paused, still nothing. "This is Amy Wirth. Who is this?" There was still no response, so I tried something different. "Is this Jenae? Is it you? Is this Jenae Malmo?"

There was another long pause, then a very hesitant, "Yes."

It was as if I were trying to lure Mister Bones indoors— no sudden movement and a steady, calm tone. This was hard because my adrenaline had just shot through the roof. My heart pounded, and my palms dampened in anticipation.

"I'm so glad you called," I said. "I need to talk to you about your old friend."

"Friend."

A few more words were said, perhaps a question, but I couldn't understand what she was saying. The background noise was too loud, and Jenae was speaking too softly. Her voice trailed at the end of every word, getting more and more quiet.

"Kasi Barnes," I said. "I'm trying to learn more about what happened, and who's responsible." There was silence. I waited patiently, then, "Jenae, are you still there?"

A pause. "Yes."

"Can we meet today?"

"I don't know."

"I'd like to meet," I said. "Anywhere you want is fine, anytime."

There was another long pause, then, "The North Pond," she said, "by the Arch."

"Okay, when?"

"Eleven, tonight. Come alone and bring some money."

"I'll see you there."

I hung up the phone, then whooped and spun around, clapping my hands and pumping my fists in the air. I felt redeemed, and I was sure my dad would've been proud of me.

Crash was watching and smiling. "I'm assuming you found her."

"Yep," I said. "Meeting her tonight at eleven by the Arch." Then I walked over to Crash and gave him a little hug. "Thank you for all of your help."

He feigned modesty. "It was nothing."

I disagreed. "No, it was everything. I would've never found her without you."

"The right tools help a lot."

I walked back to the table where I had been working and sat down. "I need to call Schmitty and Perelli to let them know what's going on."

"Good idea," Crash said. "Is everyone going to meet down

here, or do you want to go off-site? Planning might be easier with a little alcohol to get the creative juices flowing."

When I didn't respond right away, the smile on Crash's face faded as he realized my plan. "Wait," he said. "You're going to do this alone. No backup? No help?"

"This is something private, Crash. It's my deal, something my dad asked me to do for him."

"*Your* deal." Crash's face folded into a look of disgust. "You just told me you couldn't have found this girl without *my* help. I got skin in the game, Mrs. Butterworth. I can't even tell you how many laws and internal policies I broke tracking down these people. I want to see it through to the end, just like you do."

I crossed my arms over my chest. "I can't let you come with me. It's about proving myself, finally proving I'm really good enough to do this. It's something I have to do on my own."

"It's too risky."

I shook my head. "She's just a junkie, Crash. I've handled a lot worse, and I can handle her."

"What about your dad's old partner? You know who I'm talking about. It wasn't just your dad's case. It was his case, too. You should have him come along with you."

"He wanted to be kept in the loop, and I'm going to call him and Schmitty on my way home and keep them in the loop."

"But leave them and me on the sidelines?"

"That's how my dad would've done it," I said. "Sometimes you have to take all the risk onto yourself. I don't want collateral damage. If this fails, it needs to be my failure, and my failure alone. I can protect you that way."

"So you're doing the same thing you did with that judge. You did it all by yourself, and look where that got you."

I stared at him. Anger boiled inside me that was fueled by embarrassment and shame. "You know about that?"

"Of course." Crash gestured to his bank of computers. "I've got access to everybody's file, Mrs. Butterworth."

"Well, good for you." I turned away, gathered my things, and left without saying another word.

<hr>

JOHN MADE DINNER THAT NIGHT. It was pasta primavera with salmon. Ordinarily, I would have eaten my portion and stolen most of his, but not this time. I was in my own head.

I didn't like how I'd left things with Crash, and my conversation with Perelli was almost as bad. Perelli told me he knew the cops who were working the dog shift along the river and it wouldn't be a problem for them to provide a little unofficial back-up.

But I declined. I imagined my dad in this exact same scenario, and he wouldn't call for back-up. This wasn't a hostage situation or some negotiation with a terrorist. It was just a drug addict, one person. That's all, and I could handle it.

I'm my father's daughter, through and through, I told myself. *This is for him. I am his legacy.*

After dinner and doing the dishes, we moved over to the sofa to kill some time before I had to go. When John turned it on, there was a live news special about the Doomsday glacier. A couple more pieces had fallen, and scientists were predicting its total collapse within days, if not sooner.

I didn't want to watch that. "Can you give me the remote?" I whined. "I can't handle this end of the world stuff."

"It's a big deal. They say it could change weather patterns, like the jet stream would look totally different than what it is now."

"I know it's a big deal, but I just don't want to talk about it or read about it or watch television news stories about it all the time. There's nothing we can do."

"Fine." John handed me the remote. "Sounds like you need a comedy special or something."

"Baking," I said, "How about a food show?"

"Okay."

He clicked around and found a baking show neither of us had seen. It was hosted by an actor we both recognized. He was famous, but not super famous. Neither one of us could name a movie or show he had starred in, but he and an older woman were pleasant enough to watch as six contestants created elaborate gingerbread houses and French pastries in a tent somewhere in the English countryside.

After watching three episodes in a row, it was time. I turned off the television and went back to the bedroom to change clothes. I also strapped on my gun, got my badge, and grabbed my Maglite.

When I came out, John was waiting for me.

He said, "I don't want you to go." I began to protest, but he held out his hand. "From what you told me, everybody you've talked to about this has said you shouldn't do it alone, that it's too risky...I don't know, maybe you should listen to them. Call Matthews, he knows what he's doing."

"Matthews knows what he's doing?" I was insulted, but mostly it hurt because I knew he was right. "John, I can't have this conversation. I need you to support me."

"I do support you," he said. "I love you, and I don't want anything to happen to you."

"Nothing is going to happen to me." I looked at my watch. "I need to go."

"Call me as soon it's over."

"I will," I said. "I promise."

I wrapped my arms around him and gave John a tight embrace as he kissed the top of my head. When I made that promise, I meant it. I had fully intended to stay safe and call as soon as I was done talking with Jenae Malmo. As I left the apartment, I was convinced that I had everything under control.

I did not.

EVELYN

The old woman with dreadlocks, now the color black, watched Amy get in her car. She was about a half-block away, hiding behind a hedge, hoping John would've convinced her to abort the plan. Obviously, he had been unsuccessful.

There was still time to stop it. Not much, but there was time. As the car pulled out of its parking spot, Amy headed toward her. Evelyn knew she could reveal herself, coming out and flagging Amy down by waving her arms or even jumping into the middle of the street. Maybe if she threw herself in front of the car, Amy would have no choice but to stop. She wouldn't drive off. She'd stop and render aid. That was the type of person she was.

All of these options were going through Evelyn's mind as the car came closer, but she did nothing. She remained hidden and allowed Amy to pass, knowing her failure to act would cost people their lives. She looked down at her birds. She loved the birds, and Pike was right. She couldn't imagine never speaking to them again, losing her gifts and having everything she loved taken away.

The old woman bowed her head. They had won. There was

no point in remaining there. There was no point in tracking the man any longer. That would just be an exercise in futility. If she wasn't going to act, it was better not to know how much stronger he grew.

She began to walk back home, deciding the best thing she could do would be to pack her bags and leave.

26

I parked on the street at Laclede's Landing, a nine-block historic area just to the north of the Gateway Arch. It was originally a bustling shipping hub along the Mississippi River, but those days had ended a long time ago. Laclede's Landing now catered to tourists. Its many warehouses and factories had been converted into hotels, restaurants, and shops.

I walked under the Eads Bridge. The Arch was in front of me, unobstructed. Having always lived in St. Louis, it was easy to take the iconic structure for granted. Its image was ubiquitous, featured on T-shirts, mugs, posters, and countless corporate logos. The Arch was inescapable, but in these quiet moments, it could still take my breath away.

Lit from the bottom by powerful lights, its silver skin practically glowed, a marvel of engineering and human aspiration. It was as if it had been teleported to this place from the future, out of time. Marking the land as forever sacred, just as it had been thousands of years before.

Unlike Laclede's Landing, the large park surrounding the

Arch was mostly deserted and quiet. I followed a paved walking path, past the Explorer's Garden toward the North Pond.

I saw a man running along the river and noticed two people in a grove of trees. The two under the tree were sharing a joint and didn't seem to be much of a threat.

Still, I felt my heart beat a little faster and started to second-guess myself. Maybe John and the others were right, I thought, maybe I was taking an unnecessary risk. My hand reached down to my side, and I touched my gun. That made me feel a little better, knowing it was loaded and ready.

I arrived at the North Pond about five minutes early. Jenae Malmo was not there; nobody was there. I stepped off the path and walked over to the edge of the water, figuring that would be safer. I'd be less likely to cross paths with another. If somebody wanted to get to me, it'd take some effort and wouldn't be a surprise.

I checked my watch again while scanning the grounds and continued to wait. Five minutes after eleven, my phone rang.

I expected it to be Jenae, but it wasn't. A man said, "Just want to let you know we've got eyes on you."

"Who is this?"

"It's your boss, Agent Wirth."

"My boss?"

"Yes, your boss, Bob Cook. Remember me? As of a couple weeks ago, I became your direct supervisor."

Confused. "What are you...what are you doing here?"

"Crash told me you were being an idiot and he was worried about you. If you noticed a jogger down by the river, that's him. I'm directly behind you on a bench near the street."

In a whisper, I said, "If she spots you, then she's gone. She told me to come alone."

"They always tell us to come alone, Agent Wirth," Cook said. "But we don't ever go alone, because that's a good way to get killed."

"So you know what I'm doing?"

"I know enough," Cook said. "I've been keeping an eye on you. Security flagged some of your Internet usage when you started in the unit. You aren't as good as Crash in covering your ass."

"You need to leave."

"Sorry, Agent Wirth," Cook said. "You don't get to make that call. Plus, I'm having a lot of fun. It's been a long time since I wasn't behind a desk, and I'd forgotten how much I love it."

"I can't—"

Cook cut me off. "Stop it," he said, "this is non-negotiable. Plus, I think you've got a visitor coming up the walk from the east. Keep your head up and eyes open."

I turned back toward the river, and Bob Cook was right. A thin woman with long black hair was walking unsteadily toward me about a hundred yards away. I disconnected the phone, put it in my pocket, and waited.

———

SHE WANTED MONEY FIRST. It was obvious Jenae was going through withdrawal and was desperate. Even in the dim light, I could see her body tweak. Her fingers picked at the scabs on her face, and I was doubtful she even knew what she was doing.

"Give me some money, or I'm gone." Her head jerked a few times, as if being shocked by a small bolt of electricity. "Whatever you got in your wallet."

"How about we start slow? Like, how about you tell me about your friend, Kasi?"

"What's to know?" Jenae asked. "She died doing something she loved, gettin' high. Nothing wrong with that. Could've been worse."

The answer surprised me. Kasi and Jenae were supposed to be close friends. The comment was cold, almost cruel.

"If you don't start handing me some cash real quick, I'm leaving."

"Who told you to call me?"

Jenae turned and started to walk away, and I started to panic. "Wait." I reached into my pocket and pulled out a small purse. I had about seventy dollars in cash. "Here's a ten." I held it out. "Let's start with that."

Jenae smiled, and I noticed some of her teeth were missing. Whatever spark had been captured in that yearbook photo was long gone. This woman was hard, her empathy stolen away.

"Now you get it." Jenae took the ten-dollar bill from me. "I ain't got a lot of time, so let's get to it." She licked her cracked lips with a renewed urgency in her eyes. It was like the cash was on fire. She wanted to use it — *had* to use it — already figuring out where and how soon she could score a hit.

So, I laid my cards on the table. "I want to know who sold Kasi the drugs she overdosed on. I want the name of the dealer. That's what I want."

"How much you got in there?" Jenae looked at the cash in my hand.

I felt like Jenae was about to try and grab it, so I put the money back into my pocket. It was like I was at the casino, reading the expressions of the other players and calculating the odds.

When I didn't answer Jenae's question, she raised her chin in defiance. "I want five hundred dollars right now."

"I don't have five hundred dollars."

"Then go get it."

I sighed and put my hands on my hips, hoping to convey a sense of annoyance. "No," I said. "I don't think I'm going to get anything helpful from you, because I don't think you know anything. Why waste any money at all?"

It was a bluff, but Jenae, in her current state, was not a complex person. "Ain't true. I know plenty, and I know you got the money. There's a cash machine right over there." She pointed. "We can walk together, and along the way I can tell you whatever you want to know about Kasi."

"I'll give you fifty dollars, final offer."

"What I know is worth a lot more than that, lady."

"I don't think so," I said. "You're a homeless junkie. At the end of the day, I need credible people I can put on a witness stand and testify in front of a jury. Do you understand that? Credible people. Witnesses some guy from the suburbs is going to think is telling the truth." I waved my hand, dismissing her. "What you have to say is worth something, but not five hundred dollars."

Now it was time to play hardball and call the hand. I started to walk away. I took two steps, then three. On my fourth, Jenae folded.

"I'll tell you." I heard her say, voice trembling.

Without turning around, I kept up the tough guy act. "And you'll tell me where I can find him?"

"Of course." I heard her take a step toward me.

"Okay, it's a deal." I pulled a twenty out of my pocket and walked back toward her. "You get this now, and the rest when you've told me everything you know."

I held out the money, and Jenae took it from my hand as if it were a million dollars. Her face, along with the rest of her body, relaxed, practically melting.

"Thank you," she said softly, while clutching the twenty-dollar bill.

I felt sorry for her, and I even considered taking that trip to the ATM with Jenae when we were done talking. "Let's sit down over here."

I pointed to a nearby bench, and we began walking that way but never made it. There was a burst of light in the distance, and a shot rang out, then another. Jenae Malmo spun as the first bullet hit her upper right chest. Her arms flew into the air like a dancer. It seemed to happen in slow motion. Around she went, gracefully, until the second bullet hit. That brought her down. It entered on the side and blew out the back of her head.

I screamed as I crawled toward her lifeless body. There was nothing I could do for her. I looked over my shoulder. Crash was running toward us from the river. I then looked behind me to see if I could find Bob Cook.

"Did you see him?" I screamed at Crash. "Where did he go?"

Crash shook his head. "Who?"

I screamed back. "The shooter, where did he go?"

Crash didn't have a clue, so I got up and started running across the grounds toward where I'd seen the muzzle flash. It was probably too late, but I had to try and catch him. It was the least I could do.

It felt like I was running in sand. In the distance, I heard a siren. I still had the Maglite in my pocket, and I took it out and turned it on. When I finally got to the spot, there was nobody there.

The area was heavily shaded, so grass didn't grow. The rain from the day before had softened the ground. I shined the light and saw tracks and followed them. If I was right and these were the shooter's footprints, he headed toward the Old Courthouse.

I put the flashlight back in my pocket and got out my gun, then started to run in that direction. I made it about twenty yards, then I heard a groan and cry for help.

I turned and saw somebody on the ground. It was too dark to see who exactly it was, but then he called out to me. "Wirth, it's me, Bob. I'm in trouble."

I ran to his side and crouched. "Were you shot?"

Bob Cook shook his head. Through clenched teeth, he said, "I ran over here, wanting to cut the shooter off from any escape, but I…" His breathing became even more labored. "My heart," he said. "It hurts. My heart."

"Help is coming." I took his hand. "I promise they're

coming. Stay with me." I pulled out my phone and called 911, directing the ambulance to our location. "Hang in there."

Cook nodded, but the pain looked like it was getting more intense. He screamed in agony and rolled over on his side. He was fighting it.

"Wirth," he said, "this is important." His eyes closed for a few seconds as he tried to catch his breath. Then, "This is important," he said. "Important. That guy. The shooter. He's... not, he's not normal. He's not. He touched me. He did this to me."

"Did what to you?"

"He came," Bob said. "He touched me, touched my...and I fell."

"What do you mean? Like, hit you?"

Bob shook his head. "No, he came from nothing...out of nothing."

With that, Bob's eyes rolled up, and his body shook. He wasn't breathing anymore, so I started CPR. I blew air into his lungs and pumped. I kept on for what seemed like an eternity, never stopping until the EMTs arrived in the ambulance with oxygen and a stretcher.

27

———

I sat with Crash in the hospital's waiting room, watching a parade of the injured and sick. Medical privacy laws gave us no right to know what was happening with Bob Cook, but neither one of us wanted to leave.

"I shouldn't have told him," Crash said. "That was stupid."

"You did it for me," I said. "This is all my fault. Jenae is dead, and who knows what's going on in there with Bob. When they put him in the ambulance, he didn't look good, Crash, not good at all." I buried my face in my hands. "This was a total and complete disaster."

Crash put his hand on my back. I thought it was an attempt to comfort me, but I was wrong. It was a warning. Crash wanted me to look up and see who had just come in the door.

"Agent Wirth and Agent Krashnae, I think we need to go someplace quiet to talk."

I knew that voice. It was the Carrot. I dropped my hands from my face and unfolded myself. She stood in front of me. It was well past midnight, but the Carrot looked the same. She wore a full suit. Her face was made up. Her hair was perfect and nails painted. Her expression was that of a parent coming to bail their teenager out of jail.

Matthews stood next to her. He said nothing, but his eyes were locked on me, glaring. I hadn't just disappointed him. I'd embarrassed him. I didn't even want to imagine what he was going to say once we were alone.

I felt sick to my stomach but kept quiet. All of us went inside a small conference room typically used by doctors to talk privately with family members.

As Crash and I sat down, the Carrot said, "This is going to be quick."

And it was.

Both the Carrot and Matthews remained standing, glaring at us. "Here's the deal," she said. "You all screwed up so bad, I'm not sure exactly how to untangle it. As of right now, you are both placed on administrative leave with pay. Don't expect that to last. As soon as I get the green light from HR, you will be terminated. In the meantime, you are not allowed on the FBI premises. I want your badges. I want your guns, and I want whatever keys or magnetic cards you have. In the morning, somebody will clean out your desks and remove any personal items. They will be dropped off at your homes in the afternoon."

The Carrot paused, shifting her weight from one foot to the other. "Any questions?"

Neither Crash nor I had any questions. It was what we had expected.

"Good, now I'm going to go home to bed, and Agent Matthews is going to confiscate any and all FBI property. When he is done, I suggest that both of you go home. I do not want you to have any contact with Bob Cook's wife, because if she sees you, she will likely kill you, and I wouldn't blame her, but it'd be yet another mess for me to clean up. Is this understood?"

We both nodded, then the Carrot left the room.

"Okay," Matthews said. "Put it all on the table."

We did as we were told. When we were done, I looked at Matthews and apologized. "It was for my dad," I said.

Matthews shook his head, frustrated. "You keep telling yourself that as if it's some type of excuse, but we both know it wasn't for your dad. It was about you. It's always been about you. Once again, you're trying to prove to yourself that you're good enough, trying to live up to some standard that is not rooted in reality and that nobody, not even your father, could meet."

He shoved the pile at the center of the table into a black duffle bag. "Goodnight to the both of you," he said, then added, "and the Carrot was right about Bob's wife, stay the hell away from her."

WE ENDED up at the casino, because neither one of us wanted to go home. The Expedition was nearby and one of the few places open in the middle of the night. It also had free booze if you were gambling. Despite my pledge never to gamble again, I didn't hesitate. I pulled all the emergency reserves out of my account and hit the tables.

It did not go well. Within an hour, I was down $600, but I wasn't going to stop. As the drinks kept coming, I kept playing. Hours passed. At some point, Crash left, but I remained. The chips in front of me had grown, providing a false sense of hope, then more and more they were pushed to the center of the poker table and taken away.

When I was sure I had a good hand—a guaranteed win— I'd given the cashier my credit card. I punched in my PIN and pulled a cash advance from one of my credit cards. It was just like old times. I was ready to go all-in.

There were no windows in the casino or clocks. I had no

idea what time it was when John found me. "Amy, I'm so glad you're okay. I've been worried sick about you. I must've called a hundred times."

I should've stopped playing then, but I didn't. I kept going. "The battery on my cell phone went dead." This may or may not have been true.

"Cheryl called me, the bartender," John said. "She asked if I knew you were here."

"Why does she care?"

"Because Cheryl's my friend. We've worked together for over a year, and she knew we're together."

"Is that right?" I threw $100 into the pot.

John pointed at the cards in front of me. "I thought you were done with this?"

"Obviously not."

To the dealer, I called it, and everybody revealed what they'd been holding one at a time. The guy next to me won, and I threw my chips into the pot for the next round.

This made John angry. He stepped in front of me. "Can you stop this and just talk to me? Tell me what happened."

"There's a short version and a long version," I said. "The short version is, I got fired and the girl I met with is now dead."

"Wait," John said. "What happened?"

"I don't want to get into it right now, Johnny Boy," I said, "Do you mind?" I then pushed him to the side so I could see what was going on at the table.

John stepped in front of me again. "Yes, Amy, I do mind. I mind very much." He took my arm and tried to pull me away, but I wouldn't leave.

The argument escalated, and soon two security guards arrived. John saw them coming. "I work here," he said. "She's drunk, and she needs to go home. You can't keep serving someone who's obviously intoxicated, and you can't keep taking their money."

"I'm not intoxicated." I looked at the dealer and all the other players at the table. I stood up and pushed all my chips in the center. "I call."

The couple to my right folded immediately, but the man to my left matched me. "Let's see what you got, pumpkin."

I laid my cards on the table, and the man smiled. "That's good," he said, "but not good enough."

His three of a kind beat my two pair, and all my money was gone. I stood and turned to John, rolling my eyes. "Thanks a lot."

"Let's go." He nodded toward the door.

"I'm not going anywhere with you."

"What are you talking about?" He looked crushed. "Who are you?"

"This is the real me," I said. "This is who I am."

"I don't believe that." John tried once again to take me back to my apartment, but I refused.

"I'm good, John," I said. "Just leave me alone. I'll find another ride."

"I'll give you a ride home," a man said as he passed. "Is this guy giving you problems?"

To John, I said, "See, I've got plenty of options."

I woke up to see the same man who had offered me a ride the night before hastily gather his clothes off my floor. He was very tall, well over six feet, with short hair and a Marine Corps insignia tattoo on his arm. As he pulled his shirt over his head, he noticed I was looking at him.

"Hey." He walked over to the bed, kissed my cheek, and sat down next to me. "Had a good time last night, or this morning, whenever it was. I didn't want to wake you up, so I was going to write you a note."

I realized I was naked and had no idea how we ended up together. My stomach roiled up, and I tasted a bit of vodka. I must've blacked out.

"What's your name?"

"Nathan," he said. "Nathan Lake."

"Okay, Nathan Lake." I felt anger and shame as the words spat out of my mouth. "Why don't you get out of here? Like right now before I call the police."

"What are you talking about?" He looked genuinely confused. "Police? Are you crazy? You're the one who insisted I come home with you."

"Get out."

"Fine."

He buttoned his pants, grabbed his shoes, and left the room, leaving his socks behind. A second later, I heard the apartment door open and close as he left the apartment. I then closed my eyes and tried to piece together everything that had happened, but that was like shoveling mud. My only coherent thought was the obvious: what happened was that you fired Dr. Dan and stopped taking your medications, then you screwed everything up.

I rolled over and buried my head in my pillow, feeling like a fool, as well as a slut, psychopath, and piece of garbage. The list could go on, but the picture should be clear, and I won't belabor it.

I took a deep breath, then another as the past 24 hours came back into focus. I remembered the phone call and the Arch, and I remembered Jenae Malmo, dying on the ground with half of her skull sprayed across the pavement, and then there was Bob Cook, and the hospital and the Carrot. She suspended me or fired me or both.

Was Matthews there? I think so, pretty sure. Then there was the casino.

How long was I at the casino? How much did I lose? I'd pushed all my chips to the center and called the hand. I remember that. I'd lost it all, and then I lost John, too.

It took another hour for me to get out of bed. It was my bladder that ultimately forced the move. If I didn't have to use the bathroom, I probably would've stayed under the covers the entire day.

After using the toilet and being fully upright, I decided it'd be best to get out of the bedroom. I fed Mister Bones, then looked for my cell phone. I found it on the kitchen table. The battery was dead. I knew that, but somehow forgotten.

I plugged it into the charger and made some coffee while waiting for the battery to have a little juice to at least allow me to turn it on. I had a good idea of what I'd see, but it was even worse than I thought.

John had called me dozens of times, calls that went unanswered. The initial messages were gentle and sweet, then grew more concerned, and finally panicked. He hadn't wanted me to go. He was worried before I'd even left the apartment. I'd promised John I'd let him know I was okay, but I never did. It never even crossed my mind to call him.

It was then our final conversation at the poker table fully came back to me. I hated myself for everything I'd said. I wasn't just oblivious and self-absorbed. I was cruel. I began to cry, and once I started, it was difficult to stop.

28

———

Around five, I decided I shouldn't be alone. I needed to go someplace else, anyplace. I even wondered if I should check myself into the hospital. I grabbed my keys and purse. Then I walked out the door.

Much to my surprise, my car was right in front. I didn't remember driving home from the casino, much less scoring a prime parking spot. I took it as a sign from the universe to go see an old friend.

The bakeshop wasn't that far away. Although it would be closed, I knew Gray would still be there. He was skeptical of modern mixers and preferred to allow the passage of time to do the work instead. He swore it gave his breads a deeper, richer flavor. So, he always stayed late and mixed the dough for shaping the next morning.

When I arrived, I walked around to the back. Gray's white cargo van was still there, and the lights were on in the shop. I knocked on the back door.

"Sorry, we're closed."

"That's okay," I said. "I'm not here to buy, I'm just here to talk, and to get the famous baker's autograph."

There was silence. If Gray had chosen to ignore me, I wouldn't have blamed him at all. We'd grown close after Merchants Bridge, bonded by our shared experiences with wrinkles in reality. There was comfort in being with someone who assured you that what you felt and what you saw was real, even if there were still doubts.

We never had sex, but we kissed once. Our intimacy scared me. I couldn't handle being around somebody who saw the real me, and I couldn't handle being around somebody who constantly reminded me of what happened at Merchants Bridge. So, after the kiss, I told him we were done. No further explanation given, and that was it, until now.

He stood in the open doorway, wearing an apron. I didn't know if his hair was turning gray or if it was flour. It didn't matter. Gray looked good either way. He'd lost weight, and his arms and chest looked strong. I guess that's the difference between being a lawyer pushing paper and being a baker who lifts and shapes hundreds of pounds of dough every day.

"This is a surprise," he said. "Come in." Gray turned and walked back into the kitchen. "I'm just finishing up, but I can get you something. What do you say, eat or drink?"

The offer surprised me. I wasn't sure what I had expected, but I'd prepared myself for hostility. In fact, that was what I deserved, but Gray was gracious as always. "If it's not too much trouble, I'd love anything you've got," I said. "I haven't eaten."

Gray turned and smiled. "I can tell." He pointed toward a doorway that led to the front of the shop. "Why don't you go up there, and I'll put a little something together." And so I did.

I sat at the counter, while Gray shaped the dough in the back. He'd made me a panini with pesto, tomato, and burrata, along with a from-scratch sparkling lemonade. As I ate, I felt my head clear and some of my energy start to return.

On the wall, Gray had framed clippings from local newspapers and magazines about his bakery, along with a profile in

Bon Appetite. The headline was "Former Lawyer Makes The Case For Best Bakery In The Midwest."

Gray caught me looking at them. "Don't believe the hype. It's just flour, water, and salt."

"I don't know." I popped the last bit of the panini into my mouth. "This tastes amazing."

"Thanks." Gray took off his apron. "Do you want to hear something strange?"

"Always," I said.

"I've been thinking about you lately. Thinking I should reach out, but I didn't because you made it pretty clear you didn't want me to, and I understood why."

"You understood?"

"Sure." Gray leaned under the counter and grabbed a glass. As he filled it with water, he said, "You wanted to be normal, and you can't be normal with me always around you, reminding you that you're not. We are freaks." He paused and took a sip, obviously thinking about what he was about to say, and how it would be received. "To be honest, I had those same thoughts. It's like this weird tension. Your brain wants you to accept reality as it presents itself, but you know there's something else...something bigger out there. There's something behind the curtain that you don't understand."

I nodded. Gray had managed to pinpoint the issue within a half-hour of my arrival. Something Dr. Dan hadn't managed to do in over a year of therapy.

Gray sat down beside me. "So, what's up? I assume something happened, something bad. Otherwise, you wouldn't be here."

"That, my friend, is an understatement."

I took a deep breath, then told him everything. There was no filter, and I readily acknowledge it wasn't fair to dump all of my baggage onto Gray after ghosting him for nearly a year. But he didn't seem to mind the one-way conversation. Gray listened and asked questions. At some point, we moved into the back kitchen so he could do his bread stuff, which I still didn't understand after countless times watching him make and shape the dough.

It was dark by the time I ran out of gas. We were now back at the counter, sitting on stools. Gray had lit a candle and found a bottle of wine. I leaned over and kissed him on the cheek. We pressed our foreheads together, eyes closed.

"You're my best friend," I said.

Gray responded in kind. "And you're my best friend."

"If we had sex, that would really screw this up, wouldn't it?"

Gray pulled away and opened his eyes. His expression tightened. "That would most definitely screw this up."

I felt a tear escape from the corner of my eye. "Then what am I supposed to do?"

Gray took my hand. "When you're lost, Amy, you need to go home."

I pulled away. "I need to go back to my disgusting apartment?"

"No," Gray said. "You need to go to your mother. She's grieving, just like you. She needs you, and she feels alone, just like you. You need to talk. I mean, when was the last time you spoke to her?"

More tears fell. They were of sadness, of course, but also guilt. As soon as Gray had said it, I knew he was right. In the weeks that had passed since I'd put my mother on the plane back to Florida, all I had thought about was my father and being his legacy, his eternal life. I never thought about her. I never called. I didn't even send a text or email. Nothing. I was completely self-absorbed.

"She's all alone down there," I said. "I've got to be the worst daughter in the world." I stood up and wiped my cheeks dry. "I better go. You have an early morning."

"Always, early mornings are the life of a baker." He walked

me out to my car, and as I was about to say goodbye, he added a parting piece of advice. "And call John, too, just let him know you're okay, and perhaps an apology." He smiled, a bittersweet smile. "I say this from personal experience. It would mean a lot, and...who knows what'll happen if you keep the door open just a crack. Somebody special just might walk through."

29

———————

My flight to Fort Meyers was scheduled to depart at 10:30 a.m. the following day. I planned on staying with my mother for a week. I figured that I could stay longer if I wanted or I could also cut it short if necessary.

As I was packing, the phone rang. It was Perelli. He asked if I was okay. "Heard some beat cops say there was a murder down by the Arch last night. I'm assuming that was you."

I figured Perelli already knew the details, but I told him anyway. "The meeting just went sideways. It was bad."

"You should've let me be there with you," Perelli said. "I feel awful. Should've insisted."

"It's not your fault," I said. "I actually wasn't alone. There were two people from the FBI there as back-up. I didn't invite them, but they came."

"And I should've done the same thing." There was a pause. It was obvious the conversation wasn't over, then Perelli asked, "Besides these two from the FBI, who else knew about it?"

"Just you and Schmitty."

"Schmitty, that's interesting," Perelli said. "So Schmitty knew the time, location, and everything else?"

"Not everything, but he knew what was going on. What's this about? Are you trying to figure out who wanted Jenae dead?"

"No," Perelli said. "I'm trying to figure out who wanted you dead. Everybody around here thinks this junkie was the target, but that doesn't make sense to me."

"Well, it makes sense to me," I said. "She could finger the guy who sold Kasi Barnes the drugs, so she got shot to keep her quiet."

"I get that," Perelli conceded, "but why do it last night? I mean, that chick was a hard-core junkie. Why would he kill her in front of an FBI agent? That's just dumb."

"Maybe he didn't know I was an FBI agent."

"He knew. He had to know about that meeting, otherwise he wouldn't have staked out that park. I think this guy made Jenae Malmo call you and set up this meeting so he could take you out, but he screwed up. Do I have proof? No, but that's my feeling."

"Why?"

"Because you're the only person looking for him," Perelli said. "You're the only person who cares about Kasi Barnes and anybody else who's buying what he's selling. He kills you, and the investigation is done. Am I wrong? If you were hit by a train, what happens to this little investigation you got going on?"

"It'd be over," I said as a chill ran down my spine. "But it doesn't matter now, Perelli. I think it's over. I'm done chasing this case. It's hurt a lot of people."

"Do what you want," Perelli said. "but I don't like people messing with my partner's family. Let me keep thinking and poking around. In the meantime, lay low."

"I will," I said. "I'm going to Florida to see my mom tomorrow, so that should be good."

"Yes," Perelli said. "That should be good, and if you could stay down there for a year or so, it'd be even better."

THE PLANE TOUCHED down at the Fort Myers airport in the late afternoon. It was a pretty easy flight, but I was still ready to take a hot shower and wash the gross airplane air off my body. Mister Bones was also ready to get out of his little carrier.

My mother met us at the baggage claim, and soon we were on I-75. I'd actually only been there once before, the week she and my father had first moved into their townhome. So, I didn't really remember how far away from the airport they lived. I'd also never seen the townhome completely decorated. They were both still living out of boxes when I had left.

As she drove, my mother made small talk about the weather and how the people who lived in the Fort Meyers area had gotten screwed after the last hurricane. "The politicians are so crooked down here," she said. "Naples is always first in line for everything, while the rest of us just get the crumbs." Mister Bones must've agreed, because he meowed at that with quite a bit of conviction.

In the moments of silence, I could tell she was curious about what had prompted my visit. I'm sure she wanted to know about work and how I'd managed to get away as well as whether I was dating anybody. I wasn't ready to have those conversations yet, but there would be plenty of time.

I spent most of the first few days at the community pool, reading romance novels and mysteries. When I wanted to just chill, I closed my eyes and listened to music. It was like I was in an emotional detox. Under the Florida sun, all of my St. Louis problems baked away.

My mom and I talked, but nothing of substance. In the morning and evening, we'd walk the streets of the subdivision when the temperatures were less oppressive. Along the way, she'd comment on the landscaping and decor and which neighbors were friendly and which neighbors were not.

Thursday night was when it changed. I was lying in bed, having a hard time sleeping, and that's when I heard it.

I quietly opened the bedroom door. A light was on in the kitchen. As I approached, it became much clearer. The sound was that of my mother crying.

My appearance startled her, and she quickly attempted to hide the tissue in her hand. I asked, "Are you okay?"

"I'm fine." This was the response I had expected. This was the standard response to that question given by any Midwesterner, regardless of what was happening. A person could literally be on fire, and if asked, he or she would say, "I'm fine." Likely followed by, "Everything will be okay" or "Don't worry about me" or "I don't want to cause you too much trouble, but if you see a bucket of water anywhere, that would be great."

I sat down at the table next to her. "I'm sorry I haven't called," I said.

"You're busy with work and everything else," she said, "I understand."

"Doesn't make it right, Mom," I said. "I should've called, but things were getting pretty complicated up there at work and stuff...and then there's Dad."

"What about him?"

"Remember at the airport? After the funeral, I wanted to talk about what Dad and I were fighting about."

She nodded her head. "I wasn't ready for that conversation."

"Did you know why he came back to St. Louis, Mom?"

My mother remained silent, as if to answer the question would be a betrayal. So, I decided to tell her what I knew. "He was working on an old case. It's weird, because it isn't a prominent case, or even really a complicated case. It's about a young woman who overdosed about fifteen years ago."

My mother looked at me. Her eyes told me everything. She knew the case, and she knew why it was important to my father.

She said, "You're talking about Kasi Barnes."

"That's right. Who is she?"

My mother rubbed her chin and avoided meeting my eye. Eventually, she declined to answer. "I think you should leave it alone, Amy. Just let it be."

"Well, I can't do that," I said. "He asked me to find out what happened to her."

"In the hospital?"

"Yes, in the hospital, and it's already cost me my job."

"And you still want to honor that request?" My mother now looked at me with incredulity. "I assumed you'd be mad at him if you found out the truth."

"About what?"

"About the fact that..." She looked away again, then said it. "Kasi Barnes was your sister."

———

THE AFFAIR HAPPENED EARLY in their marriage. The adjustment was difficult for both of them, because neither my mother nor father had ever lived independently. Casual dating didn't exist, at least in the world they knew. They both continued to live with their parents until their wedding night.

All of a sudden, they were on their own in a small apartment filled with things they didn't need. They both had unrealistic expectations of what married life would entail, and they had no money. They were scraping by. My dad expected steak, and all they could afford was a tin of SPAM. He thought the apartment was claustrophobic and looked for any excuse not to be home. While he went to the police academy, he kept playing in a half-dozen bands of varying degrees of proficiency, while my mother remained in the apartment where she was supposed to be raising a family that didn't exist.

On their fifth anniversary, there was still no family. My dad was now a cop, making decent money but with horrible hours. My mom was still home alone. On their seventh anniversary, they were separated, but not completely apart. Then my dad met Heather Barnes at a bar, and it got complicated.

My mom and dad saw each other, even went on dates, but he would always return to Heather Barnes. One day, my dad brought divorce papers to my mother. He had expected to go back to Heather that night as a free man. Instead, he learned he would soon be a father.

My mom was pregnant with me.

He broke up with Heather Barnes, moved back into the apartment, and they remained together for the next fifty years. Except, my dad didn't really stop seeing Heather Barnes. Somewhere along the lines, Kasi was born.

"So you knew about Kasi?"

My mom shrugged. "Not at first," she said, "but I knew about Heather Barnes. I knew your father had a girlfriend. He told me he had ended it that night. But I knew it hadn't ended, not right away. By the time you were going to elementary school, your dad was mostly done with Heather Barnes, romantically, but who can really say."

My mom pressed the tissue to her eye. "I found out about Kasi because I saw our bank account statement years later. Every month, your father wrote Heather Barnes a check. I went to her house. I was going to confront her, and when I arrived, I saw a little girl in the front yard. She even looked like you. Younger, but there was a resemblance."

My mother shook her head. "And that was what the money was for, but I just pretended I didn't know, and your father and I never discussed it. We never talked about Heather Barnes or his daughter...it was a different era. I couldn't conceive of getting a divorce. And why should I? I loved Jack, and I still do."

———

IN THE MORNING, after breakfast and coffee, my mother brought me into my dad's office. "His passwords are written on a sheet of paper in the top drawer of the desk. Those will get you into Jack's computer." She pointed at the file cabinet. "He has a bunch of binders in there, and other documents."

"I already have the file," I said. "I got it from Perelli. So, I don't think I need that."

My mother shook her head. "That's the official police file, dear. All this stuff, he did on his own. He's been working on it for years. It wouldn't be in the police file."

She started to leave and then paused. "Take what you want," my mother said, "and if you don't mind, I'd like you to throw the rest away before you go back to St. Louis."

"You want me to throw it away?"

Her shoulders slumped, and she turned back. "It's all very painful, as you can imagine...like a little sliver stuck in your foot, always reminding you that a big part of your life was a lie, no matter how much you love each other or how much you try to be the perfect wife or the perfect mother or the perfect family...there's this thing— evidence, as you cops would call it — proving that it's not true."

My mom began to cry, again. "I know it's not Kasi's fault, and it's unfair, but that's who she and her mother are to me, an annoying little sliver." She took what seemed like a final look at the office, surveying it.

Then she added, "You should also know that toward the end...your dad...I think it was all the chemo and painkillers and all of those pills. Well...he started talking about things that didn't make any sense. I think...I don't know, but I think he was so desperate to get justice for Kasi, or maybe he simply felt guilty for never being there in the way that he was for you—he was coming up with all these crazy theories. I had to listen to them, because I was the only one he could talk to at the end. I'm sure it's in here somewhere."

She then walked to the door. "If you could take care of it, clear this office out for me, I would really appreciate the help." Then my mother nodded and left me alone.

I just stood in the middle of the office for the longest time, unsure of where I should even start, or even whether I should start. I'd made a promise to my father, but didn't I also have a duty to my mother? She suffered in silence as big Jack played the hero. The perfect guy who'd saved her from sitting alone in the lunchroom. He was the best at everything. He was a big and powerful man who commended the room, whether it was at home, or the police station, or on a stage with his guitar.

If my father would've told me who Kasi Barnes really was, would I have made that promise to him as he lay dying in that hospital bed? If I had known about his affair and my secret sister, would I have even become a cop? Would I have been so disgusted with him and his hypocrisy that I would've moved out at eighteen and never spoken to him again?

Since his death, I've run through walls because that was what Jack Wirth would do. In the process, I stopped taking care of my mental health. I tarnished the reputation of a respected judge. Jenae Malmo is dead, and a legendary FBI agent is in critical condition in a hospital. Because I was trying to emulate my father, I lost my job, and I destroyed the best relationship with a man I'd ever had, because "you can't win if you don't play."

Maybe Perelli was not a lazy cop. Maybe Perelli wasn't working behind a desk in the evidence room because he wasn't good at his job. Given what I now knew, he had probably also gotten burned by my father, flying too close to the sun. Hadn't he tried to warn me about Kasi Barnes? He had to know who she really was, and he also had to know it was 100% unethical for my father to be the lead investigator of his daughter's death. Yet they both worked that case.

I sat down on the carpeted floor, cross-legged, and surveyed my father's office, just as my mother had just done. I didn't know what to do. Usually I just went with my instincts, but this was different.

30

—————

I got a big plastic tub and box of garbage bags. I was tempted to trash it all. I figured I could clear out the office in a few hours and be at the pool by noon. There was nothing wrong with that. It would certainly please my mother, and it would also be a good way to channel my anger, but I couldn't.

That harsh judgment, categorizing a person as either good or bad, was something my father did. He routinely wiped away the entire value and accomplishments of an individual because of a single mistake. With a snap of his fingers, a man or woman could become worthless, scum.

I see that now, and how this influenced my life, creating constant anxiety in me from a very young age. The pressure to be perfect and pure. Interacting with the world with a belief that whatever good I brought to it could be rendered moot in an instant by a single bad decision.

I've made a lot of bad decisions, and now I know my dad made a lot of bad decisions, too. It's complicated. A person can be both good and bad. Everybody compromises, and I couldn't simply erase my father.

I had to do it my way, not his. Perhaps I would ultimately throw away everything in his office, but maybe not. Perhaps I'd give whatever he'd discovered about Kasi Barnes to Perelli, or maybe I'd keep it. I didn't know. The first step would be to sort through his things, all of it, and give each a modicum of respect before deciding what to do.

I wandered over to my dad's bookshelf in the corner. Most men my father's age had biographies of presidents, maybe a memoir by a famous coach, or a collection of novels by Tom Clancy or Robert Ludlum. That's what I expected to see, but instead it was filled with books about the early church, ancient myths, and folklore.

I picked one up and flipped through it. In places, there were barely legible scribbles in the margins, and the corners of a few pages were folded over. I looked at one such page.

It was a crude drawing of a black body hovering over another, grabbing its neck, or maybe they were wrestling. Whatever it was, the image was creepy. It was also vaguely familiar, but I couldn't quite figure out why.

I decided to temporarily categorize this book and my father's entire bookshelf as "crazy stuff." I knew my mother didn't want to read these types of books, and neither did I. My intention was either to donate them or throw them all away.

With the bookshelf done, I went over to the computer, turned it on, and entered the password that had been written down. I opened the electronic folder containing my father's files. I clicked a button, and the files were sorted into chronological order. At the time, I remember bracing myself for more things I could categorize as "crazy," and I was right.

The file most recently opened by my father was entitled "Mtoza." It was a media file, a video. I double-clicked it. The media player opened, and the video began to play. It was a very old film. In a college class, I'd watched a movie called "A Trip To The Moon," by a Frenchman named Georges Melies, and I also watched the first true American film called "The Great Train Robbery." Both of these were made in the early 1900s.

This movie seemed to be of that vintage, but even more raw. It was almost as if it had been filmed in secret. The image was grainy, black and white. There was no sound. The camera was unsteady, and within a few minutes it was done, but what I had seen left me feeling cold.

It was a puppet show with haunting marionettes carved out of wood. It began with a family in the forest, a mother and father and a little girl. Day became night. A paper moon appeared in the sky. The mother bent over and kissed her daughter goodnight. Then the parents left, and the child was all alone.

That was when Mtoza came. It was a person, but not really a person. Mtoza had no skin. It was like a skeleton, but with bloody muscles instead of just bone. The Mtoza danced around the child as the forest turned into a giant fire, growing bigger and bigger with each circle Mtoza made.

And then, in the final moment, Mtoza jumped on top of the child, rode it for a second or two, then the film ended with a kiss.

That was it.

In addition to feeling cold, my other reaction was disgust. Without context, it was easy to assume this was a sexual act by Mtoza, perhaps the first child pornography ever made. But I felt like there was something more to it, because the Mtoza or something like it had haunted my own dreams since Merchants Bridge.

I got out of the chair and went back to my father's bookshelf. I pulled the book I'd previously categorized as crazy and turned to its index. I found the word "Mtoza" and then the passages in the book that explained what or who it was.

Mtoza was Swahili for a "collector," and that was what I'd seen the figure doing in the film. The monster was not riding the child for sexual pleasure. The Mtoza was smothering it, and the final kiss was not a kiss at all. The Mtoza was stealing the child's last breath, collecting it before the child died.

I flipped through the book and found that my father had also flagged the story of the "boo hag," a mythical creature from South Carolina's Gullah culture. The boo hag didn't just steal a person's last breath to give it strength, the boo hag would also steal the person's skin if they resisted and wear that skin to travel freely and gain entry into homes to steal the breath of others.

I put that book back on the shelf and pulled another. In this one, my father had flagged similar stories in Roman mythology. It was a story of Prometheus, stating that he not only stole fire from Mount Olympus, but also the breath of Apollo while Apollo slept. He snuck into the room and "placed his hand upon Apollo's chest and stomach, forcing the god's breath into his own." Apollo's breath was necessary to ensure that the fire would forever be fed with the oxygen it needed, never to be extinguished on Earth.

I flipped to the next section marked by my father. It was about a Greek myth involving Hermes, who was often considered among the most mischievous of the ancients. He was not just the protector of thieves, in this story Hermes stole the last breaths of humans to help guide their souls into the afterlife. With each soul delivered, Hermes was rewarded by the creatures of the underworld. They gave him power, and he became more clever and even more devious.

This continued until his father Zeus grew wary of Hermes' antics and allowed Hermes to die. When his son passed away, bacteria-carrying insects swarmed out of his body. Each insect was one of the breaths he'd stolen, which then caused disease and plague to spread across Mount Olympus and the Earth, killing many.

I closed the book and walked over to the file cabinet. My

mother was right, it was much more than the official file. There were about fifteen binders. The first few contained some of the things Perelli had given me, the remainder was entirely different.

One binder was filled with maps. There must've been sixty or seventy different maps in the binder. Most of them were of St. Louis and across the river in East St. Louis, but he also had maps of Missouri, Iowa, Tennessee, and Arkansas. There was also a map of the United States with a line going up from Miami, Florida, through Atlanta, Georgia to Nashville, Tennessee to St. Louis, and then down from St. Louis to New Orleans.

My father had also made dots on these maps, and each dot had a number. In the back of the binder was a list of names associated with each number along with a date. Some of the dates went all the way back to the 1920s.

This also didn't make a lot of sense, because if my father believed all of these deaths were connected, then that meant he also believed the killer was over a hundred years old or there was some type of cult killing people, maybe both. My mother did say my dad was talking crazy, and by the look of it, he wasn't just talking crazy.

I closed the file drawer, thinking all of these binders should be thrown away in the same way all of the books on that shelf were going to be thrown away. It was difficult to imagine what my colleagues would think, if I ever tried to explain this. It also made the death of Jenae Malmo even more tragic. If my dad would've just left it alone, then I would've left it alone, and she'd still be alive. I'd also probably still be working with Matthews at the FBI. I'd be solving real cases involving real crimes, not chasing my father's delusions.

I felt like a fool. When the Carrot suspended me and Matthews took my badge and gun, I was convinced I was a failure. I was the one who didn't work hard enough or have the mentality to run through the wall to get to the justice on the other side. My father remained on a pedestal. I thought if only I was as good as him, then I wouldn't have failed.

Now I knew better.

I walked over to the computer and sat down at the desk, fairly convinced that I would simply find more of the same, that I'd continue to discover the desperate ideas of a dying man, attempting to bring some sense of order to tragedy. I was sure that my dad had convinced himself that his other daughter couldn't simply be a statistic, one of thousands who die of an overdose every day. Her death had to be special, because he was special, and therefore his children were special.

I clicked, and the next file opened. It was a document consisting of random words, locations, and questions. It was like he was brainstorming, attempting to marshal facts like an Internet conspiracy theorist. It wouldn't have surprised me to see a question asking, "Why has nobody ever seen Michael Jordan and Barack Obama in the same room?"

I was reaching the end of my patience, no longer curious. I'd done what I said that I would do. I hadn't jumped to a conclusion or dismissed my father's work out of spite for what he'd done to my mother and me. The sun was out. The sky was blue, and the pool beckoned. I was ready to be done.

For no reason at all, I clicked one more file at random. It was somewhere in the middle, and up popped an autopsy photo. This surprised me. I wasn't prepared. It was as if I'd invaded a sacred space without permission, and I instinctively turned around to see if anyone else was in the room.

Then I looked at the photograph in front of me, really looked at it. The image was of a man from the waist up, pale and naked. His arms were bruised from countless needles, vestiges of failed attempts to find a vein that did not want to be found. That was what caught my attention at first, but then I noticed the other bruises.

There were two, both in the shape of a hand. One on the stomach, and one on the heart. It was like a person had dipped their hands in a mottled bucket of yellow, blue, and purple paint and pressed that onto the wall of a cave.

It was so clear.

I closed it and opened another. This photograph was of a woman, perhaps Hispanic. She also displayed the markings of an addict, and she also had the handprints on her chest.

My heart beat faster as I opened the third photograph. It was another man. He had tattoos all over his body, but the handprints were still visible, just like the others.

I stopped, closed the image, and scrolled down the screen, studying the directory of file names and types. My quick estimate was that there were at least two dozen photos similar to these. Each one likely had an autopsy photo of someone's chest from the waist up, and each one likely had handprints in the same locations.

I thought about what I was seeing. Was there another explanation? I'd heard people were often bruised after CPR. It was even possible for ribs to be fractured or even broken. This was, in part, the reason why so many states had enacted Good Samaritan laws in the early 1990s. People were getting sued for saving another person's life.

I found an electronic folder with the autopsy photos of Kasi Barnes and clicked it open. The image of her naked from the waist up was halfway through the series, and the bruises on her chest and stomach were the same as the others.

I closed my eyes and wondered whether any of this mattered. It was all insane. Even assuming that there was, in fact, a person collecting the final breaths of dying men and women, who was I to track down the Mtoza?

Everything that I had ever done had resulted in disaster for either myself or others. I just needed to walk away. I knew that was the right decision, and I also knew I couldn't. Perelli was right. Jenae Malmo wasn't the target at the North Pond; those bullets were meant for me. The Mtoza wasn't going to stop until I was dead.

I'd seen it in my dreams, and I'd seen those handprints in my dreams as well.

31

———

I stayed in Florida for an extra two weeks. I didn't have any specific plans to leave, but I was preparing myself. I was now back on my medications. I had started exercising every day, and I kept reviewing the materials in my father's office over and over again.

My mom and I also got into a routine. It started with morning coffee on the back deck, followed by a walk in the neighborhood. It ended with dinner and another walk at sunset.

I was tempted to rush back to St. Louis many times, but I knew that I wasn't ready. The only plan that I'd come up with was to use myself as bait, and I didn't like the odds of dangling at the end of a string and holding a tiny hook in my hand, hoping to catch a monster. The days of blindly running through walls on my own were over. I knew that if I was patient, a better opportunity would come along, and I was right.

It was late when my burner phone rang. The noise was a complete surprise. My emotions had been so chaotic when I had left St. Louis, I'm not even sure why I brought it. With Jenae Malmo dead, there wasn't any reason to be expecting another call. I had forgotten it was even there. It lay on the floor in the corner of the guest bedroom, silent and unused. I had plugged it into the wall when I had first arrived out of habit, not expectation.

"Hello."

"Yes." It was a woman's voice. "Is this Agent Amy Wirth?"

"It is. Can I help you?"

"I don't know. I think you wanted to talk to me about Kasi Barnes."

"Of course," I said, cautious. "How did you get this number?"

"My public defender told me to call," she said. "He told me that a cop had contacted him and said that the FBI was looking for me. My lawyer kind of freaked at first, but then whoever it was said that he shouldn't worry, said I wasn't in trouble. You were just looking for information. My lawyer thought that cooperating with you might help with some of my pending cases, like get a better plea deal."

"And who are you?" Now I was genuinely curious.

"Jenae," the woman said. "I'm Jenae Malmo."

The response was automatic, blurting out of my mouth with no filter. "But you're dead."

The woman laughed. "I don't think so."

We spoke for another ten minutes, confirming a little bit about her background and relationship with Kasi. I was careful to avoid anything too direct. I didn't want her to know exactly why I wanted to talk, because I was afraid that she might disappear. I needed time to figure out a real plan.

When I hung up the phone, I called Perelli. He picked up after three rings, and I jumped right into it. "Guess who I just talked to?"

"I have no idea."

"Jenae Malmo."

"You sure about that?" Perelli said. "Last time I checked, she was in the morgue with a tag on her toe. The medical examiner was trying to track down her family to clear some space, but no luck."

"Did they run fingerprints or DNA?"

"Probably not, since the cops who brought her in told the examiner her name," Perelli said. "Are you sure the person you talked to was telling the truth?"

"No," I said, "but she knew quite a bit about Kasi Barnes."

There was a long silence before Perelli spoke. "Hey kid, I thought you were done with this, at least that was my hope. You went down to Florida, and I was happy for you. It's already caused so much trouble."

I thought I knew why Perelli didn't want me to come back. He didn't want to have to keep my father's secrets anymore. "I know she was my sister or half-sister or whatever you call it, if that's what you're concerned about," I said. "My mom told me when I got down here. She's known the whole time."

Another long pause. "I'm sorry," Perelli said. "I was trying to protect you, protect your mom, protect everybody. I even tried to keep your dad away toward the end, too. It was a bad idea, but he was obsessed. That wasn't how he was supposed to be spending his last days, you know? But Jack was Jack. He was the hammer, and everything else was the nail."

I thought about all the people who probably knew about Kasi: other cops, guys in his band, and Schmitty, definitely Schmitty. These people, like Perelli, who had convinced themselves they were protecting me from getting hurt or protecting my mother, but they were really only protecting my dad from the consequences of his actions. It would've been easy for me to get angry at them, and there were moments that I was, and there have been many moments since then, but I'd likely have done the same thing. That's the truth, if I'm being honest with myself, and that's what I told Perelli.

"It was a difficult situation that my dad put you into," I said, "but that's done, and I need to finish this so I can move on." I felt my hand tighten on the phone as I asked a second time. "Can you just check for me? Confirm that this person is really Kasi Barnes and confirm that the person who's in the morgue is somebody else."

I gave Perelli the name and number of the in-patient treatment facility where Jenae Malmo was supposedly living. "Verify her, and maybe get the medical examiner to finally run those fingerprints. I'm sure whoever they have in the morgue has a record, prints on file."

Perelli agreed. "I'll try, because it's you who's asking, and I care a lot about you and your mom. Your father was like a brother to me," Perelli said. "I'm not gonna make no promises, though, because as you recall, I work in the evidence room. I don't exactly have a lot of juice around here."

"But people like still you, Perelli, and that counts for something. Everybody likes you."

"Thanks," he said. "I'll get back to you real soon, Little Jack in a Dress, but I gotta say it. This doesn't change my opinion. It's nothing but trouble."

"Maybe," I said, thinking about the Mtoza who had come to me in my dreams, "but I can't live with a target on my back, always being afraid when I close my eyes at night."

"Fair enough," Perelli said, then hung up the phone.

32

It took two days for Perelli to confirm that the young woman in the morgue was not Jenae Malmo. The finger-prints, once taken, came up with an immediate match and identified her as Angie Prater.

Perelli told me that she was a girl who grew up in Illinois farm country. As a kid, she sold her family's corn out of the back of a pickup truck until she hit puberty; that's when the big city started calling for her. Selling corn for a few dollars along the highway or hanging out at the Dollar General on a Friday night smoking weed wasn't enough. She wanted more, desperate for more.

I thought about that as I packed my father's books and files into boxes, remembering the look in her eyes as she tried to negotiate with me near the North Pond. Angie wanted to drive a hard bargain, but deep down we both knew she had no leverage.

I wondered what she'd been told, how someone had convinced her to meet me that night. My guess was that Angie was given a little bump of heroin or cocaine to make the phone call, just a little. Then she was told I'd be bringing money for information and she could keep whatever she hustled out of me.

"I don't want you to go."

I turned. My mother was there in her bathrobe. She'd been watching me pack the boxes that I'd ship back to St. Louis that afternoon. "I know you don't," I said. "We've already had this conversation."

"So you really believe this? You believe that there's a monster, some ancient creature that travels around, killing people so that he can steal their final breath. That's what you think?"

"I don't know." I turned my attention back to the bookshelf. I picked one up. It was *Primitive Mythology*, written by Joseph Campbell. Published in 1959, it was the first of a four-volume series called *Masks of God*. Based on the scribbles in the margins, this was the book that really sent my father down the rabbit hole.

I put it in the box. "It's crazy, Mom. I agree. All of it is crazy." I picked up another book off the shelf, put it in the box, then another, continuing as we talked. "But I really do think there are things that happen that we don't understand. They happen all the time, and our brains don't allow us to accept it, or it's dismissed altogether. It's sort of like a safety valve for our sanity, the key to maintaining a sense of safety and control."

I took the final four books off the bottom shelf, filling the box. My mom picked the roll of packing tape off the carpet and brought it to me. The corners of her eyes were drawn down, concern appearing to have deepened every line in her face.

I took the tape, and without me asking, my mother closed the top of the box and held it shut. As I anchored one end of the tape, then sealed it, I tried to reassure her. "I'm in a good place right now," I said. "The meds are working, and my head is clear. I also want you to know that you might be right, maybe all of this is just something I want to believe because I want to believe in Dad again. I want to stop thinking about him as somebody who cheated on you and kept secrets from me, and, most of all, I want my hero back."

"He was a hero, Amy." My mom held down the tape as I cut it. "He was an honorable man who made a mistake, that's it. He was a great husband, the love of my life." She put her hand on my shoulder. "But even so, you don't have to do this, not for him, and not for me."

"I'm not." I spread my arms, gesturing at the now half-empty office. "I'm doing this because even if it turns out not to be true and there's no connection between all of these people, I'm still a target. I was still the person who was supposed to be killed at the North Pond. Those bullets were intended for me. Whether it's this or something else, it has to be bigger than just Kasi Barnes. That's what I have to figure out."

"Alone?"

"No." I picked up the box of books and stacked it on top of the others. "I have people who will help me."

"But you're suspended."

"That doesn't mean I won't have support. I'm not going it alone."

"Like who?"

"Perelli," I said, "Perelli is going to help."

My mother shook her head. "I don't know about him. Your father—"

"Dad trusted him enough to be his partner for over a decade, Mom, and I think he's a lot smarter than he lets on. He gets it."

———

MISTER BONES STAYED with my mother. I wasn't sure how long I'd be in St. Louis, but the cat didn't like traveling, and he'd grown accustomed to the Florida lifestyle. The constant supply

of treats from my mother didn't hurt the transition. I promised
Mister Bones that I'd be back and soon boarded a plane.

The trip gave me plenty of time to think about what needed
to happen. What started as a loose plan had solidified, and I
felt ready. The weather was just a bonus. It was early fall in St.
Louis, and the humidity was gone, which was a nice change
from Florida.

It made me think of sitting in the cheap seats with my dad
at a Cardinals game with a bag of peanuts as the playoffs
approached, wondering if this would be the year that we'd win
the World Series. It was always possible; some years the odds
were better than others, but all you needed was to get hot at the
right time.

As I picked up my car from a long-term parking lot a couple
miles from the airport, I knew that I needed the same thing as
the Cardinals this time of year. My team had to come together,
and we needed to get hot. It didn't matter to me whether things
clicked because of skill or luck. I just needed everything to
click.

Jenae Malmo was at an inpatient treatment facility on the
outskirts of Troy, Missouri. It was about an hour drive. I exited
Highway 61 and followed Northstar Drive west until I arrived at
a gate with a small sign that said, "Evolve."

I told the attendant who I was and who I wanted to see. He
checked a list that he had on a clipboard, then radioed somebody about my arrival. The gate opened, and he pointed at a
parking lot about a hundred yards away. It was a small, squat
building with several golf carts off to the side.

When I parked, a second attendant greeted me with a smile
and led me into the building. She was a large woman with
frizzy hair. She had me sign a confidentiality form, and then
she asked me to empty my pockets.

By way of explanation, she said, "No drugs or alcohol are
allowed in the facility. It needs to stay in your car."

After I turned my front pockets inside out, she put on a pair of rubber gloves and stuck her hands in my back pockets. Then she frisked the rest of me and followed that with a black plastic wand that beeped at my watch and earrings.

The attendant then asked to see my bag. "You'd be surprised at what people do to 'help' their loved ones." She shook her head as she poured the contents of my bag on a plastic table. "Sometimes I think they can be the biggest obstacles for change." She worked through all the items, including flipping through my paperback book and opening my mascara to look inside. "I know that was what prevented me from getting clean. Now I'm seven years sober."

"Good for you," I said.

She smiled and nodded, then finished her examination. When she stepped away from the table, the frizzy haired woman said, "I'll let you pack it up the way you like it while I bring the golf cart around. I got a garbage can over there if there's stuff you don't want, usually there is."

I wasn't given a chance to go back to my car. I figured that if I had, the search would need to be repeated. The attendant patted the seat next to her on the golf cart, and we drove up to the main building.

It was just under a half-mile from the entrance and overlooked the Fork Cuivre River. There were lots of trees. People were in hammocks, reading. Another group was playing kickball, and some were just lying on the grass, soaking up the sun.

"Pretty nice," I said as we stopped.

"Miracles happen here," the attendant said, then appeared to reflect on her statement. After a moment, she added, "Just not every time."

———

I MET with Jenae Malmo on the second floor of the building, off the library. One balcony overlooked the river, but there were people sitting there, and so Jenae led me to the other balcony that overlooked a pool and a wooded area with hiking trails. We had that one to ourselves.

"Before we get started, Jenae, I have to be honest with you." I settled into an oversized, wooden rocking chair. "I want to find this guy for personal reasons."

This confused her. "I thought you we an FBI agent."

"I am, sort of," I said, "but this isn't just a case. Kasi was my half-sister. I didn't know that until very recently, and it explains why my dad asked me to do this before he died. He had worked the case when he was a cop, then kept working it after he retired."

"Kasi's dad was a cop?" It was obvious that Jenae didn't know this information, and it was unclear how she felt about it. Then, "She always said he was 'out of the picture,' which I understood, because my dad wasn't around much either. We didn't dwell on it, because there wasn't anything we could do. It just is what it is."

I nodded. "I only wanted to let you know that this isn't an entirely official investigation, if that makes sense. I've got a personal stake, and I'm not sure whether your attorney is going to be able to use your cooperation to get you a better plea deal or not. It's possible, but I want to be straight. I'm not interested in tricking you, because I think this guy is really dangerous."

"I *know* he's dangerous," Jenae said. Then she sat there, obviously thinking about everything that I'd said and everything that had happened to her and her best friend. It took a while, but I wasn't going to press. I'd wait as long as it took, because that was the right thing to do. That's how you built a team.

And Jenae eventually opened up.

"After she died, it was awful. I went to some pretty dark

places, but do you know what I didn't do? I didn't quit using, and I kept buying drugs from this guy, because if he got arrested and went to jail...poof, there goes my source."

Jenae shook her head, then continued. "But that isn't the only reason. I mean, it's not like I couldn't find somebody else. There are lots of people selling, but he was different. He had this, I don't know how to describe it, energy that you were drawn to. He had power over me, and I knew that if I turned on him, it was going to be trouble." She paused, then looked at me. "Did you know he's a cop?"

———

WE WALKED the paths around the campus and along the river, together. I asked her questions, logistics. I wanted to know everything about the dealer. I wanted details. I had to know how contact was made, what was said during a typical exchange, and where a typical deal went down.

Then we talked through my plan and the role she could play. Jenae understood and offered ideas as to how to make it work even better. We continued to walk and talk.

It was obvious Jenae was lonely, and I was happy to listen to whatever she wanted to say. We had time, and I was curious about the sister I never had an opportunity to meet. Growing up as an only child, there were many times that I imagined having a brother or sister. As Jenae spoke, I felt myself grieving for Kasi, and also for myself.

At a bend in the river, there was an overlook. We stopped and admired the remarkable view. "I feel lucky to be here," Jenae said. "I've done inpatient treatment before, not sure how many programs I've gone through, but this is different."

She looked around and took a deep breath. "A lot of them are dumps, but this place is spectacular. I can't believe the county is paying for this. Nearly everybody else here has a rich parent or something like that. I heard there was a famous actress earlier this year and a guy in my group was in a band, a one-hit wonder, but evidently the royalty checks keep coming."

We left the overlook and got back on the path. "No charge?"

"None that I know of." Jenae picked a leaf off a tree and twirled it between her fingers. "There was this social worker, one of those people who wander the streets at night doing outreach. I couldn't believe she was out there at three in the morning. She was this old woman, very old woman with dread-locks, and when I first met her, I assumed she was homeless, just like me. Anyway, she told me that this was the last time I'd get this chance, and if I blew it, I'd be dead. So here I am."

As soon as Jenae Malmo said it, I thought about the woman who lived behind my apartment with the birds but quickly dismissed the idea. There was no way, but maybe.

33

As I drove back to St. Louis, I made the big decision to call Matthews. We hadn't spoken since that night at the hospital when I had surrendered my badge and gun to him. I still remember the look of disappointment on his face. The fact that it wasn't the first time that I'd let him down made it even worse.

On my list of people that I wanted on my team, Matthews wasn't somebody I planned on asking. It wasn't that I doubted he could do the job. He was the best agent I knew. I just assumed he wouldn't be willing. The identity of the dealer changed that. If Jenae Malmo was telling the truth, then Matthews would want in on it, and I owed him that opportunity.

Every agent had something that motivated them to go above and beyond. For some, it was terrorism or sex trafficking. For Matthews, it was government corruption. Whether it was crooked politicians or dirty cops, I knew that he deemed this to be the most "righteous" of all our work. He couldn't stand the hypocrisy. These were the people who were supposed to be protecting society and working for the common good. Instead, they were abusing their positions of power for personal gain. They were a cancer, weakening society's foundation from the inside.

The dirty cop's name was Nick Lund. I didn't plan to tell Matthews I thought he may be a mythical creature more than a hundred years old. I also did not plan to tell him that my father suspected that Lund had killed dozens, stealing their last breath to prolong his own life and give him strength. I knew enough to keep those ideas to myself. Such talk would likely end the conversation before it started and probably lead to an involuntary trip to a mental hospital.

So, as I sped down the highway pushing close to eighty miles an hour, I played it straight. "I'd brought the burner phone down to Florida, for reasons that I still don't understand. One day it rang, and things went from there," I told him. "My dad's former partner checked her out and confirmed that she was real. The prints off the person in the morgue matched someone else."

Matthews was skeptical. "So you flew back, just for that?"

"I think you already know this case is personal." I wanted to be as honest with Matthews as I could. He deserved that. "My dad asked me to find out who was responsible for killing Kasi Barnes before he died, and while I was visiting with my mom, I found out that she was my father's other daughter."

Matthews didn't say anything, then asked, "Where are you right now?"

I told him, and we agreed to meet at the Waffle House near his house. It was the same one where we had met after Judge Griggs committed suicide. That now seemed like a very long time ago. My dad had still been alive, and I had no idea the secrets he carried.

———

MATTHEWS PICKED up a piece of bacon and started eating it, clearly thinking about all the implications and angles as he took in the vista. There was a guy changing a tire at the gas station across the street, while another paced around him with a cell phone to his ear. Finally, Matthews turned his attention back to me.

"I'd be pissed at your dad if I were you," he said. "I mean, I'd be really pissed at him. I knew you were already in the doghouse before the Carrot sent you down to the task force, but people do get out of there. I checked around, and it wasn't a death sentence. Bob Cook was right, a little contrition and maybe some tears, and you could've come back."

"Trust me," I said, "I've thought about that, but I understand why my dad did what he did, but I can't help wondering if things would have ended differently, if he'd just let it go."

Matthews scooped up some scrambled eggs with his fork. "From what you've already told me, Lund's been dealing for a long time. He was dealing before he was a cop, and it's continued through the years. And you figure that when he heard about you poking around, he sets up this meeting to take you out."

"Right, Schmitty and my dad's old partner let the patrol cops know who I was looking for, and I gave them permission to spread the number around. I was just fishing, never totally confident it was going to work. Then it all went sideways. I thought he was just eliminating a witness, but Perelli—"

"Perelli?"

I nodded. "That's the name of dad's old partner." Then continued. "He thought I might've been the target right away, and the fact that the woman who got shot wasn't actually Jenae Malmo makes it clear that it was a set-up of some sort."

"And now you want a controlled buy with Lund?"

"I do. The case against him for selling Kasi Barnes tainted heroin is weak and old. All we've got is one witness, Jenae, who could testify that Lund was her dealer, but there's nobody who can say for sure that's where Kasi got the drugs or saw Kasi with Lund on the night she died. As bad as I want Lund locked up, I know we're never going to get proof beyond a reasonable doubt for killing Kasi. Instead, we need to do it the right way, build a fresh case together."

"Is Jenae willing to do it?"

"She's willing to help, but I'm hesitant to put her at risk. It seems like she's just starting to get her life together."

"We may not have a choice." Matthews raised his hand as the waitress passed, and she gave him the check. "Let me poke around a little and get back to you."

Matthews took out his wallet, put some cash on the table, and slid out of the booth. When Matthews was upright, he looked down at me, still sitting at the table.

"And Amy," he said, "you did good work on this, and you look good, too, healthy." He knocked on the table twice. "Glad you called."

"Thanks."

Matthews began to walk away, but I called him back. I got out of the booth and with some hesitation asked about Bob Cook. He'd been on my mind the whole time that I was down in Florida, but I'd been afraid to ask.

"What happened? Is he okay?"

"Alive and out of the hospital, I know that much. I talked to him on the phone a week ago. He's officially retired but says his wife is still pissed at him."

"That's a relief," I said, "the part about him being alive at least."

"It was a close call, but it worked out," Matthews said. "I'm sure he'd appreciate hearing from you, but I'd still avoid his wife."

"Good advice."

"It's worth the price you paid for it." Matthews smiled. "When I get back to the office, I'll text you Cook's number."

—————

AN HOUR AND A HALF LATER, I was on Bob Cook's deck, sipping an Arnold Palmer and watching his grandchildren swim in their pool. Bob had something harder, and it obviously wasn't his first. His overall change in demeanor compared to when I had first met him was dramatic.

Back then, he was bitter and hated his job but insisted on squeezing every penny out of the government pension plan. Cook now seemed to be embracing retirement with gusto, proving that a major health scare was an excellent way to recalibrate priorities, assuming you didn't die in the process.

"Can you believe they're doing this?" He pointed at the two smallest ones bobbing to the bottom, sitting cross-legged, then springing back to the top. Then he pointed at the oldest lounging on an innertube at the far end of the pool with gigantic headphones on her head. "They always want to swim, doesn't matter how cold it is outside. That's why my wife made us get this thing. I thought it was a waste of money, but she insisted, and now I get it, making memories in the pool. These kids will remember swimming at our house for their whole lives, happy times. The cold doesn't matter."

"Kids are just warm blooded, I guess."

"Is that true, or are you just making stuff up?"

"I don't know." I shrugged. "Might've seen it on the Internet."

"The internet." Cook shook his head in disgust.

We talked some more, then the conversation transitioned to my dad and Jenae Malmo. I told Cook about my surprise phone call from her and my trip to the inpatient facility over in Troy.

"Matthews is going to talk to the Carrot," I said. "My guess is that they're going to want to wire her up."

Cook didn't say anything at first. The two littles were now trying to make him laugh by pretending to fall into the pool, as if they didn't know it was there. At some point, singing and dancing became a key component of their comedy routine. He smiled at them, chuckled, and gave his granddaughters a thumbs up.

Then he said, without looking at me, "Seems risky. This cop is not dumb. He obviously knows that you and the feds were looking for her, and by extension him. After that night by the pond, it wouldn't surprise me if he stopped dealing all together and he's just waiting to see it play out."

"I agree, but I'm not in the room anymore. I don't have any say in it."

"Too bad," Cook said. "I mean it. You've got guts. The bureau got way too cautious after Waco." He took another drink and added, "That's what happens when things are run by politicians."

"But I trust Matthews," I said. "He knows what he's doing."

"I agree." Cook nodded, then cheered and clapped after one of his granddaughters retrieved a plastic ring from the bottom of the pool. Then to me, "But I'm not sure Matthews really understands what we're dealing with here." There was something in the way he said it, a suggestion. He wanted to know what I knew.

I thought of that night as Cook lay on the ground and we waited for an ambulance. *I was fine, and then he touched me, touched me, and I fell,* he had said. *He came from nothing.* I thought about all the books my father had collected, many of the stories mentioned the creature's ability to cause paralysis in its victims, rendering them unable to resist.

"Did he get on top of you?" I asked. "After you fell, did he get on top of you? Not like trying to give you CPR, but more like trying to push the air out of you, not allowing you to take another breath?"

Cook's eyes widened. He looked at me. The smile was gone, and his face had turned pale. "So you do know.... I had wondered." Now his eyes were cast down. "I never told anybody about that, nobody, because...I'm not crazy."

From the pool came, "Grandpa. Grandpa. Grandpa."

Cook forced a broad smile as he called back, "What is it, sweetie?"

"Swim with us." She bobbed up and down. "You promised."

"In a minute," Cook said.

"You promised." His granddaughter wasn't going to give up. "Promise. Promise. Promise."

"You should go swim." I stood, gesturing to the adorable little girl begging for her grandfather to swim with her. "I need to go. I just wanted to stop by and say hello, but I'll let you know if I find out anything more, but, to tell the truth, I honestly don't think they're going to keep me informed or ask for advice."

"But you'll warn them about this guy?"

"I'm out of the bureau, Bob. It may not be official, yet, but I'm out. They took my badge and gun."

"I know that," Cook said. "But you'll try, right?"

"Yes," I said. "I'll try."

———

When I arrived, Gray was in the back, loading loaves of bread into large plastic trays to be delivered to local restaurants. The bakery wasn't busy. The morning coffee and pastry crowd had all gone to work, and I figured the people who were looking for fresh bread to go along with their dinner wouldn't start showing up for another hour or so.

"Who's the woman working the counter out front?" I sat on a stool in the corner of the kitchen.

"Helena." Gray opened one of the oven doors and started to pile fresh baguettes onto cooling racks. "She's from Germany."

"She's cute, maybe a little young for you, but within the acceptable range. It wouldn't be totally disgusting."

Gray stopped. He tried to act serious, but I could tell that I'd gotten to him. His cheeks flushed bright pink as he said, "She's my employee, Amy."

"Obviously, but I'm just making conversation." Actually, I was doing more than that, I was teasing him. *Was I jealous?*

Gray changed the subject. "How was Florida?"

"Much better than I thought it would be. I had some good talks with my mom."

"And what about your guy..." Gray searched for the name. "Jim?"

"John," I said.

"That's right, Johnny Boy." Gray boxed a half-dozen loaves, checked the name on a sheet of paper, then wrote the name of the restaurant on top. "What's going on with him?"

"Nothing," I said. "I sent him a text, but no response."

"A text?" Gray made a gagging sound as he began to box the next order for another restaurant. "No wonder he hasn't responded. You have to do it face-to-face, in-person."

"Maybe," I said, then ended the discussion regarding my love life, "can we talk about something else? I came here for advice."

"And I'm giving you really good advice about John."

"Not that kind of advice."

"Fine." Gray laughed. "You just sort of opened the door by encouraging me to have an inappropriate, and likely illegal, workplace romance with one of my employees, so I figured anything was game."

"Well, you were wrong." I crossed my arms across my chest. "I can give it, but I can't take it."

"Very true." Gray wrote a name on the box and placed it on top of the other. "So if it's not personal, then it's professional."

"How about both?

"Nice." Gray rubbed his hands together, then retrieved a chair and sat down. "Tell me more."

And I did. I told him everything, including my father's secrets. I described all the things that I found in his office, my conversation with the real Janae Malmo, and Bob Cook's experience at the North Pond.

"Do you think I should call Matthews off? Tell him about Cook and what was in my dad's books?"

"I don't know," Gray said. "And that's the truth. Speaking for myself, I hold it inside of me, tight. I know what happened. I know it was a miracle or supernatural or whatever you want to call it. I know it's true. I accept it, but what do I have to gain by trying to convince others? I think about that desire we used to have to find the Irish Santa, and I think it was rooted more in a need to convince myself, getting some sort of validation than anything else." Gray got up and began to pace. "But this is different. It isn't just a wrinkle in your reality or Bob's reality, Matthews could die if he isn't prepared, others, too."

"That's what I thought," I said. "I just...I just want to be normal. I want everything to be normal."

Gray nodded. "I know, but you have to call and tell him."

I agreed, but Matthews called me first.

34

I hadn't expected to ever to step foot in the FBI field office again, but there I was. The very next morning, the Carrot's assistant led me from the front desk to the main conference room. He pretended that he didn't know who I was, but I'd met him multiple times. His coldness irritated me more than it should have.

When he opened the door, I saw that Matthews was already there, waiting, but he wasn't alone. The conference room was full. There were two other agents, along with Colton Steele and a couple people that I didn't recognize. As I took a seat next to Matthews, the Carrot's assistant announced that the Chief would be with us shortly.

When the door was closed, I leaned over to Matthews. "What's going on? I thought that it was just going to be you and the Carrot?"

"That's what I thought, too, but evidently this got bigger really fast."

Before I could ask another question, the Carrot arrived with another man, and the room went silent as she took her place at the head of the table and the other man sat beside her. "Good morning," she said. "I thought it was important for us to all come together so that we could coordinate our efforts. Since I'm not sure everybody knows the people who are here, we'll take a moment for brief introductions."

Each person around the table proceeded to state their name and the division that they were working in. The man who had entered the room with the Carrot was Aiden Douglas, Deputy Bureau Chief out of Chicago. He'd brought along Agent Darnel Fischer. The other person that I hadn't recognized was Maddie Sloan, a field agent from the New Orleans bureau. All of them had flown into St. Louis that morning just for this meeting, which suggested that this was no longer simply about Nick Lund.

When it came time for me to introduce myself, I was unsure of what to say. I figured that identifying myself as a probationary agent currently suspended for running an unauthorized investigation would not be a good first impression, but I didn't want to lie. Luckily, the Carrot came to my rescue. She must've sensed my hesitation and thought it best to save me from embarrassing the both of us.

"Agent Wirth is relatively new to our office," the Carrot said. This was a little deceiving, since it sounded like I'd just finished Quantico a few weeks ago. "She came to us from the St. Louis Police Department. Her father was a well-respected detective for many years as well and worked on the Kasi Barnes case. That's how she connected with Jenae Malmo. Before her father died, he wanted her to look into it."

Douglas nodded and gave me a reassuring look, as if to say that he knew the truth and it was all okay. He was mid-forties, with a square jaw and anchorman hair. "I get that," Douglas said. "Some cold cases haunt you."

"Exactly," the Carrot said, clearly putting an end to any further conversation about me or my dad. The others probably didn't sense it, but it was obvious to me that the Carrot was uneasy with my presence and wanted me to keep my mouth shut. I was more than happy to oblige, but I have to admit that I was also a little uneasy. It wasn't until the very end that I understood. I was there because the Carrot and others had no choice.

————

"OPERATION TRADE WINDS" was an absolutely stupid name, but the FBI needed to give every large, multi-district investigation a name. This, I guess, was the best that some bureaucrat in Washington, D.C., could conjure. I think the other people around the table agreed with my assessment as well, because whenever it was mentioned, they just used the acronym, "OTW."

Agent Sloan from New Orleans was tasked with summarizing OTW for those unfamiliar. "We're about six years into this operation," she said. "It involves a network of police officers in different jurisdictions. Most of them work in specialized units targeting gang activity, guns, and drug dealing. Often they're accused of harassment and use of unnecessary force, but that isn't what we're investigating. Those are just means to an end, what we are really investigating is a criminal enterprise that steals drugs and guns from individuals and crime scenes in order to sell them later. The cops obviously don't want any direct connections with it locally, and so they trade the drugs and guns with other cops doing the same thing out-of-state."

"It's like a hub and spoke," Douglas said. "They spin this stuff through multiple cities, making it hard to track exactly where it came from. That's where the gun tracing task force has come into play." Douglas nodded at me, as if I was a star agent executing a cutting edge assignment rather than one of a handful of misfits that the Carrot had relegated to the basement. "We know stuff is coming into and out of St. Louis. Its central location is perfect, but we haven't been able to nail it down."

"But you think Nick Lund is part of it?" Matthews asked.

Douglas nodded. "We do. We've been able to turn quite a few people, and his name has come up multiple times, but we have no proof. We believe he works in and through cities mostly in the southeast."

"And New Orleans," Sloan added. "He's down there four or five times a year."

As they talked more about how the network of dirty cops trafficked guns and drugs across state lines, I thought about the maps I had found in my father's office. Although these maps were documenting something entirely different, the routes were the same, or close. My guess was that if I laid out my father's map of the United States—the one with the line from Florida to St. Louis and then down to Louisiana—it'd be identical to any maps created by Agent Douglas for OTW, documenting the cities where Nick Lund is suspected of unloading his goods.

"How many people are we talking about?" Matthews asked.

"We don't know exactly, over fifty for sure," Agent Sloan said. "Nobody is doing this alone, that we're aware of. It checks all the boxes for racketeering, like the mob or a street gang. In Chicago and New Orleans, they have initiations and tattoos. The lead cop, usually a sergeant, pulls you in by doing something small, then once the line is crossed, it's tough to get out. They're afraid. These cops are terrified of going to prison. That's both good and bad. It's bad because they're incredibly loyal and understand how to cover their tracks. It's good because if we manage to get direct evidence against them, they flip easy. They know how an ex-cop is going to be treated in prison."

Then the Carrot stepped in. "That's why Nick Lund is important. OTW hasn't been able to get a handle on what's happening in St. Louis and how the organization operates in our city. They've been able to identify Lund as a target, but nobody else."

"Now we have him potentially tied to the overdose death of Kasi Barnes and the killing of that girl last month," Douglas said. "That'll be our in."

The other agent from the Chicago office, Darnel Fischer, spoke. "I went out to talk with Janae Malmo last night with Agent Matthews, and she refused to speak with us." Then he turned to me.

That's when I realized that everybody around the table already knew my situation. My guess was that there had been a conference call. I pictured agents from all the jurisdictions across the country, along with the various bureau chiefs and prosecutors, debating the pros and cons of my involvement. In the end, they must've all concluded that I was necessary, but I was also potentially toxic to any prosecution.

It's called a *Brady* disclosure. The name comes from a 1963 decision by the United States Supreme Court, requiring prosecutors to disclose any evidence that may be favorable to the defendant. This not only includes evidence that could prove a defendant's innocence, it also includes evidence that would allow defense counsel to impeach the credibility of a government witness.

If one of these cases went to trial, my background file would need to be disclosed to the defense by Colton Steele or any other U.S. Attorney who was assigned to prosecute it. In that file would be documentation of my suspension, and likely my termination after my probationary review hearing. I'd be cross-examined about everything that I knew, including the information in my father's office and how I'd first come into possession of Kasi Barnes's police file from Perelli. I'd also have to disclose my personal interest in the case. I was not a neutral fact-finder.

I was a daughter fulfilling her father's dying wish to obtain justice on behalf of my sister.

I felt myself sink a little lower in my seat, embarrassed. I could imagine what one of those slick defense attorneys could do to me, and I did not want to be humiliated in front of a jury. That was not what I had signed up for.

It took everything in my power not to run out of that room as fast as possible, but I didn't. I realized that the answer wasn't to run, whether it was running away or running through a wall. Sometimes I just needed to be present, remain in one place, and listen.

We were on the same team and had the same goal: arrest Nick Lund. None of these people was interested in setting me up to fail. They did not want me to be humiliated in a courtroom or hurt their case any more than I did. They just wanted to get enough information to arrest him, so they'd have leverage to make Lund one of many of their cooperating witnesses.

"I'll do as much or as little as you need me to do," I said. "If you think it'll help for me to vouch for you with Jenae Malmo, I'd be happy to do it and then step aside." I felt a palpable sense of relief in the room. Who knew what horrible stories the Carrot had told about me, but I assumed the worst: unsafe, unstable, stubborn, unpredictable, lacks discipline. I'm sure they all feared how I'd react, whether refusing to cooperate or using the situation as leverage to get my job back. I did none of that. "How about I let you all have a private discussion about next steps? I can either go home and you can give me a call, or I can go and wait in the lobby. Like I just told you, I'm happy to help, but I'm also fine stepping aside."

"I don't think that's necessary, Agent Wirth." Douglas, once again, gave me a reassuring, gentle smile. It didn't matter that the Carrot was glaring at me. It was now obvious that Douglas was in charge of OTW, not the Carrot. It was his call to bring me back and he wanted me to be a part of the team. "Let's just take this one step at a time. The first step is for you to talk to Jenae and see where she's coming from. Since Matthews and Fischer weren't successful, I'd like you to go out with Agent Sloan."

The rationale behind Douglas's decision to send Sloan to chaperone me instead of Matthews or Fischer wasn't exactly subtle, although it had been left unsaid. Both of us were women. He had to have figured that if two guys in suits were unsuccessful, perhaps two women could get the job done. It was the same reason Matthews had asked me to talk to Christine Griggs, and not him.

Douglas was right.

During the drive from St. Louis to Troy, Sloan and I talked about our backgrounds, where we grew up, and what drew us to law enforcement. Sloan was an army brat, moving every two or three years as her father got transferred to different military bases all over the world. When I told her about growing up and living in the same house where my parents had brought me home from the hospital, Sloan couldn't imagine it.

"I'm jealous," she said, and I think she meant it.

At the Evolve Treatment Center, we went through the same procedures as I'd done before, and soon we were back up on the balcony overlooking the grounds.

"I wasn't expecting to see you so soon," Jenae said.

"That makes the two of us." I introduced Sloan. "This is Maddie from New Orleans. She's also with the bureau."

Jenae's greeting of Sloan was not as warm as the one given to me, but we were already doing better than Matthews and Fischer. They never made it past the guard station.

As Sloan and I had discussed, I took the lead in our conversation. "You probably know why all these people suddenly want to see you."

"Pretty much," Jenae said, "and I didn't mean to be rude to

those other guys or nothin', but, after you left, I began thinking about what comes next. I get discharged this week, and the treatment facility has me lined up with a sober house in Southern California. Can you believe that?"

Jenae looked off into the distance. "I'm thinking this could be a fresh start. I've never really been out of St. Louis, and I've got no reason to stay."

"They really need you," I said. "They need you to make a buy from Lund, maybe two."

Jenae shook her head. "People, places, and things. That's what they preach in here every day. When you're sober, you can't go back to the same people, go to the same places, and do the same things you did before. It's too tempting."

"But if you don't, he'll never be held accountable."

"I've been in the system since I was a teenager, Amy. They don't lock drug dealers up for life. It's a revolving door. Selling a little something to me, maybe thirty days in jail at most."

"But there's more going on here that we can't talk about," I said. "I promise you that he'll go away for a long time. He'll pay for what he did to Kasi, and to all the others, too."

Jenae began fidgeting with the cuff of her shirt sleeve, buttoning and unbuttoning it. "I'm scared, Amy. I'm really scared. Lund told us that if we ever crossed him, he'd kill us, and I don't doubt it. He's a cop. He can do whatever he wants."

"Sloan will keep you safe."

Her demeanor changed, as if she'd caught a sleight of hand. "What about you?"

"I...I can't be involved in this anymore. I'm too close. It's not appropriate, not when it's my sister."

Jenae's face hardened. "Well," she said, "if you aren't with me, then I won't do it. I'm going to California and getting out of this place." She looked at Sloan, then got up and left.

35

———

The debate happened behind closed doors with the Carrot, Douglas, Colton Steele, and another U.S. Attorney from Chicago. I was not invited to participate, and neither were the other agents. Frazier and Sloan went to get something to eat, while Matthews and I sat in what was our old office.

It could've been awkward, but it wasn't. I had accepted my fate. This decision wasn't in my control, and although I wanted to see it through for myself and my father. I also didn't want to jeopardize a multi-year, multi-jurisdictional investigation. This was much bigger than me or Kasi Barnes.

"I met with Bob Cook the other day after we met," I said. "He seems to be really enjoying retirement, says he wishes he'd done it sooner."

"I hear that a lot." Matthews tossed a rubber ball from hand to hand. "The bureau becomes your identity, and it's scary to imagine what happens when that identity is stripped away."

He tossed the ball over to me, and I caught it. "I think my dad was like that. He didn't want to let go, and even after he retired, he couldn't let it go." I threw the ball against the wall, then back over to Matthews, just like old times.

"That's not typical, though," Matthews said. "The vast majority are like Cook, confused as to why they didn't pull the pin sooner."

I thought about that as I caught the ball. It wasn't just the old-timers who hung on too long, maybe I fought too hard to stay when I should've realized that my services were neither wanted nor appreciated. My old priest used to talk about that. It was in one of the gospels, something like, "If anyone will not welcome you or listen to your words, shake the dust off your feet and leave."

I tossed the ball back to Matthews. "Bob Cook wanted me to warn you, warn everybody."

My toss was high and wide. Matthews had to stretch his arm out for a one-handed grab. He nearly fell out of his chair, but he got it and managed not to hurt himself in the process. "About Lund?"

I nodded. "Says that Lund appeared out of nowhere and touched him, paralyzed him. He thinks he's much more dangerous than we know. He thinks we're underestimating Lund and we're at risk."

"More...dangerous...than...we...know," Matthews stretched those words out quietly as he tossed the ball from one hand to the other. Then to me, "What do you think?"

It was time to be honest. "I think my dad thought that whoever killed Kasi Barnes was not just a drug dealer. He had all sorts of books on myths and legends, and by the way that Cook was talking, I think he came to the same conclusion."

Mathews stopped tossing the ball and put it on his desk. "Like a demon."

I shrugged. "I guess."

"Lund could've also had a stun gun," Matthews said. "He is

a cop, after all, and there's lots of stories about people having cardiac arrest after being shocked with a taser."

"That's the more likely scenario," I said.

"But it's not what you think."

There was a long silence as I thought about how to answer Matthew's question. I thought about Gray and what he'd do in this situation. We'd often discussed our belief in the wrinkles in reality, and how others perceived them and us.

I was not, however, going to lie to Matthews. I was committed to the truth. We may not be partners anymore, technically, but I owed him that. "There are some things that we can't explain or understand," I said. "Lund may be one of them, or he may just be a dirty cop. Either way, I think Bob Cook gave us some good advice. Lund is very smart, and if we're not careful, people are going to get hurt."

———

IT WAS JUST me and the Carrot in the room. The lack of any witnesses as to what was about to be said and done was not lost on me. I was on my own, and nobody would ever believe my word over hers.

"Sit." The Carrot pointed at the chair across from hers. "You have put the bureau in a very difficult position, Agent Wirth. And I will tell you that I disagree with the ultimate decision that has been made. I think you should've been fired immediately and not just suspended, but I was overruled. And now, I believe that you are a liability and should remain suspended until your review hearing next month, and then I will let you go."

"I understand," I said, "and I accept—"

The Carrot held out her hand to cut me off. The look in her eyes made it clear that this was not a two-way conversation. This meeting was going to be her talking, and her alone.

"Your job is to babysit Jenae Malmo. The bureau has access to a furnished condominium, and when she is discharged from her treatment facility, that is where she will go. The bureau will provide her with a daily stipend, and you are going to live in the condominium with her. Your job is to lower her stress and ensure that she can perform. That's it. You are not to act as an investigator or field agent." The Carrot paused, holding her gaze. "Am I making myself clear?"

I waited for the Carrot to nod, thus granting me permission to speak. "Yes," I said. "Perfectly clear."

"Good." The Carrot pursed her lips. Then, as if about to perform an odious task, her nostrils flared when she took a deep breath and held it as she opened her desk drawer and removed my gun and badge. She placed them in front of me. "You will need these," she said, "but just so you understand, nothing that I am doing here changes anything. My opinion of you remains the same, and I have been promised up and down the line that I get the final decision as to whether you stay or go." Then she leaned forward and whispered, "I guarantee you, Agent Wirth, that your time in the bureau is coming to an end."

———

THE FORCES MARSHALED against Lund were impressive. During my time at the FBI, I'd only worked cases with Matthews. Some of them were high-profile, but nothing like this. In addition to Matthews, Douglas, Fischer, and Sloan, there were dozens of others brought in to help. They were from bureaus all over the country. Whether they worked remotely or came to St. Louis, each agent was putting Lund under the microscope, examining every part of his life. The resources dedicated to OTW were unlike anything I'd ever seen.

The bureau threw a net over Lund, 24/7 surveillance. Warrants were quickly issued by judges friendly to law enforcement. Known phone numbers were tapped. Subpoenas were issued for Lund's bank account records, cell phone records, emails, and internet browsing history.

Each morning, agents reported new information and discussed patterns. Humans were creatures of habit, and Lund was no different. Soon, we knew the route he took to work, where he liked to eat, how often he went to the grocery store, his love life or lack thereof, and what time he typically went to bed.

As I listened silently in the corner of the conference room, day after day, I thought it was all good information. The bureau was working quickly, but not rushing. We were being careful, just as Bob Cook had told us to act. The problem was that none of what had been reported was incriminating in any way.

I pulled Matthews aside in the hallway as the meeting broke up. "Can we talk for a minute?"

"Of course," Matthews checked his watch, "I gotta be some place in fifteen, but I have a minute. What's up?"

"Where's the evidence?" I asked. "Doesn't that worry you? All we have is Jenae Malmo and some rumors. You'd think we'd see something suspicious with the surveillance or find something in all those records by now."

"I had the same thought," Matthews said, "but Douglas is convinced this is the guy. You have to remember that we're dealing with dirty cops. They know how investigations work. They've seen how people get caught, and Douglas says Lund is smart. He not only knows how to cover his tracks. He also knows how to create false trails and false alibis. Douglas says he even faked a body cam video."

This did not make me feel better. In fact, it made me feel worse, like Lund was playing us for fools, but what could I do? "Okay, I'd better go," I said. "Jenae is getting discharged, and I'm praying she gets in the car with me."

"She'll come." Matthews put his hand on my shoulder. "You've got this."

———

DOUGLAS MADE the decision to send only me to pick Jenae up from the treatment facility. He didn't want to scare her or give the impression that she was under arrest. They wanted Jenae relaxed and unaware of just how important she was to the entire operation.

The discharge was scheduled for 1:30 p.m. She'd told me that there was a final group meeting. This was when everybody was given an opportunity to say goodbye, and Jenae Malmo could talk to the newer members of the group about her journey.

I arrived early and waited in the front lobby. It shouldn't have been a big deal. If Jenae Malmo backed out, it didn't really impact me. The Carrot had made her intentions quite clear. She was going to terminate me, regardless of whether Nick Lund was arrested or not.

But it did matter to me. It mattered because I felt, for the first time, I was doing things the right way. I gave my opinions, but I was also willing to let them go. I trusted my colleagues. I followed directions, and I finally felt confident in myself and who I'd become for the first time in my life.

I wasn't trying to prove something to my dad or be a miniature version of him. I wasn't sneaking around or keeping secrets, and when the Carrot terminated me from the bureau, she could take my badge, but she wouldn't be able to take my new confidence away. I just needed to see this through, I thought, and deliver Jenae Malmo to the condo without incident. So, I waited.

At 2:00 p.m., my phone rang. It was Douglas. He wanted an update, and I told him I was still waiting for her. He asked me to check the front desk. He wanted me to confirm that she hadn't left the facility.

I did as instructed, and the lady at the front desk informed me, "For privacy reasons, we cannot disclose that information."

It was relayed back to Douglas, and I went back to my seat, because that was all that I could do. A half-hour later, Douglas called again, and I still had nothing to report. He didn't yell or scream, but I could hear the concern in the sound of his voice.

If it had been the Carrot, this would be the moment that she lay all blame at my feet. "I knew you couldn't do it," she'd say. "All you needed to do was be a taxi, and you couldn't even do that."

Douglas was different. He was the captain of this ship, and he carried it on his shoulders. "Agent Wirth," he said. "You know this girl better than any of us. I know you can think of something, and if you need some help, give me a call. You've got my number."

I hung up the phone and walked outside for some fresh air. Douglas told me to think of something, and he was right. I couldn't just sit on the couch waiting.

———

THE LADY at the front desk was a little more annoyed to see me the second time, but I had decided to take a different approach. "I know, for privacy reasons, you cannot confirm whether Jenae Malmo is still here or not. That's not my question. What time does the group meeting end?"

"We have a lot of meetings here," she said. "I'm not trying to be difficult, Agent Wirth, but there are." She reached into a drawer and removed a piece of paper and slid it across the desk. "I'm not sure if that is one hundred percent current, but it's pretty close. You can see that there are about five cohorts. It's staggered so that everybody isn't trying to use the pool or other facilities at the same time."

I looked at the sheet of paper, and she was right. The cohorts were staggered, but my stomach dropped when I saw that none of the five groups had a meeting that ended at 1:30 p.m. "Okay," I said, knowing it was time to be creative. "Tell me this," I said, "where's the closest dive bar?"

The edge of her lips curled into a knowing and wicked smile. "Now you're talking, sweetheart."

———

I REALIZED that if Jenae Malmo had decided to go to a sober house in California, then she would've just told me that. She knew that the FBI couldn't force her to do anything. Jenae also knew that she could've just left. Douglas had told me that I knew Jenae better than anybody else, and he was right. When she asked me to come to Evolve Treatment to pick her up, she had her own plan. It took me awhile to figure it out, but I understood what Jenae really wanted. She wanted me to save her from herself.

Skinner's Road House was about three miles down the highway. It was a long, squat building with a gravel parking lot. In front, there were two pick-up trucks and five motorcycles. If somebody wanted to get drunk or score some dope, this would be the place.

I walked through the door, and it took a second for my eyes to adjust. It was dark and mostly empty, which wasn't surprising for the middle of the afternoon.

Although the music had not come to a screeching halt, the talk in the bar had gone silent. All eyes were on me. They may not have fingered me as a cop, but I certainly didn't fit in. I half-expected the bartender to direct me to the nearest Starbucks.

I thought the bartender might say something like, "No oat milk lattes here, ma'am. You best be moving along."

I circled the room, looking for Jenae and hoping that I wasn't too late. I was convinced I was in the right place, but I didn't see her. On my second pass around the room, the bartender finally asked, "Can I get you something to drink?"

I hesitated, considering whether or not I should show him the photo of Jenae Malmo that I had on my phone. I walked toward the bar, trying to convey a sense of purpose and authority. I took the phone out of my pocket, and I was about to begin searching for the photograph, when I saw a pint of beer half-full on the bar. Next to it was a plate with what remained of a cheeseburger and onion rings. A jacket lay on a stool.

Then I turned, and saw Jenae Malmo coming out of the bathroom.

36

The bureau's condo was nice. It was a two-bedroom unit on the seventeenth floor of a downtown building. Originally it was the headquarters of a life insurance company, but the historic building was converted into residential lofts in 2002.

From the balcony was a partial view of the Arch. The distance from the street softened the noise, and its height made me feel safe and hidden, as if I were a kid up in a treehouse. I hoped that Jenae Malmo felt the same.

Her brief disappearance had spooked Agent Douglas, and he didn't want to wait. He couldn't give Jenae another opportunity to back out. The buy was scheduled for the next morning. My job was to make sure that she stayed in the condo, and then get her to the bureau on time.

As I slid the glass door closed, I sat down on the couch next to Jenae. "Are you doing okay?"

"Not really." She looked around. "I can't believe I'm back here, back in the city."

"Not for long," I said. "The guy who's running this operation, Douglas, he's really smart. He knows what he's doing. He's not going to take any risks, and it'll be quick. You'll be fine."

"I should be in California."

"You will be," I said, "but you didn't run to California. You ran to a bar just up the road from the treatment facility. There are going to be lots of bars in California, too. It doesn't matter where you are, Jenae, you're still going to be you. And staying sober is going to be hard, wherever you're living."

"I know I'm an addict."

"True, but the good news is that you didn't completely relapse. You had a beer. You didn't shoot heroin."

"But I would have."

"But you didn't." I picked up the remote and turned on the television. "That's a victory, Jenae, just take it one day at a time, okay?"

She nodded. "One day at a time."

———

IN THE MORNING, we ate some cereal, showered, got dressed, and then were transported to the bureau's headquarters in a large black SUV. Douglas met us in a conference room. On the table, there were doughnuts, coffee, water, and a bowl of fruit.

The absence of other agents was part of the plan. Douglas still didn't want to scare Jenae or increase the pressure that she may be feeling, so other than me, he was the only other person interacting with her for now. I knew, however, that we weren't really alone and nothing said was truly private. A camera recorded everything, and there were at least five agents watching us from the other side of a mirrored panel of glass.

"I can't thank you enough for doing this, Ms. Malmo," Douglas said. "I hope the accommodations were comfortable last night."

Jenae nodded. Her arms crossed tightly over her chest, as if she were physically preventing herself from falling apart. She managed to utter, "It was nice."

"Good." Douglas looked at a clock. It was ten minutes to nine. "Here's what's going to happen. I'm going to tell you when to initiate the phone call. Lund is being followed, and we want you to call just as he arrives at his neighborhood coffee shop. When he steps out of his car, I'll be notified, and then I will tell you to place the call."

"Why can't I just call right now and get this over with?"

"Because he uses burner phones, so they're hard to trace and hard to tap. We have agents in place with an LDL, which stands for Long Distance Listening device. Essentially, it can capture conversations up to three hundred feet away, but it's not quite as effective going through glass or through a car. We want him outside when you call."

Jenae looked at me for assurance, and I nodded my head. Then she looked at Douglas, "Okay, fine. Let's do it."

"Excellent." Douglas poured himself a cup of coffee, and he got the go-ahead a few minutes later. To Jenae, he said, "We're ready."

With that, Jenae took out her phone and called a number. As expected, it rang three times and went to voicemail. Then she left a message, "Hey, this is Jenae. Just got out of sobertown, and I'm ready to party. Give me a call."

That was just step one, now we had to wait for Lund to call her back. It was all an elaborate system created by Lund to hide identities and avoid wire taps.

The phone number that Jenae had called was connected to a burner phone that was purchased with a stolen credit card. Nobody knew where the phone was located. It was simply a conduit, notifying Lund that there was a voicemail message, which he would access with another burner phone. If he recognized the name or number, he'd return the call. If not, there were more hurdles the potential customer would need to overcome.

Luckily, Jenae was well-known to Lund, and her phone rang a few minutes later. Agent Douglas nodded, and Jenae answered.

The conversation was short and to the point. "Where can we meet?" A pause, then, "Good."

When she hung up the phone, Douglas pumped his fist, as if he just hit a home run. "Nice work," he said, "very nice work."

"What's next?" Jenae asked.

"You tell me," Douglas said. "When and where are you meeting?"

"There's a park behind the Central Library, downtown."

"Lucas Park?" I asked.

"That's it," she said. "That's where we're going to meet."

"Have you and Lund ever met there before?" Douglas asked.

"Plenty of times. We meet on a park bench near the playground equipment. I give him the money, and then he tells me where he stashed the drugs. That part is a little different every time. Sometimes it's in a McDonalds bag, looking like garbage. Sometimes it's taped under a mailbox, could be anything or anywhere."

"Okay," Agent Douglas said. "That means we need to get video surveillance on that park right now. I want pictures of this guy hiding those drugs."

That's what Douglas wanted. That's what everybody wanted, but that wasn't what we got.

FORTY-FIVE MINUTES BEFORE THE MEETING, a kid who was not much older than twelve arrived at the park with his mother and a baby in a stroller. The kid did what kids do at a park. He swung on the swings and slid down the slide.

When he was done, the kid talked briefly with his mom. Then he took a gigantic, reusable plastic cup—like the ones that truckers buy at a gas station for discounted soda—and removed it from the stroller's bottom basket. Then he put it next to a boulevard tree, and the family walked away.

I was sitting next to Douglas in a van parked down the block. He looked at the screen with a combination of disgust and disappointment, then relayed an update to the team over the radio. "Looks like we got no video of Lund with the drugs. Somebody pick that family up and get a statement from them." Then to me, Douglas said, "Nothing ever goes perfect. Now, let's just hope he shows."

As if on cue, Lund arrived. The video was in high definition, perfect. He was dressed in his blue uniform. His badge sparkled. In his hand, Lund carried a paper bag from a local sub shop.

"The drugs might be in that bag," I said. "Jenae told us he used stuff that looked like trash. We might be wrong about the kid."

"Maybe." Douglas kept his focus on the screen. "I hope."

Lund sat down and removed a sandwich from the bag and began to eat it. Agent Douglas, over the radio, set the car in motion. "Deliver to target," he said.

A response crackled back, "Delivering to target." I recognized the voice. It was Matthews. I thought of Bob Cook's warning and felt uneasy.

Why did it have to be Matthews?

I wanted him safe, far away from Lund.

On the monitor, I saw a white Toyota SUV arrive at the park, stopping on St. Charles Street. It had a pink furry mustache on the front, and the logo of an app-based rideshare company. Matthews was driving.

The door opened. Jenae got out, took a few steps, and

stopped. She watched Matthews pull away, and her body appeared to tense when she was alone.

The radio crackled again with the sound of Matthews's voice. "Package delivered." I was relieved that Matthews was no longer in danger, but now my concern grew for Jenae.

Douglas had said this was a large criminal enterprise. I'd always assumed that Lund was the person who took the shot at me and killed the woman at the North Pond, but that was just an assumption. It could've been somebody else. There were lots of tall buildings around the park, plenty of places for a sniper to lay in wait.

Jenae walked over to the bench. Douglas sent a message to Team 2. "Check audio."

The speaker crackled in response. "Team Two, audio good, recording." A decision was made for Jenae not to wear a wire. Instead, agents set a recording device underneath the bench and were also recording from distance with the LDL.

When Jenae sat down next to Lund and began talking, their voices came through the van's speakers. Unlike the radio transmissions between the agents, this audio was clear, free of static.

Lund said, "For whatever reason, I didn't expect to see you again." He wasn't looking at Jenae as he spoke. "Thought that fancy place they sent you would be different, fix you up, but I guess not."

Jenae rolled her eyes. "My lawyer told me I could get a better deal if I went, so I did the dog and pony show for thirty days, and now I'm here."

"That's sad. All that taxpayer money flushed down the toilet." Lund packed up the remainder of his sandwich. "Well, good luck, Jenae." He stood and began to walk away.

"Wait." Jenae quickly took the money out of her pocket and held it out to him.

Lund raised his hands in the air, acting confused. "What are you doing?" He shook his head. "I don't want that." He lowered his hands, then came to her. He touched her cheek. "I care about you, Jenae." Lund's head moved, slightly to the side. "Call me if you need any help." Then his hand moved from her cheek, to her neck, and then down Jenae's back.

"I'll always be there to help you." Lund then walked away in the same direction from which he came.

Douglas looked at me. "What just happened?"

"I don't know," I said. "His head...at the end of their conversation, did you see that? It looked like he directed Jenae to the cup by the tree. Right?"

"I don't know." Douglas ran his hand through his hair, concerned. We both watched as Jenae went to the tree. She picked up the plastic cup, removed the lid, and retrieved a plastic bag from inside.

"Looks like a little baggie of heroin," I said.

"Looks like it," Douglas said, "I'm just not sure if this is good enough. It's not clean. He didn't sell it, so there's no sale."

"Maybe possession?"

"When did he possess it?" Douglas's frustration was turning into anger. "We'll have to bring in the lawyers." He got back on the radio and instructed the teams to pack up and meet back at the bureau to debrief. "Nobody enters the park until Jenae Malmo is out. I want whatever is in that bag tested immediately, and I want her taken directly back to the condo."

Douglas then turned to me. "We're probably going to have to do this again. You need to prepare her for that."

"She wants to go to California."

Douglas laughed. "So do I."

37

Jenae was not happy. She'd been promised that after making the buy, the bureau would put her on the first flight to California. That was the deal. Yet she remained.

"When are we going to know?"

"We just have to wait." I walked from the living room into the kitchen and began to heat water on the stove for tea. "Douglas needs to review all the recordings with the lawyers, and then there will be a meeting to decide what to do next."

"They're going to ask me to do it again, aren't they?"

"I don't know, but probably. Has that ever happened before? Just giving you the stuff like that?"

"No, it was all weird," she said. "He's always given me bad vibes, but this was different."

"Do you think he's suspicious?"

"Lund is always suspicious," then added, "so probably."

"How about when he touched you, ran his hand down your back. Has that ever happened before?"

"Not really." Jenae turned away from me, now a little ashamed. "I mean, sometimes when I was low on cash, we'd... barter, if you know what I mean."

"Maybe that's what he was after." I thought about Lund's hand moving, touching her cheek, then her neck. I opened a cabinet and removed the chamomile tea. "You want some of this?" I showed Jenae the box.

She nodded. "That's supposed to relax you, right?"

"That's what they claim," I said, waiting for the pressure to build and the teapot to whistle.

———

THAT NIGHT, I had difficulty falling asleep. Agent Douglas had decided to do a second buy with Jenae, as expected. I called my mother. Even though it was late, she answered on the second ring. We did the dance. Each assuring the other that we were just fine, when we both knew that we were absolutely not fine.

The nights were the hardest. The absence of anyone else to hold. The empty space on the other side of the bed, a confirmation that you were very much alone.

"When will you be coming back?" she asked. "I miss our walks."

"I miss our walks, too," I said. "We're wrapping up here. I think we got him, the guy Dad was looking for. I think we got the dealer, and this will be done." As soon as I uttered those words—*this will be done*—I regretted it, like it was a jinx.

"Your dad would be proud of you."

"I know, but it's still a little early to do a victory lap."

"Amy," she said, "I was a cop's wife for forty years, and I know that it's never really done. There's always going to be another bad guy to catch. That's not the point. Your dad would be proud of you for how you've handled yourself. It doesn't matter whether this man goes to prison or gets away. It's how you've grown."

"I'm scared, mom," I said. "Everybody's so confident, but I

know who this man really is and what he's done, and it doesn't feel right. Somebody's going to get hurt."

There was a long silence, and I heard Mister Bones begin to purr on the other end of the line. I pictured the cat on my mother's lap, snuggling with her. Then my mother said, "I think that's a good thing, Amy. It means that you are alert, and you're always much safer when you're alert."

"I don't feel safer."

"I know," she said, "but pretty soon you'll be back here with me and Mister Bones." A jingle of his collar could be heard, as well as another purr.

"He's getting fat, isn't he? You're spoiling him."

My mom laughed. "Very much so."

I wished her goodnight, hung up the phone, and turned my light off. Maybe it was the conversation, or maybe it was that my nighttime drugs had finally hit my brain, but I now fell asleep quickly and hard.

This dream was different. I was not at Merchants Bridge. There were no flames or men touching me. I was just running. It was dark. I ran down one hallway, then another. I ran down the stairs and then up the stairs. I tried every door, and they were always locked.

This continued on a loop, until I finally made it to the bottom of the stairwell. That's when I stopped. There, I saw her on the ground. It was the old woman with dreadlocks. Her skin was pale white. Her lips were blue. Her stomach moved barely, not really breathing. It twitched.

Around her were dozens of birds. All of them were dead. Each with their necks broken, bent unnaturally to the side. I stepped closer, paused, then stepped closer.

I wanted her to be alive. I wanted to save her. The twitching beneath her cotton dress grew more active. It was a sign of life. It should have made me happy, but it didn't, because it wasn't a sign of *her* life, but something else entirely.

I took one more step, then knelt down close to her. I reached out to touch her, but before my hand made it all the way, the fabric of her dress tore. Her body exploded in front of me. Thousands of insects swarmed into the air, just as thousands of insects swarmed out of the body of Hermes as told in one of my father's books. They pelted my face like buckshot. I couldn't close my mouth fast enough. I gagged as some continued down my throat as others began to sting.

I rolled over as my tongue swelled. I gagged. I could not breathe. I tried to spit the bugs out but couldn't get them clear. Some were trapped. I could feel their tiny legs pricking me from within. I was choking, struggling for air.

That's when I woke. There was a loud argument in the hallway outside the condo, and then it got even louder as it came back into the apartment. I must've looked crazed, because Jenae stopped yelling at Sloan and Matthews the moment I came out of the bedroom.

"What is going on?"

Jenae pointed. "They're holding me hostage. That's what's going on."

I rubbed my eyes and tried to orient myself. I looked at the window, and it was still dark outside. The clock on the wall indicated it was just past 4:30 in the morning. Then I looked at the suitcase next to Jenae.

"You're leaving?"

"Trying to."

"You weren't going to say goodbye or anything?"

Jenae's face looked at me with disgust. "You're not my friend." She looked at Sloan and Mathews. "None of you are my friends." Then back at me. "You're just like them, keeping secrets, or am I just supposed to believe that you failed to mention to me that there were guards posted outside our door at night?"

"I didn't know about that." This was true, but Jenae rolled

her eyes as if I'd taken her for a fool. Then I asked Sloan and Matthews to leave. "Give us a minute."

Neither of them moved.

"Seriously," I said, "I want to talk with Jenae alone."

This time Matthews nodded, and then the two left. I pointed toward the living room. "Can we sit down? You all woke me up from a wicked dream."

Jenae Malmo now examined me. Before, it was just surprise at my appearance, but this was more. It was like she put everything together. It wasn't just that my hair was stuck out in a hundred directions, dark circles under my eyes.

"Damn, girl, what's wrong with you?"

"A lot," I said as I sat down on the couch. "So don't try and give me a hug. I'm sweaty, and I stink."

"No chance of that." Jenae's demeanor appeared to soften, and she walked over to an easy chair and sat down. Then she settled, and I began.

"Can I ask you a question?"

"I guess," Jenae said.

"Were you leaving to go to California, or were you leaving to go get high?"

"Why does it matter?"

"Technically, it doesn't," I said. "You're right. You're not under arrest. You can walk out the door. We can't stop you."

"Sure seems like you can," Jenae said. "Your boyfriend pulled a gun on me."

"Matthews is...or was my partner, but never my boyfriend."

"Whatever," Jenae said, "he did what he did."

"I get that, but you've got to understand. This isn't just about Lund and Kasi. For me it is, but for them it's not. There are lots of dirty cops and lots of people who've died...and we're close. Agent Douglas thinks Lund is the final piece, and then they can bring down the whole network across the country. That's why I asked about why you're leaving, because if you're leaving to go to California, I get it. You're moving on with your life, and you should go. But if you're leaving just to get high, you should stay, because that means that you're not moving on with your life at all. You're just going back to the familiar."

She said nothing, but I knew I'd gotten to her. I think the technical term was that I had a "successful intervention," but that sounds too manipulative. I really meant what I said. If she wanted to move on, then who were we to stop her? I just didn't want her to go back to what she was.

We talked for about an hour. I told her about some of my struggles, and she told me more about hers. After our conversation, Jenae Malmo decided to stay. Although I still stunk, we hugged one another and went back to our rooms and fell asleep. In a few days, we'd try and bring Lund down. I say "we," but really it was only Jenae. It all depended on her, and in hindsight, I wish she would have left that night, even if it was to get high. She would've been better off.

38

The second buy was attempted two days after the first. A few minutes after Jenae left her voicemail, Lund called back. Much to everyone's surprise, he hadn't switched burner phones yet. So, the bureau was able to get a recording of Lund's conversation with Jenae, as well as recordings of him setting up multiple other deals throughout the day.

Douglas was ecstatic, but this streak of luck only increased my concern. I was a gambler, and I knew that every streak came to an end at some point. The house always won.

Lund arranged to meet with Jenae on the eastern edge of the St. Louis University campus. There was some greenspace wedged between a parking garage, an arena, and a baseball field. As Agent Douglas and I watched the video feed in the communications truck, I said, "I don't think he's going to show."

But I was wrong.

Lund appeared right on schedule, and unlike the first deal, he hid the drugs himself. The video was perfection. The camera that the bureau set up on the top of the parking garage zoomed in close and captured Lund removing a small plastic bag from his pocket and putting it into an empty potato chip bag. He took the bag over to a garbage can and set it on the ground. Passersby would have no idea. It was just a wrapper that just didn't quite make it to where it should've gone.

Lund then sat on a park bench about a hundred yards away and waited. Agent Douglas used the radio, directing Agent Sloan to deliver Jenae to the site. A few minutes later, Jenae was dropped off in a black Prius. This one had a sticker of a different rideshare company on the door.

I was surprised as I listened to their conversation. There was nothing coy about what was said between Lund and Jenae. "Back for more?" Lund said. "Must've been good."

"Always," Jenae said.

"But this one isn't going to be free."

"I figured that." Jenae took $40 cash out of her purse and handed it to Lund. Each of the twenty-dollar bills had been previously photographed by Agent Matthews and the serial numbers recorded. Lund put them in his front pocket without looking and pointed at the garbage can.

"It's in the potato chip bag," he said. Then Lund got up from the park bench and began to walk away. "Until next time, Ms. Malmo, always a pleasure. You know how to reach me."

Agent Douglas commanded everyone to hold their positions, and then he looked at me with a huge smile. "That was beautiful."

And it *was* beautiful. The knot that had been in my stomach began to loosen, and I felt the muscles in my back and neck unwind.

Maybe I was wrong, I thought, *maybe Lund isn't special. He's not a monster. He's nothing more than a stupid, dirty cop.*

We all headed back to the bureau's headquarters. By the time we arrived, a technician had confirmed that the substances that Lund put in the potato chip bag had tested positive for heroin, but that was just the rapid test. The technician had sent them on for a more thorough examination of its weight and purity.

Jenae went with Agent Sloan to make a sworn statement about what had just occurred, as well as her history and knowledge of Nick Lund. Matthews and I went into the large conference room with the others. The mood was upbeat, with lots of small talk and laughter.

Agent Douglas and the Carrot sat together at the head of the table, and Douglas called the meeting to order. "Okay, folks, let's settle down," he said. "The U.S. Attorney is drafting a warrant for Lund's arrest as we speak. We're hoping to get it approved, internally, and signed by a judge by close of business today."

There were smiles and nods from around the table. "Agent Matthews, I want you to pull a group together to brainstorm the best way to initiate Lund's arrest. We know he's got firearms, and we have to assume he won't come voluntarily. I've already notified our SWAT team."

"And where is he now?" Matthews asked.

"On patrol," Douglas said. "We have eight agents working out of six different vehicles tracking him. We've also tapped into the police department's GPS, so we know where his squad is located at all times, along with the closed-circuit traffic cameras. It's a tight net."

"Agent Wirth, I need you to take Jenae Malmo back to the condo. She needs to be packed up, and we'll make arrangements to get her to California. An agent will be meeting her at the airport when she arrives, then transport her to the sober house so that she may continue her step-down program."

Douglas looked around the table. "Any questions?" When there were none, we were dismissed.

We all began to gather our things and head to the door, except the Carrot called me back. "Agent Wirth, I'd like a moment, if you don't mind."

I looked at Douglas, and he gave the Carrot a quizzical look. "Mind if I stay for this? I wouldn't mind debriefing a little with Agent Wirth. We have worked closely together over this past week or so."

"I do, in fact, mind," the Carrot said. "Now that Agent Wirth is done with OTW, I believe she is once again reporting directly to me."

"But she's not exactly done," Douglas said. "She's in charge of Jenae Malmo, and Ms. Malmo is still here."

"True, and you can certainly debrief with her all you want at some other time, but right now we need to speak privately."

"Fine," Douglas said, then to me, "Call when you have a moment, Agent Wirth. Good job today." Then he left the large conference room, and I was alone with the Carrot.

She pressed her fingers together, index to index and so on, like she was a cartoon villain hatching a plot to ignite the atmosphere. "Having fun?"

"Fun?" I shook my head. "No, ma'am."

"Ma'am." Her brows arched. "Such formality all of a sudden. Why not just call me the Carrot? That's my nickname, right? That's what you all call me?"

I said nothing.

"I want you to know that I appreciate what you've done to assist in the investigation of Officer Lund. I'm serious about that, but it doesn't undo everything else. I believe you remain a risk to the safety of yourself and others in the bureau, and now that this phase of OTW has wrapped up, I've scheduled your probationary review hearing for next week."

"And you're going to terminate me?"

"Yes, that's still my intention," the Carrot said. "I also don't want you at Lund's arrest tonight or at any further meetings related to OTW. You were activated for a limited scope of duty. That is what I agreed to with Agent Douglas, and now I'm putting you back on suspension with pay until next week's review."

"And there's nothing I can do?"

"No."

"Okay," I bowed my head slightly. "I disagree with the decision, obviously, but it's your decision, and I accept it."

39

———

Back at the condo, both Jenae Malmo and I packed up our things. The bureau had bought Jenae an economy-class ticket to San Diego, but Agent Douglas personally upgraded her to First Class with his own money.

"Don't tell her," he texted me. "I want it to be a surprise."

"I won't," I said. "And we're leaving now." I hung up on Douglas and called back toward Jenae's room. "Ready?" I was standing at the door with my hand on the light switch.

Jenae emerged from the room with her suitcase. "Ready as I'll ever be," she said.

Then I turned off the lights, and we took the elevator down to my car. "One of our agents will be meeting you at the airport after you land in California," I said. "I'm sure Agent Douglas will provide you with updates, but if you don't hear anything, I wrote his cell phone number on a sticky-note. It's in the envelope with your boarding pass. He told me that you can call whenever you want."

Jenae thanked me as the elevator door slid open. We stepped inside, and the elevator began to descend. "Do you think I'm going to have to testify?"

"Most people don't think so," I said. "They assume Lund is going to take a plea deal and cooperate with the investigation."

Jenae sensed my apprehension. "Most people, but not you?"

It wasn't the time or place to talk about my father, my dreams, or my gut feelings. Rather, I said, "It's just better not to make assumptions."

"Well, I don't ever want to come back here."

"I understand, and I hope you never have to." The elevator doors opened with the sound of an electronic bell, and we stepped out. We loaded our stuff into the trunk of my car, and I drove Jenae Malmo to the airport. It was a quiet ride, neither one of us talked much. I remember that, how incredibly quiet we were.

As I exited I-70, she said, "You can just drop me off."

"Not going to happen." I turned into the parking garage. "This is door-to-door service, Ms. Malmo."

I found an open space and parked the car, and then we walked together into the airport. At the security gate, Jenae gave me a hug. "Thank you again." She started to cry. "Thank you for everything. Sometimes I don't think I deserve this, but it's really happening, isn't it? I'm getting out. I'm getting out of this place, and to think that I almost screwed it up." She shook her head. "Multiple times."

"But you didn't," I said as Jenae hugged me again. "You better go. You don't want to miss your plane."

"I won't," she said, and I believed her.

I watched her walk to the back of a line of people that snaked toward a series of metal detectors and X-ray machines. I could've left, but I didn't. I stayed. I watched her progress as she shuffled forward, a few steps at a time. Eventually, she made it to the front. Jenae showed her boarding pass to the agent, and I continued watching her until she disappeared down the terminal.

I left the airport feeling good. I reported to Agent Douglas, and that made me feel even better. He was upbeat, and the successful delivery of Jenae Malmo to the airport seemed to lift his spirits even higher. The FBI had established a tight net of surveillance around Lund, and our star witness was off to California. She was safe. We succeeded, or at least we thought we had succeeded.

———

No longer living in luxury at a fancy downtown condo, I returned to my little apartment on Cherokee Street. With Mister Bones in Florida and all of my plants brown and wilted, there wasn't much life in the place. I set down my bags and immediately began opening windows, trying to circulate the stale air. It helped, but not much.

I poured myself a glass of ice water, then sat down on my little balcony, overlooking the courtyard below. The shack was dark, and I wondered if the old woman had moved while I was away. It wouldn't have surprised me if she had.

I pulled out my phone and called Matthews, giving him an update about Jenae and squeezing him for information about Lund. He told me the warrant was signed less than ten minutes ago. He and Fischer wanted to immediately arrest Lund, but Douglas was more cautious.

Although the arrest was unlikely to result in a hostage situation, Douglas decided to put a negotiator on standby. He also decided that the arrest would be made by the SWAT team, believing that overwhelming force would ensure success and impress upon Lund that he was in serious trouble.

"So what time is this happening?"

"Douglas will brief the team in about an hour," Matthews said. "So, I figure it'll go down about nine or ten."

"I wish I could be there," I said, and that was the truth.

"You *should* be here. Everybody wants you here, including Douglas, but the Carrot made the call."

"Yes, she most certainly did," I said. "She made her thoughts about me very clear, and I am suspended once again. She scheduled my probation review hearing for next week." I felt a little ball form in my throat, and I cleared it with a cough, trying my best to sound cheerful. "Wish everybody good luck from me, okay?"

"I will do that," Matthews said, "And what are you gonna do?"

"Celebrate," I said. "I'm going to call some friends and hang out at a new bar that just opened downtown about a block off Washington. They've got a great patio, of course, bocce, and free popcorn. You know I'm a sucker for a bar with free popcorn."

"Sounds good," Matthews said, "Depending on how late this goes, I might join you."

"Excellent. The more, the merrier."

———

AND A MERRY BAND of misfits we were indeed. A table near a large, free-standing, stone fireplace was where we gathered. The small white lights that were strung above our heads twinkled in the cool night as classic songs from the 1970s kept the mood lively and fun. It was one hit after another from bands like the Eagles, Fleetwood Mac, Deep Purple, Steve Miller, Queen, and the Rolling Stones.

As the old-timers, Perelli and Bob Cook got along great, sharing war stories and complaints about arrogant defense lawyers and incompetent prosecutors, but that was just the beginning. They must've talked for an hour about the growing number of highly paid middle managers in law enforcement. At one point Cook, slammed his hand down on the table and declared, "There's always more money for a paper pusher, but no money for people doing the actual work." He then stood and raised his pint of beer. "Long live the beat cop."

"To the beat cop," we called back.

Crash and Gray delved deeply into the craft of fermentation in all its forms. Both had begun dabbling in making their own cheese. Crash compared it to his early attempts in brewing kombucha, and Gray talked about his sourdough.

I ate basket after basket of free popcorn. Occasionally I chimed in, whenever I felt like I had something to contribute, but mostly I listened and enjoyed the company. I couldn't remember the last time I'd gone out like this with friends.

It was fun. I laughed so hard, I cried at times. Being around a group of people who also had a hard time fitting into the roles they were expected to play allowed me to feel lighter and less alone. The only piece missing was Matthews. I wanted him to come and laugh with us.

I had expected an update, and as the evening progressed, I found myself watching the door that led from the bar to the outdoor patio. I thought that maybe he'd just show up rather than call. Every time it creaked, I hoped that he'd be among the new arrivals, but he never was.

I also kept checking my phone. Even though it never rang or vibrated, I still thought there might be a good chance that I'd missed a text or phone call, but I hadn't. The only notification that I got was that my battery was running low.

Gray was the first to notice my distraction. "What are you doing there, Amy? Expecting your lover boy to come and give you a ride home?"

Crash laughed hysterically. It wasn't that funny, but he was on his fifth pint. "Johnny and Amy sitting in a tree, K-I-S-S-I-N-G." The song got the other's attention.

Perelli's eyes sparkled. "Little Miss Amy has a boyfriend? Tell us more."

I shook my head, I didn't want to tell them all that I hadn't seen or heard from John in quite some time, but my reluctance only seemed to fuel Crash's desire to create more of a show. "Booty call," he said. "She's trying to make a drunken booty call, and I think that's an excellent decision, which we should all encourage her to do." He began a quiet chant of "booty call" while clapping his hands, which caused the tables around us to also start chanting.

"Stop." I raised my voice, and everybody quieted down. "First, I am checking for a message from Matthews. I just want an update. That's it. That's all I'm doing."

Gray tilted his head to the side. "But what about John? Are you back together? You should've invited him so we could decide whether or not we approve. Please tell me that you are not ashamed of us?"

"No, I am not ashamed of you, and I've left a couple messages for him, but we haven't connected."

"All the more reason for you to make that booty call right now," Crash said. "Seriously, I've had many a dead relationship revived after a late night call like that, and I highly recommend it."

"No, thank you," I said, "but I do appreciate all of the unsolicited advice." I got the server's attention. "Another round for my friends, please, but only if they shut up."

"You got it," she said, and that seemed to calm the mob.

"Please continue your merriment," I said. "But in exchange for the alcohol, I hereby declare any discussion of my personal life to be off-limits."

Crash and Perelli booed the decision, but everybody complied and settled back down. I checked my phone again. There were still no calls or messages. So, I decided to send Matthews a text, and the evening continued.

Bob Cook was the first to fade. He'd lasted longer than I had expected. When Cook decided to leave, Gray left with him. "It's going to be a little rough in the bakery tomorrow morning," he said, "but it was worth it." He gave me a hug and pecked my cheek.

That left Perelli, Crash, and me. We talked for another hour. Perelli complained about the constant auditing of the evidence warehouse, and Crash talked about his new job at a private cyber-security firm. "It pays double with stock options," he said, "and they absolutely love the fact that I got kicked out of the FBI. I thought it'd kill my application, but it's like some weird selling point to potential clients, as if I'm a bad-boy hacker turned good." Crash shrugged. "But I can't complain about the money."

We settled the bill, then Perelli and I waited until Crash's ride arrived. We said goodnight to him, and off he went.

"How about you?" Perelli asked. "Need a ride home?"

"No," I said, "I nursed a couple beers and then switched to club soda quite a while ago."

Perelli looked around the way cops always do, scanning the street for trouble. "Where you parked?"

"Down there." I nodded toward a parking garage. It was a block north, next to the convention center. A large sign was brightly lit with an arrow pointing at the entrance.

"Me, too," Perelli said, and we walked together. I didn't mind the company at all. The entire downtown area was in a weird place. Unless there was a game, the streets were often vacant and abandoned, then suddenly they'd explode in activity. Sometimes it would be good, just a group of friends leaving a bar. Sometimes it would be tragic. The randomness of it all was what created fear.

We rode the elevator up together. I got off on the third floor, and Perelli was parked one above me. "You okay?" he asked.

"I'll be fine, thanks." I stepped out of the elevator. "I'll talk to you soon."

"Good," Perelli said. "And I still want to know what's going on with this guy, Lund. Keep me in the loop."

"I will." The doors closed. Perelli disappeared, and I walked to my car. It was one of only six on the otherwise empty level. I got out my keys, unlocked the door, and got inside.

As I was about to start the engine, my cell phone rang. I looked at the screen, and it was Matthews. "Finally," I said to myself as I accepted the call.

Matthews skipped the pleasantries. "Where are you?" There was a bit of panic in his voice, which was unusual.

"I'm about to go home. What's going on?"

"So, you're still at the bar? That's good. Stay there until I can come pick you up."

"I'm not at the bar. I'm in my car, about to leave the parking garage." I looked around. The garage suddenly felt darker and more empty than it had moments before, a trick of the mind. "Tell me what's going on."

"Lund wasn't at home," Matthews said. "We raided it, but he wasn't there."

"But he was under—"

"There was a tunnel," Matthews said. "When it was built a hundred years ago, the owner built a tunnel to a detached garage. He was a mechanic or something, and he worked out there. It was his shop, and nobody knew about it."

"But how'd he slip past?"

"I don't know, but you need to get out of there and some-place safe, someplace with lots of people."

"Okay, I will."

"He might be coming for you, Amy. I'm almost sure of it."

"That's crazy," I said. "I'm the least of his problems. What would that accomplish?"

"I don't know," Matthews said, "but Jenae never arrived in California. The agent waited over an hour. We checked with the airline, and she never boarded that plane."

"I stayed and watched her go through security," I said. "She was happy to leave. She never wanted to come back."

"We're working on it," Matthews said, "just come to the—" He cut out.

"Matthews. Are you there? Are you still there?" I took the phone from my ear and looked at the screen. The battery was dead. I tossed it aside and then turned the key.

The engine didn't roar to life. It clicked instead, like a loud clock marking the seconds. I stopped, fearful that I'd burn it out, then I tried again.

Nothing.

Twenty feet away, I heard a car door open and slam shut. My heart rate spiked, and a wave of panic rolled up my spine. Every hair on my neck stood on end. My eyes widened.

I heard the footsteps. A person was coming. I quickly pressed the button to lock the doors, just as a man lifted the handle to come inside.

I had no place to go, trapped. When I turned to look out the window, I saw a spike pressed against the glass and the hammer come down. Shards of glass exploded into the interior of the car as I turned away.

A hand reached for me but couldn't hold on. Then I heard the push of a button, and all the doors unlocked. I risked a glance back and saw Lund. He was coming for me.

I reached across the center console to the passenger seat, found the edge, and pulled myself over. Then I kicked the driver's side door open, hard. It caught Lund by surprise as he was about to enter. I heard him scream in pain, then I crawled out the other side.

It wasn't graceful. I toppled headfirst onto the pavement. Then I felt Lund grab my ankle and twist. It felt like a vice, and I began to kick in a wild fury.

Lund let go, and I was out, running toward the stairwell as

fast as I could. The metal door slammed into the wall, and I descended the stairs two or three at a time.

I did not look back. I knew he was behind me. I heard him coming, gaining ground. I pushed myself to get away. I needed distance. Instead of two or three steps at a time, I let go of the railing and just started jumping, flying down the stairs.

Lund couldn't keep up. The sound of his steps grew more distant as I rounded the stairwell again and saw the door below. There was a large "G" painted on it, the ground floor. If I could get outside, I thought, I could make it, so I jumped, but when I landed, my ankle turned, and I heard two pops as ligaments snapped.

I curled into a ball and rolled in pain.

Then he was on top of me. His eyes were now all black, and I swear his skin was red, a cartoon devil. He pressed down on my stomach, forcing every bit of oxygen out of my body. I tried to fight it, but he was too strong. I couldn't breathe. I was suffocating.

I felt dizzy, and I saw Lund lean toward me. His mouth was open, and his black eyes were growing even darker in sweet anticipation.

Then a woman said, "Get off her, demon." I turned and saw the old woman who had lived in the shack behind my apartment. She pointed, and a dozen birds flew at Lund. Their claws were out. Their high-pitched screeches echoed in the stairwell.

Lund tried to bat the birds away, but they kept coming. In the distraction, I was able to take a breath, then I tried to get out from under him. This did not last long.

Lund caught a pigeon and threw it against the wall. The bird's neck snapped, killing it instantly. He swatted two more away, and then he grabbed my head, slammed it down on the concrete, and everything went black.

40

When I woke up, I was flat on the ground, frozen. Just as I had read in my father's books, and just as Bob Cook had described, I was paralyzed, helpless. The old woman was crouched in the corner, blood streaming from her nose. All of her birds lay dead on the ground. It was just like the dream. Lund, no longer red, paid no attention to me. He knew I was no threat. He was focused on the woman.

"Evelyn, when will you learn?" he asked. "This is what has been foretold, and you are too old and weak to stop us."

"We will never stop fighting."

"We?" Lund laughed. "You act as if you have an army, but we both know that those in the resistance are few."

Then he moved toward her, and the old woman he called Evelyn sprung from her crouch. She tried to jump toward me. She was right there, inches away, but I couldn't help her. I could not move.

Lund pinned the old woman down, and I saw his hand pressed down, beginning to squeeze out her last breath. She bucked and tried to claw him off her but could not. Lund was too strong.

Without air, she was dying before my eyes. Lund leaned forward to collect her last breath. His mouth touched hers, and just as she was about to die, Evelyn turned to me and released it at the same moment that I inhaled.

It felt like I was being sucked into a black hole, time and space collapsed onto itself with unimaginable force. It pressed against me, broke me apart, and then brought me back together in less than a second.

My eyes cleared, and I felt like the world was suddenly in high definition. My brain was electrified, and I could hear, smell, and see everything. It all came at me as if it was under a microscope, but it wasn't overwhelming. I understood exactly what I needed to do.

I spun my body around and caught Lund's neck between my legs. My upper body strength wouldn't be enough, but my legs could do it, regardless of my ankle. Now, I was the one choking him.

Lund tried to hit me, but his arms only flailed, unable to land a punch or pull my legs off his throat. I squeezed as hard as I could, and I felt him begin to drift. Like a 1980s wrestler, I was putting him to sleep.

Just a little more, I told myself. It's just me and you. My legs trembled as I constricted Lund's access to air, tighter and tighter. Finally, I felt him go limp. I'd done it. I pushed him off me and crawled toward the old woman. I felt for a pulse, even though I knew that there would be none. I then pressed my forehead to hers, knowing the sacrifice she'd made for me.

That was when the shot was fired, echoing in the narrow stairwell like a bomb. I looked up the stairs. Perelli was on the landing, holding a gun. I saw his lips moving. He was yelling, but I couldn't hear anything he said. Finally, Perelli came down. He put his arm around me and took me outside, letting

Lund bleed to death on the floor, a gunshot wound to his chest.

———

It took a day for the ringing in my ears to stop, and another few days before I felt like my hearing was close to normal. My mind was something else. I can't say that it was fine. It wasn't. Any human being would be affected by what had happened. I certainly was, but I didn't regress in the way one might expect. I didn't go back to how I reacted after Merchants Bridge, or even the suicide of Judge Griggs.

Perhaps the fear, depression, and anxiety would come— all of these wrinkles in reality were enough to throw anyone for a loop— but first there was an overwhelming drive to finish what had been started. Sure, I admit that part of my motivation was fueled by anger, but it wasn't a blind rage or desire to prove something to my dad.

It was driven by the fact that I knew that Lund had not acted alone. He evaded surveillance by some of the best law enforcement agents in the country. He had known exactly where I was that night. He had even known the car I drove and where I had parked. Someone had been feeding Lund inside information, not just about the investigation, but about me personally.

I had a theory. I thought I knew who it was, but I didn't have any real proof. For that, I needed help from my merry band of misfits.

Crash provided the technical support, hacking into cell phone records, bank accounts, and GPS. Bob Cook leaned on his old contacts in the agency, passing along rumors and calling in favors. I got copies of old anonymous tips, personnel files, and internal investigations. All the while, Gray kept me supplied with copious amounts of bread.

I worked the file. When I skipped my probationary review hearing, Matthews called, "The Carrot was looking for you."

"I have no doubt she was," I said, "but we both know it wouldn't have made a difference." The Carrot was clear about that. Perhaps if Lund would've been arrested and had started cooperating, there would've been an argument in my favor, but even that ended badly. It wasn't possible to turn a dead man into a cooperating witness.

"That wasn't your fault," Mathews said. "You and you alone were responsible for convincing Jenae Malmo to help us. We were the people that messed up the surveillance and the arrest. Frazier and I wanted to go in as soon as that arrest warrant was issued, and I can't help thinking about how things might've been different if we'd done that."

"I'm not so sure," I said. "Lund knew exactly what we were doing the whole time."

"Sure felt like it," Matthews said.

"It's more than feeling," I said, "I just need to talk to one more person on my team to confirm that I'm right."

"You have your own team?"

"Shouldn't we all?" I laughed. "You can be on it if you want. Membership is free."

"Sounds like trouble."

"Only the good kind, my friend, only the good kind of trouble."

Matthews considered, and then nodded. "Okay," he said. "I'm in. I'm on team Amy."

41

I'd never been to Perelli's house in Edwardsville, but it wasn't surprising when he told me where he lived. A lot of St. Louis cops lived just across the Mississippi River in southern Illinois. The housing prices and schools were great, and the commute wasn't much longer than the commute from the more prestigious suburbs on the Missouri side.

It was a three-bedroom farmhouse built in the 1920s, sitting on nearly four acres not far from Indian Creek. As I turned off South Moreland Road and parked my car on the gravel drive, I realized how little I had known about my dad's former partner. He was just always there, like a distant uncle.

I knew he got divorced when I was in junior high school. I remember that because my dad complained at the dinner table about Perelli's constant rants about how his wife took everything in the divorce and how the judge was "anti-man." Looking at his house, however, it was clear that he hadn't lost everything.

I rang the doorbell, and Perelli invited me inside. "Thanks for taking the time," I said.

"No problem." Perelli pointed toward the living room. "Have a seat in there. I'm getting a beer, want one?"

"Water would be just fine."

"Suit yourself." He returned to the living room a minute or two later. Perelli handed me a glass of ice water, and he sat down in an oversized leather recliner across from me. "So, what's all this about?"

"Theories," I said. "I can't stop thinking about Lund, and I wanted your help. You know the St. Louis Police Department better than I ever would."

"I don't know about that," Perelli said. "If I was really smart, I wouldn't be working the crypt, know what I mean?"

I agreed. "It's just Lund obviously had a source. He knew things that he shouldn't have known."

Perelli held up his hand. "This is a bad idea, Amy. Your dad wanted to find Kasi's dealer, and you did that, and now that bastard is dead. Game over. Time for you to move on."

"Move on to what? I just got fired from the FBI," I said. "There's a two-year probationary period, and I didn't make it. So, if I'm unemployed with nothing to do, I figured I might as well keep digging."

"Not if you want another job in law enforcement," Perelli said. "I know where you're going, and I'm partially to blame. I never should have suggested you couldn't trust Schmitty, and you should definitely abort any plan you may have of trying to kill the king."

"So, you don't think Schmitty had anything to do with it?"

Perelli shrugged. "What I think is irrelevant. It's about what somebody can prove, and Schmitty is the master of hiding bodies and manipulating situations to further his own career."

"But can't you see it?" I asked rhetorically. "If Lund had been arrested without incident, he'd have started talking to the feds in an attempt to get a deal. Schmitty knew that this wasn't going to be good, because he's the ultimate prize. What prosecutor wouldn't agree to anything Lund demands, if Lund promises to deliver the Chief of Police for the City of St. Louis on a silver platter? That would be amazing, so Schmitty feeds Lund information. Crash got the ME records that prove that Schmitty knew, and prove that Schmitty was getting regular reports about OTW from Douglas. Schmitty is the guy. I just know it."

"I'm telling you, don't go there, Amy."

"But I am going there, and I'm trying to play it all out. In my head, trying to come up with ways that Schmitty could get away with it." I paused, then pointed at Perelli. "And I think Schmitty would ultimately blame you. After all, you're the guy who shot Lund. Schmitty wasn't even there."

Perelli sighed. "I've been patient, Amy, I have really tried to be patient," he said. "When you asked to come over to talk, I thought you wanted to talk about your old man. I thought you were grieving? I don't want to be any part of this." Perelli took another drink, got up from the chair, and pointed at the door. "I'm sorry you came all this way, but I don't want any part of this or whatever you're cooking up. Leave Schmitty alone."

"But you are a part of this, whether you want to be or not." I set my glass of water down, then I stood, too. "That's why I'm here. We must be proactive. We need to be prepared."

"Prepared for what?"

I was getting animated now. "Prepared to knock down Schmitty's defenses and misdirection. You see, he'll say you're the one with some 'axe' to grind with Lund. Schmitty will say it was your partner's daughter who was killed after taking drugs that Lund provided for her. He'll say that you knew all about the federal investigation, because you were talking to me. And here's the kicker: Schmitty is going to say that the drugs that Lund was selling were coming from the evidence room that you managed."

I waited for a reaction, but Perelli remained silent. So, I

continued to push. "He'll say you'd take the drugs out of evidence. Then they'd be sold, and you'd get a cut of the money. So, we need your cell phone records and your financial records. I'll give them to Crash, and he'll make sure they're all clear for when Schmitty makes these crazy allegations, right?"

"I don't know." Perelli shook his head.

"You could lose your job. You could go to jail," I said. "You need to protect yourself."

To this, Perelli nodded. "Okay." He nodded his head some more, as if convincing himself. "These would be totally crazy allegations, but you're right. I gotta be smart. Schmitty is savvy, and he'll do anything to save his own skin."

"I know," I said. "So, what do we do?"

"I got a lot of my financial stuff in the guest bedroom. I can get it." Perelli turned and took a few steps toward the back of the house but stopped. "So, Crash knows about this, who else have you talked to about Schmitty and what he might do to me?"

"Just you," I said. "I asked Crash if he could help me out on some things. He got the stuff on Schmitty, but he doesn't know any details."

"Good," Perelli said. "Let's keep this tight." He left me in the living room, while he went into the back to get his files. I heard drawers opening and closing, papers being shuffled. Then as he was walking back through the kitchen, "You sure you don't want a beer, Amy?"

"I'm sure."

"Okay." He came into the living room with a stack of folders. He dropped them on the table and turned to me.

Perelli had a gun in his hand.

He fired, but I was ready for it. I dove behind the couch, and before Perelli could fire again, the front and back doors were knocked off their hinges. Wood splinters flew in every direction as the SWAT team entered and Perelli was brought down to the floor.

I may not have known who Perelli was growing up, but I knew exactly who he was now. He was a dirty cop, and not a smart one either. Unlike Lund, Perelli didn't understand the electronic trail that documented his every phone call, text, email, and financial transaction. It was pure laziness. His corruption was easy to find, just somebody had to look in the right place.

When the noise subsided, I rolled over and saw Matthews holding his hand out to me. "You did good."

I took his hand, and he pulled me to my feet. I untucked my shirt, stuck my hand inside, and removed the small microphone that had been taped underneath. "How was the recording?" I asked, "Did you get it all?"

Matthews nodded. "Absolutely."

Then I saw Douglas come through the door, Frazier and Sloan not far behind. He had a huge smile on his face, giving me a thumbs up.

42

———————

The North Pond looked different in the daytime, even though all the elements remained the same: the river to one side, the city to the other, and in the center, the Arch, reaching toward the sky. It was bright. The noir was replaced by a palate of primary colors, the grass impossibly green. The emptiness was replaced by couples holding hands, families picnicking, and one generation sharing the landmark with the next, all culminating with a rickety ride to the top in a tiny elevator shaped like an egg.

Matthews arrived with the coffee and a small bag of donuts. He handed me one of the cups, then sat down on the bench next to me. "Never thought you'd want to come back here."

"Ha ha," I said, "trying to avoid the Arch in this town would be a futile effort. Plus, I've got other business down here this morning. My new therapist said I should do it before I go visit my mom again."

"You're flying to Florida?"

"This afternoon." I opened the white bag, peeked inside, and smiled. "Glazed donut holes from Old Town Donuts?"

"Made a special trip on my way in this morning, just for you."

I picked two out of the bag and popped them in my mouth. The rush of sugar was instant, and I felt the front of my brain tingle in delight. "These are the best."

Matthews nodded. "Only the best for the best." He wasn't an emotional guy, but I could tell he was having a hard time. "Talked to Douglas, and he's trying to pull strings to get you back into the bureau. He wants to offer you a job up in Chicago but says it's a steep climb. The Carrot is fighting him."

"I warned the him when he told me about his plan, so that shouldn't have come as a surprise. I also told Douglas that it'd be a lot of work for nothing, if I declined the offer."

"You'd turn him down?"

I drank a little coffee and took another donut hole out of the bag. "I really don't know. A fresh start sounds nice, but I'm not sure I'm ready to leave St. Louis. I feel like there's still some unfinished business here." I thought about the old woman with dreadlocks and the growing numbers of wrinkles in my reality, then I changed the subject. "Did you get a new partner yet?"

"Not yet," Matthews said. "The Carrot is considering a shake-up, wants us to start working in teams, like groups of four or six. She read about it in some sort of management book."

"Sounds painful."

"It would be," Matthews said. "Just when you think morale couldn't get any lower." He took the bag of donut holes from me and claimed a handful for himself. "I wanted to let you know that Perelli has a lawyer now, and he's going to start talking if the deal is good enough."

"The issue is what information he actually has," I said. "I never figured he'd be a leader, that he'd know enough about the whole operation to be particularly valuable."

"You're right," Matthews said. "He wasn't in leadership, but I think he was considered so harmless and dumb that he overheard things that he probably shouldn't have."

"What's his initial play?"

"As a gesture of good faith, his attorney has offered to tell us the location of Jenae Malmo's body and what happened to her."

I closed my eyes and lowered my head as a numb feeling began to spread. It took a minute to say anything at all. "She's dead." A whispered statement more to myself than Matthews. "I'd sort of hoped that she just disappeared and reinvented herself somewhere else, far away from everybody. That she got the new life that she had wanted."

Matthews put his hand on my back. "I'm sorry," he said. "It's not fair."

"No," I said. "It's not fair. Just a bunch of wheeling and dealing while real accountability gets pushed further down the road." I thought about poker and all the time I'd spent watching the cards get dealt, and this felt like that.

Fold or pass, raise or stand.

It was dealing justice. Different players came to the table and left, but the game continued, and the house always won.

"Thanks for telling me," I said.

"I thought you should hear it from a friend," Matthews said. "It was also a good excuse to have coffee and donuts with the best partner I've ever had."

This made me cry. "I'm going to miss working with you."

"Me, too," Matthews said, "but that doesn't mean we can't talk. You can always call, and we can just hang out, vent our frustrations, and otherwise solve the world's problems."

"A friend," I said. "I like that."

Matthews checked his watch. "I better get going, another lovely morning with Colton Steele." He rolled his eyes. "Are you going my way?"

"No, like I said, I've got another appointment this morning, just over there." I nodded my head toward the casino. "Wish me luck."

———

JOHN HADN'T AGREED to meet. He, in fact, had never returned any of my voicemail messages or responded to any of my texts. My goal was simply to apologize, but I was fully prepared for this in-person mission to fail. He owed me nothing, and this apology was more about me than him. I needed to acknowledge the people I'd hurt when I was off my medications and obsessed with running through walls, regardless of the consequences.

Assuming his school schedule hadn't changed, I knew John would be working the morning and early afternoon shift before his evening sociology class. He had a break at 11:30, and I arrived about twenty minutes early.

I walked the perimeter of the casino and saw him at the roulette wheel. It was the same one where we'd met. The same table where I'd played the lucky black chip and pulled myself out of debt. He had a beard now but otherwise looked the same.

I walked to the bar and found a table where I'd have a clear view of John. Then I waited. I felt like a stalker, probably because I was, and that was when I began to question myself. Maybe this wasn't a good plan at all. Maybe I should just write him a letter.

Above the bar was a television, showing another report about the glacier. A second large piece had fallen, but a significant cold front came in early. The climate experts now predicted that the entire ice shelf would not fall into the ocean this year. It was a reprieve, like a last-minute stay the night before an execution.

My mind drifted, then circled back to all the stories of love

I'd read or seen depicted in the movies. In the end, the beautiful person shows up unexpectedly after doing wrong, makes an impassioned apology, along with a raw declaration of love. The other beautiful person, upon hearing this, is overcome with emotion. They accept one another's faults, embrace, then kiss or even find some nearby minister or judge to marry them on the spot.

Was I looking for that ending somewhere in a subconscious brain that had been warped by decades of rom-coms?

The longer I sat and waited, the more I realized that this was going to turn out badly. I probably wouldn't even get a chance to apologize before being scolded or perhaps ushered off the property by security. Sometimes when you hurt someone, it can't be fixed. If he wanted to hear my apologies or see me, John had already had plenty of chances.

I decided to go home and pack for Florida. I'd write him a letter, and that would be it. He could make the next move if he wanted.

I finished my coffee and the last of the remaining glazed donut holes. I took a final look at John, then walked toward the door. This was the right decision, and I knew it. The guilt and shame started to lift off my shoulders. Then, out of the corner of my eye, I saw a familiar face.

It wasn't John. It was Christine Griggs.

She sat at the high stakes poker table. Her hair was immaculate. Her clothes fit just right, tailored to her exact proportions. Everything was perfect, except her eyes. They were heavy and bloodshot, with large, dark circles underneath. I recognized the look, because I'd seen it in my own face whenever I saw my reflection in the mirror during those late nights at the Internet casino.

That's when it clicked, and I realized how stupid I was. I'd gone about investigating Judge Griggs all wrong. I'd made assumptions, and I'd failed to ask the right questions.

I walked over to her and saw her body jump when I said, "Hello, Ms. Griggs." It was like she'd been awoken from a trance or maybe just surprised that somebody recognized her. She turned with a fake smile, then realized that it was me.

The smile disappeared. "What do you want?"

"I wanted to apologize," I said. "You were right. Your husband didn't have a gambling problem, you did."

"Beg your pardon?"

"I should've noticed that those were joint accounts. They weren't just for your husband. I wish you would've just told us that the cash advances were to pay off your gambling debts, not his."

She turned back to the table. "I don't want to talk to you, Agent Wirth." Christine Griggs tossed a few chips into the pot as the dealer shuffled, then began pulling the cards off the top for each of the players.

"I'm not Agent Wirth anymore, I said. I don't work for the FBI. I'm just Amy Wirth, and if you ever want some help, please reach out. I know exactly what you're going through. I know what it's like to not being able to stop."

I pulled an old card from my wallet, crossed out the official number, and wrote my cell phone number on the back. "Call me." I put it on the table in front of her. "Seriously, you need some help, or somebody is going to get hurt." I thought about the timing of when her husband took out the insurance policy. "Because my guess is that if somebody spent the time to talk to your daughter and really started to dig into her car accident, they'd probably figure out that it wasn't an accident. Right? Somebody was sending a message to you. Somebody who was probably collecting a debt?"

Christine Griggs closed her eyes, and her hands began to shake. "It wasn't my fault," she said, but we both knew that it was a lie.

____

WHEN I HEARD the intercom buzz, I hoped it was John. Even though I hate admitting that, it's true. I thought for a moment, perhaps he'd seen me at the casino or heard about my interaction with Judge Griggs's wife, then decided to stop by on his way to class.

"Yes," I pressed the button, "who is it?"

"It's the Chief of Police, unlock the door."

This was definitely not John. "You got a warrant?"

"I don't need a warrant," Schmitty said. "I knew you when you were still in your mama's belly, now buzz me up. We need to talk, and I don't have a lot of time."

"Well, neither do I."

"Good," Schmitty said. "I'm glad we can agree that we are both incredibly busy and important people. So, unlock the door."

"Fine." I pressed the button next to the intercom and opened the door, stepping out into the stairwell to see Schmitty puffing up the steps. "This is a new one," I said, "usually I'm the one calling you."

"Well," Schmitty said, "I bumped into Mathews today, and he told me you were skipping town. Sounds like the feds didn't appreciate you, and I was a little worried that you'd just stay down in Florida with your mother."

"It's a possibility." I pointed at the empty suitcase on my couch and laundry basket of clean clothes. "Mind if I pack while we talk? I have a flight in a couple hours."

"You do what you need to do," Schmitty said.

"Thanks." I went over to the laundry basket and plucked out three pairs of socks, turned them into balls, and put them in the suitcase. "But before you say anything, I have to let you know that I don't believe for one second that you just 'bumped into Mathews.' He called you and told you about how the FBI let me go."

"Okay, you're right," Schmitty said. "He called. You know we're friends, and he knows that you and I have a relationship. Nothing wrong with that."

"No, nothing wrong with that, but I don't like people feeling sorry for me, like I'm a charity case." I grabbed a handful of T-shirts, rolled them up, and added them to the suitcase. "Know what I'm saying?"

"I do," Schmitty said. "You're a proud woman, and you should be proud. You're a damn good cop, too, and that's why I'm here. I want to offer you a job."

I stopped packing and put my hands on my hips. "There is no way that I'm going back to the St. Louis Police Department. No offense, Chief, but those people tore me up, and I still haven't really recovered."

"I know that," Schmitty said. "I know about the harassment, and if I could, I'd bounce Bird and Doles to the curb, but the police union wouldn't allow it without you formally filing a complaint and testifying against them---which you have refused to do---and even then they'd probably just get a suspension or stripped of rank."

"So, what are you asking?"

"I'm asking you to come work internal affairs," Schmitty said. "This'll give you an opportunity to do what you want. I listened to that recording, the one between you and Perelli, just before he got arrested. I don't believe you're that good of an actress. I think you really do want to find out everybody who's involved and bring them down."

"And that's what you want, too?"

"I do," Schmitty said. "The shield means something to me, just like it meant something to your father. We gotta root these guys out before it's too late." He rubbed his chin. "Might already be too late. We've got our congresswoman and the mayor talking about defunding our department. It's crazy."

"I didn't become a cop to investigate other cops," I said. "It's just not what I ever wanted to do."

"But that was exactly what you were doing with Lund, and if you hadn't been fired by the FBI, that's what you'd be doing right now, investigating all the other cops that were working with Perelli."

I threw a couple pairs of shorts in the suitcase, then zipped it up. "I don't know."

"Think about it," Schmitty said. "I talked to Agent Douglas, and he was jazzed about the idea, really jazzed. You'd be working with him, too."

I checked my watch and picked up the suitcase. "Okay, like I said, I'll think about it."

"I'll give you a week," Schmitty said. "Let me know in a week, one way or another."

"How about two?"

Schmitty considered. "Okay, two." He held out his hand, and we shook.

"Deal," I said. "In two weeks, you'll have an answer."

Schmitty smiled. "Great. Have a good trip to Florida, and it'd be an honor to have you back on my team." He took a step toward the door, and then stopped. "One other thing," he said. "Matthews told me that you think that your dad pulled strings to get you into the department, and I'm here to tell you that you absolutely, one hundred percent got into the police academy on your own merit. No strings were pulled. No favors were given, and if you want me to open your file so that you can see that for yourself, I will do it for you, regardless of whether you accept my job offer. Understood?"

"I understand," I said, "and thank you."

He nodded. We said our goodbyes, and then I watched

Schmitty leave. When he was gone, I took a deep breath and thought about investigating dirty cops. I thought about Matthews and what he would think about Schmitty's job offer. Then I smiled, and thought, "It'll be righteous."

AND, in two weeks, I was back.

PRE-ORDER "TOWER GROVE" THE NEXT BOOK IN THE DARK RIVER SERIES

ABOUT THE AUTHOR

J.D. Trafford is the winner of the National Legal Fiction Writing Competition for Lawyers, has been profiled in Mystery Scene Magazine (a "writer of merit"), and written multiple bestselling legal thrillers. This includes the "No Time" series featuring Michael Collins, which was selected as an IndieReader bestselling pick, and *Little Boy Lost*, which has sold over 100,000 copies worldwide and was the #1 overall bestseller on Amazon.

He now lives with his wife and children in the Midwest, and bikes whenever possible.

For more information visit: www.jdtrafford.com

ALSO BY J.D. TRAFFORD

Little Boy Lost

Good Intentions

Without Precedent

No Time Series, featuring Michael Collins

No Time To Run

No Time To Die

No Time To Hide

Dark River Series

Merchants Bridge

Dealing Justice

Tower Grove, coming fall 2024